Other People's Stories

by
Patrick Kidd
(with a little help from some others)

To Eileen, without whose encouragement I would never have written these stories.

To Esther, whose enthusiasm after reading the first drafts pushed me to finish editing.

To my father, for whom I am grateful every day.

To my mother, whom I miss every day.

But most importantly: To everyone who suggested a story. Without you, this would quite literally have not been possible.

Contents

Foreword

At the end of 2013, I was feeling pretty unhappy with my writing. I had 'won' National Novel Writing Month[1] a couple of times in the previous few years but my output had stagnated. Also, I wasn't satisfied with what little I was putting out.

Knowing how I had been motivated by the format of NaNoWriMo in the past I decided to set myself a challenge. I wanted to see if I could write about 1500-2000 words a week for a whole year. The problem was I didn't have an idea for a novel. At least not one I was enthusiastic enough to commit to doing that for, so I went in a different direction. I decided I was going to write a short story every week in 2014. I would stick with the 1500-2000 words limit, and I would have to be done with the first draft of each story by midnight on Sunday.

So, 52 weeks, 52 stories. What else did I need, right?

Well, 52 ideas would be a start. I very much did not have that many, so I turned to the Internet for suggestions. I asked friends and family for a few to get me off the ground, and boy did they deliver. As I started to post the finished first drafts on my website other people I had never met started to read them and even suggested a few of their own. That is why this book is called Other People's Stories. Every word you see in these stories was written by me. But almost none of those words would have made it to the page without some amazing suggestions from those who contributed.

I actually ended up with 53 stories at the end of the year. For week 25 someone challenged me to enter a short

---

[1] A yearly challenge to write 50,000 words of the first draft of a novel during November.

story contest. It was with a writing group near my childhood home in North Wales, but the word limit was 1000 for the entry. Not wanting to betray my own (admittedly entirely arbitrary) word count goal I decided to write two stories that week. One was based on a suggestion from my father, and the other was the only one I came up with myself the whole year. So I did write 52 stories by other people. I am a man of my word!

The stories in this book are written in a variety of genres and styles. I am proud of all of them. But, for various reasons, some of them aren't of as high a quality as others. Even now, after several rounds of editing, there was only so much I could do to make them the best I could. But that is to be expected with such a variety of topics!

I don't say all this because I think any of them are bad. Well, except 'To Boldly Go' from week 15, which was a deliberate attempt to write a bad story. I say it because I think it's important to show every single one of these stories. They do not exist in a vacuum.

Every single story was written with the lessons of the ones that came before it in mind. Some of these lessons were happy ones, but some were things I found I needed to work on to grow. If I only showed you the stories I was truly happy with (and there are a fair few of those!) then it wouldn't be representative of the journey I took to get to them.

I hope you enjoy reading these stories as much as I did writing them.

Patrick Kidd
Author, Dreamweaver, Visionary

Ennui

John Muskett - *'A story about a circus Monkey suffering from ennui induced alcoholism, learning to love life again.'*

Barnabus puffed at his cigarette. The dull repetition of the train running over the tracks was the only sound. He was alone with his thoughts in the dark carriage.

He had been living this life for five years now. No one place to call home besides the four walls of a train car and nobody he could call his friends or family. He pawed around on the floor for the bottle, and eventually, he felt its cold, glassy exterior. He lifted the bottle to his lips. A solitary drop fell from the neck on to his waiting tongue, but no more. It seemed he was out of luck.

He shrieked in anger and hurled the empty bottle, shattering it against the opposite wall.

The loud crash raised a cacophony from the next car over. The corrugated sheet metal walls were thin after all. Excited hoots, hollers, whoops and whines flitted across the air for a moment, then died down again.

It was almost pitch black and the cabin was so hot that it stifled the air. He knew they had recently passed into South America and the heat had been intolerable. A light shone for a moment through a gap in the sheet metal. It illuminated the drops of liquid on the wall that had so recently borne the brunt of his frustration. There had been more left in the bottle after all.

Barnabus picked himself up from the floor and stubbed his cigarette out on the wall. He was careful to avoid letting any ash drop on to the dry straw that lined the floor. He did not want a repeat of THAT incident.

He edged his way closer, trying not to lose his footing on the bouncing train, but he could not quite reach the wall. He strained harder, but the chain shackled around his ankle would not allow him to get any closer.

'Eeeeek,' he screeched and was then thrown back to the floor by a particularly bumpy piece of rail.

Struggling to right himself Barnabus flung his tail upwards in desperation. He felt it catch on something solid and used it to pull himself up. He got to his feet, before climbing up on to a metal bar. He breathed a sigh of relief, though he was no closer to the delicious whiskey that decorated the wall.

Moments later a heavy box dislodged from a shelf above his head and smashed on the carriage floor. He stared in disbelief. It seemed his luck was changing after all A few seconds earlier and he would have died. Those idiots. Didn't they know how to secure their supplies? They could have lost their star attraction.

Barnabus felt a breeze on his face. It was almost imperceptible, but in the stuffy carriage it was a welcome change. It took him a moment to realise where it was coming from. He looked down at the floor of the carriage. The crate had dented the wall enough to create a gap. A gap that was big enough for him to crawl through.

He could be free. Free from this life that he had loathed for so long. Free from the other animals, whom he found so intolerable. He could get his life back.

Barnabus made to go out of the hole, but stopped, overcome by memories of the good old days. He hadn't always hated this life. Back when he was first purchased from the zoo he knew he was destined for greatness.

The circus owners had spent days look at the entire litter of infants the zoo had available to sell. After a series of tests, Barnabus had been the lucky monkey selected above his siblings to train for the big top.

He had been the star of the show, and still was, but the circus was a dying concept. Once he had wowed audiences worldwide with acrobatic feats that few could reproduce. Now, thanks to the rise of MTV and the apathy of Generation X, audience numbers were dwindling. Nobody came to the circus anymore.

This decline in attendance had led to a dip in his morale, and ultimately his descent into alcoholism. Though he felt a debt of loyalty to the circus, he could not deny that nowadays it just made him miserable.

Barnabus vividly recalled the day that he stole unnoticed in to the ringmaster's caravan. He saw what he thought was the apple juice they used to give him in an open bottle on the table. It had been a particularly hot day and he felt the need to quench his thirst. He had never looked back. Now the keepers knew to leave a bottle of whiskey in his carriage for longer journeys.

Barnabus sighed. He had made up his mind. This life had given him so much. But it was no longer giving him what he needed. He reasoned that when they reached the next station they would fix the hole. He may never have another chance to escape.

Rummaging through the straw on the floor of the carriage he dug out his battered Fez and waistcoat. Donning them for the last time he edged closer and closer to the hole in the carriage. He almost changed his mind when he saw the speed at which the ground was passing below him, but steeled his resolve.

With some effort he pushed through the gap and clung to the outside of the carriage. He tried moving off down the side of the car, using whatever handholds he could find.

But his progress was impeded. He had forgotten about one thing; he was still chained to the floor.

The scenery rushed by him as he wondered what he could do. And then it came to him. The wheels of the train would cut the chain. It was dangerous, but it was the only way. If he didn't cut through and escape, they would find him at the next station and return him to the car. He had come too far to go back now.

Barnabus took a deep breath and leaped into action. He swung underneath the train and grabbed at one of the cables that ran along the undercarriage.

For a horrifying second the cable swung away with the undulations of the train, and the ground rushed towards him at a terrifying pace. Barnabus began to fall. At the last moment the cable swung back, and he managed to grab hold. He pulled himself up to safety until his body was flush with the metal undercarriage.

Breathing heavily after his narrow escape he gathered as much of the chain as he could in his paws. He then began to let out the slack in the direction of the nearest wheel.

He tried to lower the chain on to the wheel itself, but a bump sent the links flying from his hands and on to the tracks. The wheel bounced over the chain with an audible screech, nearly knocking the carriage off course. He heard the whooping of the other animals as the train teetered briefly before righting itself.

The chain was broken. He was free. He braced himself and then let go of the undercarriage, dropping on to the ground. On landing he bounced and rolled hard. Somehow he managed to avoid ending up in the path of the wheels that had just granted him his freedom.

When the train had passed over him and the dust had finally settled, he stood up on his hind legs. He had lost his Fez in the near fall, and his already battered waistcoat was practically torn to shreds. He discarded the garment by the side of the track. He checked his body for injuries. Except for some bruising he seemed to have escaped unscathed.

Dusting himself off with his paws he checked the landscape around him. Fields surrounded him on all sides, but off in the distance he could see the faintest glimmer of green trees. Without hesitation he was off.

After the train had pulled into Lima station and all the cars had been moved to the circus site, Barnabus' keepers approached his carriage. One produced a key and after removing the padlock, swung the large door aside.

'Barney!' he yelled into the carriage. 'Where are you?' There was no response. Helped by his colleague, he clambered up into the car and looked around for the monkey. But Barnabus was nowhere to be found. He spotted the hole in the carriage and the broken chain dangling through it and turned to his colleague.

'Where's Barnabus?' she asked.

'He's gone...'

The ringmaster approached the circus sign with a solemn look on his face. A group of small children clustered around it, trying to get a glimpse of what the attractions would be that night.

With a heavy heart the ringmaster pushed his way through the group. With a marker pen he crossed out the words 'The Magnificent Barnabus defies gravity with his deadly leaps and bounds!'

A chorus of disappointment rose from the group of children.

'I know, children, I know,' the ringmaster said in reply. 'I am sad too.'

After what felt like an age, Barnabus approached the forest. When he finally reached the treeline the forest looked dark and intimidating. He began to think about what a huge mistake he had made. There would be no whiskey here, and no one to come and feed him. He was on his own now and would have to fend for himself.

But even if he wanted to go back, he had lost the train and would likely never find it again. He steeled himself and stepped forward in to the trees.

He was greeted with a high-pitched shrieking noise. He turned, startled, to see another monkey, clutching a piece of fruit. Barnabus was so astonished that his tiny jaw dropped. For the first time since he left the zoo all those years ago, he was looking at another member of his species.

Shocked by this discovery he could only stand there, mouth agape. At first he thought the other creature was going to try and hurt him in case he tried to steal its food. But after a prolonged silence the tension dissipated. The other monkey, who had decided that Barnabus was not a threat, broke off a piece of the fruit and timidly extended its arm in his direction.

Barnabus took it and was greeted with a satisfied 'EEK' from his new compatriot.

Perhaps I won't be so lonely here after all, he thought. With a smile on his face and a newfound enthusiasm for life, he followed his new friend into the depths of the jungle.

Wild Things

Edward Murphy - 'A story of someone who goes into the wilds on a geocaching expedition but runs into trouble as night descends. Inadequately prepared, with no food, they half-slide down a very steep valley only to realise that they can't get across the river and even if they could there's no way out. And then the fat one (you can call him Ed, if you like) goes hypoglycaemic from lack of food.'

'Will you just admit it already? We are lost!' Lillian said, folding her arms across her chest.

'We're not lost as long as we have this!' Edwin replied, holding up his GPS device and waving it at her for emphasis.

'Well, where the bloody hell are we then?'

Edwin fiddled with the device for a few seconds. He squinted at the screen in the fading light. He cursed that he had not shelled out the extra £40 for the model that was backlit.

'Well?' She asked. Edwin could sense the impatience in her voice.

'I, uh,' he began. 'I don't know.'

'So we ARE lost?'

Lowering his head in defeat, Edwin replied 'Yes, I suppose we are...'

'Well this is bloody wonderful, isn't it? I didn't even want to come on this stupid Geocaching trip with you in the first place. Now here I am lost halfway up a bloody mountain in the middle of bloody nowhere.'

'We could go back the way we came...' Edwin suggested.

'And do you have a torch with which to guide us back along this path?' Lillian enquired. She took her fiancé's silence as a no. 'We've been walking for hours. We would need a bloody bloodhound to find our way back!' Lillian paused and took a deep, calming breath. 'There will be plenty of time for me to shout at you later. What are we going to do?'

Edwin furrowed his brow and began to scan around, looking for a way back to civilisation. There were no towns or villages in sight, but in the fading light he could just about see a country road winding its way through the fields below. It was some distance away at the bottom of the mountain.

'Down there,' he said, pointing so Lillian could see. 'There's a road. That has to lead SOMEWHERE.'

'That's bloody miles away!' Lillian pointed out. Then she remembered that the alternative was a night on this godforsaken mountain. '...let's go,' she added.

About twenty minutes into their trek the gloomy twilight began to settle into the dark of night time.

'I can't see a bloody thing,' Edwin complained, 'And I think I'm going to pass out. I'm becoming hypoglycaemic.'

Lillian rolled her eyes.

'Oh is that so?!' she snapped. 'Well if we hadn't come up here searching for some bloody lost treasure we could be filling our faces right now. Anyway, I saw you scoffing those three Snickers on the way up the mountain. You've got enough blood sugar to last five people for a month. There's another one in your rucksack. Eat that and shut up.'

Realising that this was not the time for impudence, Edwin did as he was told.

'Look,' he said with a mouthful of Snickers after they had trudged on for a few moments. 'I'm sorry. We need to stop bickering. We have to work together.'

'What do you mean?' Lillian asked, genuinely puzzled.

'Because,' he replied, pointing ahead of them, 'of that.'

Directly in front of them, and comprehensively blocking their descent, was a scree slope.

'Oh,' said Lilian. 'We're going to have to go down that, aren't we?'

'Yep,' Edwin replied.

'And there's no way around?'

'Too dark to tell, and I don't fancy doing it when it's any darker if we don't find another way.'

'Good point.'

They turned to look at each other, and their hands met. All arguments were on hold for the moment.

'Together?' Lillian suggested.

'Together,' Edwin agreed.

They made their way gingerly to the edge of the slope. Edwin felt Lillian's grip on his hand tighten, and squeezed back. Together they took a tentative first step on to the loose rocks. Several skidded away at the slightest touch, and Lillian winced at the sound of slate crashing below her.

'I have an idea,' she said.

Edwin watched as she sat down at the top of the slope.

'Edge down slowly and you should be fine,' she said. 'It'll be much easier to control our descent this way.'

Edwin nodded and sat down next to her. Together they pushed off. The going wasn't easy, but they inched their way forwards until finally they were at the bottom. They leapt to their feet.

'We made it!' Lillian exclaimed, and they shared a triumphant embrace.

'I wish I could say the same for my trousers...' Edwin said, lamenting the now thoroughly ripped seat of his cargo pants.

'They gallantly gave their life to protect their commanding officer,' Lillian said in a dodgy American accent. She gave a stiff salute. The pair laughed for the first time since they had left the top of the hill.

The going became a lot easier the further they got down the mountainside. For a while they walked hand in hand as the darkness grew all around them. Soon they had to rely on the camera lights from their mobile phones to see. It was hard to tell how far they were from the road, or even if they were going in the right direction. After some time, Edwin heard a splash as he put his foot down.

'Oh, my bloody foot is soaking!' he shouted, hopping about in a vain effort to dry his foot off.

'A stream?' Lillian asked in disbelief. 'Why didn't you mention that there was a bloody stream?'

'I didn't see it!' Edwin replied, defensively.

'How could you not see it? It's a bloody stream! It looks like a road except it's made of water, they're not exactly known for their stealthiness!'

'It's really dark!' he protested.

Their bickering was interrupted by the sound of a car approaching from the gloom. After a few seconds the engine sounds grew louder. Headlight beams appeared across the stream, briefly illuminating it and the hedges along the road they had been aiming for. They saw the vehicle speed past a gap in the hedges.

'There it is!' Lillian cried. That's our way out!'

'But how do we get there?' Edwin wondered.

'There must be a bridge around here somewhere. Use your GPS. That must be able to tell us if there's a bridge nearby.'

Edwin rummaged around in his pocket and found the device.

'Shine your light on the screen,' he suggested. He pressed the power button and prepared to search around the local maps. Instead, he was confronted with the Low Battery symbol, and then the screen went blank. No amount of wailing or gnashing of teeth would bring it back to life again.

'Stupid thing,' he declared. 'I only put fresh batteries in this morning. What are we going to do now?'

'Did you see how deep the stream was?'

'Not really,' he replied, 'but it looked quite wide, and it's getting chilly. I don't want to risk hypothermia by wading across it.'

'Then I suppose we're stuck. We were so close too!' Lillian sat down on the ground, defeated. After a moment Edwin joined her. 'I don't want to have to spend a night in the wilderness!' she lamented. 'I want to sleep in a nice, warm bed!'

Edwin put his arm around her shoulders and drew her in closer to him. 'So do I, love, but the only other choice is to wade through that stream, and it's too dangerous.'

For a while they sat in silence, contemplating the night ahead when they heard a low rumbling sound somewhere in the distance.

'Edwin, can you hear that?' Lillian asked, lifting her head from her fiancé's shoulder. The noise was getting louder.

'It sounds like it's coming from the road, but that's not a car.' Edwin replied, wondering what could possibly make a noise like that.

Eventually, a set of high beam headlights swung around the corner and the owner, an old tractor, came in to view.

The pair leapt to their feet and began jumping up and down and shouting to try and attract the driver's attention. The headlights swept past the animated couple. They heard the engine slow down and eventually cut out altogether as the tractor came to a halt.

'Is everything alright?' the driver shouted, getting down from the cab. He was an old, wiry man with a grey beard. He wore a tweed jacket and flat cap and looked as though he would himself have been made of tweed if he had the option.

'We're stuck,' Lillian replied. 'We're trying to get back to a village or a town but we can't get across this river.'

'Well, there's a village a couple of miles down the road with a nice guesthouse. I can take you there, no problem. First of all, though we need to get you over here.'

'Is there anywhere we can cross?'

'Not for miles,' the farmer replied. 'But you may be in luck.'

He disappeared out of the glare of the headlights, fading back into the gloom. The only sign of his continuing presence was the cacophony of noise that was coming from behind the tractor.

After a couple of minutes he reappeared clutching a long ladder.

'Had a problem with one of the barn roofs earlier, so it was lucky I had this with me.' He lowered the ladder to the ground and extended it to its full length. He began edging it across the river until it finally reached the other bank. 'It'll only hold one of you at a time, and you'll have to be careful.'

It took some time but eventually, both Edwin and Lillian reached the other side of the river. They were cold, exhausted and a little shaken, but at least they hadn't taken a nighttime dip to top it off. The farmer stored the ladder back in the trailer, and they prepared to head to the village.

'There's only space for two in the cab, I'm afraid,' the farmer said as he started the tractor's engine. 'One of you will have to ride in the back.'

'You go in the cab, Lil,' Edwin said, climbing up to the trailer. 'This whole mess is my fault.'

22

After a while, Lillian recovered enough energy to strike up a conversation with the farmer.

'I'm so glad you found us,' she said. 'We could have been out there all night.'

'Yes, it was a stroke of luck,' the man replied. 'Were you up on the mountain?'

'Yeah, looking for treasure,' she laughed.

The farmer furrowed his brow.

'Well, then why didn't you just come down the other side of the mountain? The village is just down there.'

Lillian's eyes widened as she thought of everything that they had been through. How it all could have been avoided. She thought about what she was going to do to the stupid idiot when they got to the guesthouse. Maybe there would be some sharp implements she could use.

But when she turned to look at him sat, asleep, in the trailer she couldn't bring herself to be angry with him anymore. They were both here and in one piece, and at the end of the day, that was all that mattered.

Anyway, why waste years of precious blackmail material?

WEEK 3

The Mouse of Muswell Hill and the Hedgehog of Highgate Wood

Haydn Puleston Jones - *'A story suitable for a 4 year old called
Rosie and a 2 year old called Sam, set in Muswell Hill and
featuring Rosie, Sam, Highgate Woods and pain au chocolat.'*

One sunny Saturday afternoon a little girl named
Rosie and a little boy named Sam were playing in their garden
in Muswell Hill. They had been running around and laughing
all morning playing a game of tag, and now they were very
thirsty.

They sat down on a bench for a break. Just at that
moment their mummy came outside and brought them each a
nice glass of cold lemonade.

'That was a very fun morning, wasn't it Sam?' said
Rosie as she sipped her lemonade.

'Yes, it was,' Sam replied. 'But what are we going to do
this afternoon? I want to have even MORE fun this afternoon!'

Rosie thought for a moment. 'I don't know. Playing
tag is a very fun way to spend time! Why don't we see if we can
think of anything more fun?'

So Rosie and Sam sat there for a few moments trying
to think of some more fun things to do. All the time they were
sipping at their lemonade and feeling more refreshed and
ready to play.

As they both finished their lemonade they heard a noise coming from behind the bench. It was very quiet but if they listened very hard they could just about hear it.

'Can you hear that, Rosie?' Sam asked.

'Yes, it sounds like someone crying!' Rosie replied.

'But they're very quiet!' Sam said. 'I wonder where they are.'

Sam and Rosie both started to look around to try and find out who was crying. They searched and searched, but they simply could not work out where the noise was coming from. As they were about to give up, Rosie had an idea.

'I know, Sam!' she said, excitedly. 'If they are very quiet, then it must mean that they are very small!'

'And if they're very small,' Sam replied, 'then they might be on the ground!'

They both dropped to their knees, and right there behind the bench they could see a little mouse. The mouse was sat on its own and it was crying.

'Hello, little mouse,' Sam said. 'What's wrong?'

'Oh, hello,' the mouse sniffed. 'I didn't think anyone could hear me crying.'

'Well, we heard you!' Rosie said. 'My name is Rosie, and this is my brother Sam.'

'Hello Rosie and Sam, my name is Molly Mouse.'

'Why are you sad, Molly?' Rosie asked.

'I was on my way home to my mouse hole to have a lovely lunch of pain au chocolat when I saw a horrid hedgehog stealing them all from my garden. You see, I have some pain au chocolat trees, and they were just ripe enough to eat.'

'Oh no!' Rosie and Sam both said together. 'Stealing pain au chocolat is not a very nice thing to do!'

'No, it isn't!' Molly agreed. 'And now I don't have anything to eat for lunch!'

Rosie smiled and said to Molly 'Don't be sad. What if we helped you get your pain au chocolat back?'

'You would do that?' said Molly, who felt a lot happier already.

'Of course!' Sam replied. 'We've been looking for something fun to do this afternoon, and what is more fun than helping people?'

'Thank you. That is very kind of you both!' Molly said.

'Let's go have an adventure!' Rosie said.

As they were leaving the garden Molly crawled up to sit on Sam's shoulder.

'I saw the hedgehog going towards Highgate Wood. Maybe we can find him in there?' she said.

So they set off in the direction of Highgate Wood. Once they got into the wood they started to look around for a hedgehog with some pain au chocolat.

'Hedgehog!' the three took turns calling. 'Hedgehog, are you there?'

After a few moments they heard a rustling in some leaves and a hedgehog poked its head out.

'Hello?' he said. 'I am a hedgehog.'

'Did you take some pain au chocolat from a tree a little while ago?' Rosie asked.

'No,' the hedgehog replied. 'I don't like pain au chocolat. Sorry.'

'That's OK!' Sam replied, and the hedgehog disappeared back into the leaves.

So they moved on further into the wood. They looked around for other hedgehogs, and again took turns calling out 'Hedgehog! Hedgehog, are you there?'

After another couple of moments a second, much smaller hedgehog popped up from behind a log.

'Is everything OK?' the hedgehog asked.

'Did you take some pain au chocolat from a nearby tree earlier on?' Rosie asked.

'No,' the hedgehog replied. 'I LOVE pain au chocolat, but as you can see I am much too small to reach it in a tree!'

A bit further into the woods, Sam spotted something.

'Molly, Rosie! Look!' he said, pointing at a pile of pain au chocolat next to a hole in a very large tree stump.

The three ran over to the tree and knocked on the trunk.

'Excuse me!' Rosie said. 'Is there anybody home?'

A hedgehog poked its head out of the hole.

'I see you have lots of pain au chocolat!' Sam said.

'I do!' the hedgehog replied. 'Isn't it delicious?'

'Where did you get it?' Rosie asked. 'Our friend Molly the Mouse has had some stolen!'

'Oh gosh!' the hedgehog said. 'I would never steal it. Stealing other people's things is wrong! I grew it all on my pain au chocolat tree!'

The hedgehog showed them the small tree behind its stump. It looked much like the one outside Molly's mouse hole.

'I hope you find your pain au chocolat!' the hedgehog said to them as they left.

So Rosie, Sam, and Molly searched on and on, and they spoke to a great many hedgehogs in the woods. But none of the hedgehogs knew anything about Molly's pain au chocolat.

After what felt like hours they were about to give up. But suddenly they all caught the smell of something delicious. They all looked at each other and straight away they knew what the smell was. 'Pain au chocolat!' they cried out together.

They followed the smell until they came to some bushes. Behind the bushes they could hear someone whistling a very cheerful tune. As they pushed the bushes aside they saw a hedgehog warming some pain au chocolat over a small fire.

'Oh, hello!' the hedgehog said to them cheerily. 'My name is Henry! What's yours?'

Rosie stepped forward. 'I am Rosie, this is my brother, Sam and this is our friend Molly the Mouse.'

'Well it is lovely to meet you all,' Henry said. 'Is everything alright? Molly looks sad.'

'Somebody stole my pain au chocolat!' Molly said. 'I was just on my way home to have a delicious lunch and I saw someone stealing them.'

'Where did you get those pain au chocolat?' Sam asked.

'I found them on a pain au chocolat tree in Muswell Hill a little while ago!' Henry said, smiling.

'Those are my pain au chocolat!' Molly said. 'That was my tree outside my mouse hole!'

Henry stopped smiling and looked very sad. 'Oh gosh,' he said. 'I am very sorry. I didn't think the tree belonged to anyone. I didn't see your mouse hole.'

'I only need a very small hole, because I am only a very small mouse,' Molly replied.

'I am so very sorry!' Henry apologised again. 'If I had known the tree belonged to someone I would not have taken them. They are cooking at the moment but when they are done please take them all back and enjoy your lunch. I will find something else to eat.'

As the pain au chocolat finished cooking, Henry looked very glum, so Rosie took Sam over to one side.

'Henry looks very sad. Now he doesn't have anything delicious to eat for lunch!' Rosie said.

'Poor Henry,' Sam replied. 'He didn't know they were Molly's or he wouldn't have taken them.'

'Look, Sam,' Rosie said, pointing at the pain au chocolat cooking over the fire. 'There is plenty of pain au chocolat for both of them.'

'You're right,' Sam agreed.

So Rosie and Sam went over to where Molly was sitting and waiting for the delicious lunch to cook.

'Molly,' Sam said. 'We think it would be very nice if you shared your pain au chocolat with Henry. He didn't mean to take them from you and he is very sorry for making a mistake.'

'Yes,' Rosie added. 'And there is plenty of pain au chocolat for both of you, and there will still be some spare!'

'I know!' Molly said. 'Why don't we ALL have pain au chocolat for lunch? You must be very hungry having helped me search all that time, and I want to say thank you for helping me! Like you say, there is plenty to go around!'

'That is a wonderful idea!' Rosie said.

A few moments later and the pain au chocolat were ready. 'Here you go,' said Henry, picking one up and offering it to Molly. 'Enjoy your pain au chocolat,' he added, with a deep, sad sigh.

'The first one is for you!' Molly said, and straight away they all saw Henry's face brighten up.

'Really? Do you mean it?' he said.

'Yes,' Molly replied. 'After all, you cooked them for us!'

And so they passed out the pain au chocolat and they all had a delicious lunch.

When they had finished Rosie stood up and said 'That was lovely, but we should go home. Our mummy and daddy will start to worry if we're not home soon.'

'Thank you, Sam and Rosie, for all your help,' Molly said. 'I couldn't have found my pain au chocolat without you.'

'You're welcome, Molly,' Sam said.

'Remember, Henry,' Rosie added. 'In the future, you should always ask before you take something. It might belong to someone else.'

'I will always ask from now on!' Henry replied.

So Rosie and Sam walked back home, and Molly came with them.

When they got to the garden Molly said 'Thanks again, Rosie and Sam. If you ever want some pain au chocolat just look for the little mouse hole with the little pain au chocolat tree outside and come and say hello. We can have a delicious lunch together.'

'That would be lovely!' Rosie said.

'I told Henry that he can come by any time and have lunch with me as well, as long as he lets me know beforehand!' Molly added.

'Goodbye Molly, thanks for taking us on an adventure!' Sam said as they both waved to their new friend.

'Goodbye, Rosie and Sam. See you soon!' and with that Molly disappeared into her mouse hole, and Rosie and Sam went back into their garden.

When they got back into the garden their mummy was sat outside.

'And where have you two little rascals been?' she asked.

'We've been on an adventure!' they both shouted.

El Presidente's New Clothes

__Graham Kidd__ - 'A story about a despot (in a modern context, not as a fairy tale) who realises the error of his ways, and sets about reforming his country to benefit his people. How he goes about it, and the consequences are your choice.'

Juan Carlos surveyed the sunset as he sipped a cold Daiquiri.

It was the height of summer, and he appreciated the icy cocktail in the heat of the early evening. As the sun dipped below the horizon the lights in Antemacassar began to twinkle on, one by one. As if someone had laid the stars out on the ground before him. Nothing more than a man of his great status deserved.

The heat was relentless, so he took another sip of his drink before placing it on the table in front of him. Inspecting the selection of fresh fruits that lay on a silver platter he opted for a slice of pineapple.

He clicked his fingers and one of his palace servants appeared and began to fan him with a large palm leaf.

The assassin crept along the corridors of the palace. Having to dress all in black in this heat was almost unbearable. But her mission was of such vital importance that she forced herself to push on.

If her intel was correct the President would be out on his private balcony enjoying an evening drink, as he did every night. She sneaked into his private chambers and, as expected, the French windows were wide open. The cooler night air blowing through was a relief.

There was a silhouette in the doorway. Allowing her eyes to readjust to the light, she determined that it was not El Presidente. Whoever it was was waving a fan up and down. She cursed her luck.

Collateral damage was regrettable but necessary for the completion of her mission. Drawing her baton she tiptoed up behind the servant and, placing a hand over his mouth, knocked him out. She bore the body down to the ground silently, and now only her target was left in front of her. She crept forward. It was too late to turn back now. And too late for El Presidente. Almost too late.

'I say, Gilberto,' Juan Carlos said, without turning around. 'It's still quite warm, do start fanning again.'

The assassin froze in her tracks. Juan Carlos waited for a second, then turned around to see why his servant had not started fanning again. He let out a gasp.

To the assassin's surprise, Juan Carlos shrank down and cowered behind the table.

'Please don't kill me!' he cried. 'I'm too important to die!'

'You coward!' the Assassin roared. 'You have run this country into the ground and ruined her people and you don't even have the courage to face me like a man?'

'No,' Juan Carlos smiled. 'But my friends do.' The Assassin cursed and turned around.

Two large men holding AK47 assault rifles confronted her. The bastard hadn't been cowering, he had been reaching for a panic button under the table. Her baton clanged as it hit the floor of the balcony.

The butt of one of the Kalashnikovs was introduced rather forcefully to her head, and everything went dark.

When she woke up again it was morning, although it was hard to tell. Very little light came in through the barred window high up in her prison cell.

Her head was still ringing from the blow she had received, but in the gloom she could make out the cell door. She could also hear activity behind it.

She heard the sound of metal scraping against metal as the door was unlocked. It creaked open, probably for dramatic effect, she noted. That was El Presidente's style.

It surprised her to see El Presidente Juan Carlos himself enter the room, flanked by bodyguards. She wondered if it was the same two that had accosted her last night, but all goons start to look the same after a while.

El Presidente was grinning unpleasantly. He was holding the baton she had brought to his chambers the previous night.

'I suppose you are wondering why you are not already dead,' El Presidente said.

'Not really,' she replied.

'Hah! Such impudence.'

Without another word he swung the baton at her face, stopping millimetres away. She did not flinch. Still smiling, the leader of the country turned to his thugs.

'Ruben, Ricardo. You can leave THIS one to me. Do shut the door on your way out.'

The two men shared an apprehensive glance but obeyed. They had not gotten this far by questioning the decisions of their glorious leader, after all. The door creaked again as it swung shut behind them.

'You can beat me all you want, I won't tell you anything!' the Assassin said.

She spat defiantly at the man she loathed so much. Making sure to show no fear she closed her eyes as she expected a swift and painful response. But none was forthcoming.

After a few seconds, she thought she could hear a sobbing noise. She very carefully opened her eyes and saw that El Presidente was crying. He was sat, hunched, in the corner of the cell.

He wiped her spit from his face with a silk scarf embroidered with his coat of arms. She knew that he had spent a significant amount of taxpayers money designing the symbol.

'Why?' he asked, meekly. His voice was so quiet that she could barely hear him. 'Why did you try and kill me?'

The assassin sat in silence, trying to take in what she was seeing. She wondered if she was hallucinating after the bump on the head. She rearranged her hands in their bonds behind the chair to pinch herself on the arm. It was not a dream or a hallucination.

'I...don't think I understand?' she managed, finally.

'You tried to kill me last night, yes? You did not sneak into my private chambers and incapacitate one of my finest servants to deliver me a kiss-o-gram, correct?'

'Well, no. I mean yes. I did try and kill you.'

This was all a bit too much for her in her already confused state. She wondered if he was trying to trick her into giving up information, but she didn't think he was that smart. Ducking to push a button under a table was about the limit to El Presidente's cunning.

'Then why?' he remonstrated. 'What have I ever done wrong?!' At that, the Assassin let out a laugh. 'What?' the man continued. 'I genuinely don't know. The people are happy, the country is prospering. I am universally adored!'

'Are you listening to yourself?' she answered. 'None of those things are true. The people are dying. Unemployment has reached 50%. Poverty is everywhere! How can you not see this?'

'Lies! My advisors tell me that everyone has a job, everyone is gaining wealth by the day. Disease and poverty are at an all-time low!'

'Then it is your so-called 'advisors' who are lying to you, Presidente. Not I. When did you last take a trip around the city, to see your people?'

'Why only last week! The people were smiling and waving. They all looked delighted to see me!'

'They are actors. Paid by your cronies to convince you everything is OK! They smile because they fear for their lives! How many decisions do you make yourself?' El Presidente thought for a moment.

'I...' he began. 'But I tell...' he stuttered. 'I asked...' His train of thought reached its terminus as he trailed off. 'It is they who run the country, isn't it?' he said, a hint of sadness and terrible realisation creeping over his voice.

'You are a puppet, Presidente. A figurehead. Those bastards run the country into the ground and make it look like your fault. You take the blame and they get away with no repercussions! They make sure you see only good things to keep you in the dark and perpetrate crimes in your name!'

'I thought things were going so well! I thought I was doing right by the people,' he replied, slumping back into the corner. 'What can I do? I must make this right!'

'Presidente, you were having people taken away and killed by the army. You are still complicit in this.'

'I know now what I have done, and I will pay the appropriate price. But we must remove these men from office immediately. And then remove their heads from their shoulders soon afterward. Nobody, and I mean NOBODY, makes a fool of Juan Carlos!'

'Not exactly the right sentiment,' the assassin replied, 'but close enough.'

'I still have friends in the army from when I was an officer,' El Presidente said, thinking aloud. 'One of them is now a Field Marshal. I had hoped to never call on his...services but it is evident that the time is right. I must go. There are arrangements to be made.'

'And what will become of me?' the assassin asked

'You have opened my eyes,' he replied. 'You are free to go.'

El Presidente moved towards her and drew a knife from his belt, cutting her bonds.

'Stay here for 30 minutes after I am gone. Then, tap the smooth brick on the back wall three times, and you will be free. It is down in the corner.'

He banged on the door.

'I am done with this miscreant!' he yelled to the waiting guards, who opened the door a fraction to let him out.

He winked at her as he left.

Two days later she reached a safe house. It was as far away from the capital city as she could get in that short a time. She was pleased to see several of her friends were there.

'Gonzala!' one shouted as she came through the door. 'Where have you been?! We gave you up for dead!'

'I was...indisposed.' she replied.

'You've got to see the news!' her comrade said. 'Something amazing has happened!'

They turned on the television to the state-owned channel. The news ticker read 'PRESIDENTE JUAN CARLOS STANDS DOWN, FLEES COUNTRY. GOVERNMENT HIGH COMMAND IMPRISONED BY ARMY.'

Behind the ticker, a man was being interviewed. According to the television, he was Field Marshall Mikel Acuna.

'Field Marshall, is this a coup?' the reporter asked.

'No, I am operating on behalf of our now ex-Presidente. He has ordered that the army seize the country's high command on grounds of treason. Democratic elections are to be held immediately.'

'Do you have any idea who will run for office?' the reporter asked. 'In his letter to me, El Presidente mentioned that the right people would know what they had to do.'

Gonzala switched the television off.

'Excuse me, everyone,' she said. 'I have work to do.'

Two weeks later Juan Carlos emerged on to the balcony and sipped at a Daiquiri. The weather here in the Strasbourg was not as forgiving as it was in his own country. But the Daiquiri reminded him of home.

Tomorrow he would hand himself over to the International Court of Human Rights. There he would petition to be tried for the actions of his government. But for one last night he sipped at his drink and enjoyed the cool breeze on his face.

Around the World in 80 Pages

Steve Newman - 'Author can't think of a plot, goes in search of one.'

Fred sat down in front of his computer and stared at the blank document open on the screen in front of him.

His face was lit by the glow of the screen. He insisted that tonight was the night he finally started the greatest novel ever written.

But every night it was the same old story, or rather lack of story. After an hour of staring at the screen he got distracted by social media. He would close the laptop and insist that tomorrow would be the night.

This night was no different. He sat there, the cursor blinking at him accusingly. *'What are you waiting for?'* it challenged. *'Don't you have what it takes to write a novel?'* He was starting to think that he didn't.

By this stage, he was begging for another distraction. Any excuse to take his mind off writing and on to other things. A notification popped up in the corner of his screen. An email! Perfect. Better reply to that immediately. Fred clicked through to his mailbox.

It was only spam. He cursed. TravelWise with another one of their promotional emails. Cheap holidays to places he wouldn't visit if someone threatened to shove an angry ferret down his trousers.

He switched the window back to the word processor and leaned on his hands. If only he could think of a plot. He knew he had a novel in him. I mean, everyone did, right? Why would he be any different?

He racked his brain for inspiration, but his mind began to wander. Maybe he needed a holiday after all, to get the creative juices flowing. He clicked back on to the email to see what dreary destinations were on offer today.

Scrolling through the offers the idea of a weekend in a cottage in the Brecon Beacons was underwhelming. A wildlife tour of Sussex did not enthuse him, and he was downright disgusted at the thought of a Club 18-30 booze up for a week in Marbella. But at the very bottom of the email, something caught his eye.

A year-long around the world tour.

As he scanned the list of stops his interest piqued. Rome, Athens, Budapest, Prague. And those were just some of the ones in Europe.

He baulked at the price: £10,000. But it was all-inclusive and he HAD gotten a big bonus. He clicked the link and entered his credit card before his brain could catch up and change its mind. The very next day he would quit his job.

If a round the world trip didn't inspire him to write the greatest novel in history he didn't know what would.

Two weeks later Fred was all packed and ready to go. He sat in the departure lounge at Heathrow airport and flicked through a magazine. His adventure would begin in New York City.

The adrenaline was flowing. He hadn't so much as left Berkshire before, let alone Europe. And here he was preparing to jet out to the Big Apple and the USA. A tingle of excitement ran down his back.

BING BONG.

A nearby Tannoy kicked into life.

'Would all passengers for Zoom Air flight ZM9934 please head to Gate 42 as the plane is now ready for boarding, thank you.'

BING BONG.

It was time.

Fred spent the next two months in North America. He climbed the Empire State Building, swam with dolphins in Florida, hiked the Grand Canyon and camped in the wilds of Yellowstone Park. He watched ice hockey in Vancouver, went on a Moose safari in Nova Scotia, and celebrated Cinco de Mayo in Tijuana.

But in spite of all his adventures, he still could not think of a plot for his novel. Every situation he found himself in, he felt as though he had been here before. Or, rather, someone else had been there first and written about it in some way or another. The Great American Novel had already been written several times after all.

Even Mexico and Canada felt like they had been done to death already in literature, film or television. There was nothing new to write about. No new story to tell. And so he moved on.

After he left North America, Fred moved on to Japan. Here, he felt sure that a plot would present itself. After all, Japanese culture was so different from that in the West he was sure something would start his mind working.

But he was disappointed to find that again he didn't feel all that inspired. He sat on a bench in Disneyland Tokyo, looking out over the bay, where he could see Mount Fuji in the distance and sighed.

He readjusted his Mickey ears and took a bite from his toffee apple. The problem with Japanese culture was that it was TOO different. Sure, he felt that the homogeneity of

British culture had stifled his creativity. But Japan was a swing too far in the other direction.

Everywhere he turned people were doing interesting and unusual things. People having food and drink that he had never tasted, games and sports he had never imagined. As for the theatre and television, well it was a lot different to Takeshi's Castle, that's for certain.

It was too much. Someone like Fred could not relate to the common Japanese man. He did not feel as though he could tell his story. He had failed to find what he was looking for under the pagodas, so once again he moved on.

His next stop was the Asian mainland. He spent some time trekking the Great Wall, and yet more time still on the backpacker trail around Thailand, Cambodia, and Vietnam.

In a hostel in Bangkok, he found love, or at least what passed for it on the road. He spent two weeks exploring the Thai countryside with a Canadian girl. Their passion burned bright before dying out as they both had to go their separate ways.

As he prepared to move on to Mumbai he wondered if he would ever see her again. As the plane made its ascent out of Thailand he came to a realisation. In the fortnight they had spent together he had completely failed to think of a plot for his novel.

He scanned back through his memories of the previous fourteen days and they were all taken up by her. He couldn't remember anything else from his time in South East Asia. All he could think about was the girl he spent the time with.

He sat back in his seat and smiled. But a small part of him remained sad that he had still not yet found the story that he was so desperately looking for.

He mused further on his failure to think of a plot as he wandered the streets of Mumbai, and it almost cost him dearly. As he wandered around a young pickpocket snatched his messenger bag from his shoulder.

Spotting the miscreant, Fred gave chase immediately. He was glad of the parkour lessons he had taken at university. The small child was nimble and quick, and knew this area of the city well.

They leapt over boxes and street stalls and weaved between people as the chase went on. Eventually, his superior speed paid off and he caught the child, snatching his satchel back in annoyance. He looked through to see if anything was missing and cursed. His notebook, on which he had written what few ideas he had come up with, had fallen out during the chase. That would set him back another couple of weeks.

At the end of the year he returned to his parents' home in Berkshire empty-handed and despondent.

None of his friends could understand why he was so sad. He had, after all, just spent a year travelling to some of the world's most exotic locations and seeing some wonderful and fantastic things.

After a few weeks of doing the rounds of visits to friends and family he settled back down into a normal routine.

His uncle found him a job in the local supermarket while he looked for something more long term. But every night it was the same as before he had left. He would sit in front of the computer for an hour or more at a time and stare at a blank screen. All that time and all that money wasted, and he hadn't come back with a single idea for a story.

After the third night in a row of sitting and staring at the blinking cursor, he gave up. Perhaps what they all said was a lie. Maybe everyone didn't have a novel in them. He sighed and wondered what he could do next.

'Oh well,' he said to himself. 'I suppose I could write up my travel journals. Though I can't think why anyone would want to read any of that...'

Taking a sip from his mug of coffee Fred stretched his fingers out and began to type. Several hours later the sound birds singing outside his window startled him. He opened the curtains and daylight streamed inside, forcing him to blink to adjust. It had felt like he had been writing for no time at all, but he had been up all night.

He looked at the document and saw that he had written ten thousand words. Maybe he didn't have a novel in him, but he had inadvertently found his muse after all.

Paw of the Worlds

Sophie Green - *'A sci-fi story featuring at least one alien spaceship. Oh, and I'd like it set in Harrow. And during the 1930's.'*

The disc-shaped craft spun silently over the dark streets of London. Its progress went unnoticed on the ground, in part because of its cloaking device. Mostly, though, it was because radar was a nascent discipline. It had yet to be adapted to detect alien spacecraft. Anyway, with the situation on mainland Europe as troubling as it was, all dishes pointed firmly in the direction of France and Germany.

The extraterrestrials within observed that the city was quieter and calmer than others they had observed.

Some were hives of activity. Bustling centres that never slept, or busied with the industry of wartime. This hustle and urgency had not yet reached the city below them, but they expected that it would, given time.

It seemed to the creatures like a good place to test the waters of interplanetary communication. They directed their craft downwards and landed on a green, open space. It happened to be Harrow Recreation Ground.

The ship disengaged its cloaking device. The disc-shaped craft was made from a material that glimmered even when no light was present. There was little detail to the exterior of the ship. It was largely smooth, excepting the spindly little legs that protruded from the bottom.

The ship began to hiss and lines appeared in the previously smooth exterior. A metal ramp lowered slowly to the ground, and the creatures emerged.

There were four of them in total, and none looked alike. In contrast to humanity's dominance of earth, they came from a planet where several species had developed at a similar pace. Between them, they ruled Frolix IX amicably.

One was a humanoid, roughly seven feet tall and thinly built with blue skin and six eyes. Another was an eight-legged horse-like creature with two heads. The third was no larger than a human baby and floated about five feet from the ground. The last alien creature seemed almost reptilian and crawled around on four legs.

Of course, none of this was relevant to the welcoming committee that greeted the landing party from Frolix IX. As it was 2 o'clock in the morning on a Tuesday this comprised of a trio of stray dogs that lived in the park.

Until the craft revealed itself they had been foraging for scraps of food in a nearby bin. When they saw the ship appear in front of their eyes, they were not amazed. At least, no more amazed than if they had spotted a new rabbit to chase. Or found a new and interesting odour to investigate before replacing it with their own.

They were, after all, dogs. Everything is amazing to dogs.

The lizard-like creature crawled down the now fully extended ramp. It studied the three dogs. The canines' interest was piqued such that they had discarded the remains of the sandwich they had been chewing on.

Looking directly at the dogs, the creature opened its jaw. It emitted a fast burst of speech in a language that had never before been spoken or heard on planet Earth.

The closest of the dogs, a mongrel, who had understood none of it cocked its head slightly. It gave an exploratory bark.

The lizard creature turned and looked at its compatriots at the top of the ramp. They began to descend to ground level. When they reached the floor the humanoid alien began to tap away on a screen that was attached to its wrist.

'Detecting language,' it informed its friends in their shared native language. A few seconds later the results came back. 'Language unknown. The closest approximation is Canin language from Barkulus IV. Patching in translation field now.'

The alien pressed a button on its wrist screen, which caused a holographic field to appear around the landing site of the craft.

'Translation field active,' the alien added.

'What does 'translation field active' mean?'

The aliens who had been communing amongst themselves, turned to face the source of the question, which it seemed was one of the earthlings. The humanoid stepped forward.

'It means that through the use of our technology we have created a field. Within the boundaries of that field we should be able to understand one another.'

'Cool,' said the dog, not having understood a word. 'Got any food, mate?' it added hopefully.

'Err...' said the humanoid. 'We have come to initiate interplanetary discussions to aid the furthering of the planet known throughout the galaxy as 'Earth'.'

'Wouldn't know anything about that, mate,' replied the dog who had assumed leadership. 'Nice trick though,' he added, referring to the shimmering field of holographic light. 'Very pretty.'

'Thank you...' the humanoid continued.

'My mate over there can sit if someone asks and he feels like it and there's a treat involved. He's clever.'

'Quite,' the alien responded, its tone becoming somewhat strained. The nuances of tone were lost on the dogs, however. Outside of loud and angry and soft and friendly what more could you need to understand?

'What is your name?' the floating creature interjected, in an attempt to save its exasperated friend.

The lead dog cocked his head and considered the question. Part of this consideration involved a quick lick of his unmentionables. Then, after a thoughtful scratch behind the ear, he felt ready to answer.

'Don't know. Don't really have one. That over there is Rufus.' He indicated at one of his canine colleagues with his head. Rufus was a bulldog. He was currently investigating the inviting smells of the space ship's small legs. He prepared to make them smell more like he did instead, which is to say not very nice. 'Nobody ever gave me a name, though. People shout 'Get out of it' at me a lot though, so maybe it's that?'

'I am Gagargaflax,' the humanoid replied. 'This is Morpu, Jajjjarsxxxe, and Lo,' he added, indicating the lizard, the floating creature and the horse-like creature in turn. 'We are emissaries from the planet of Frolia, who wish to include Earth in relations with the wider galaxy. We are here to meet with representatives of the people of Earth. We wish to form a lasting bond and bring our two societies closer together. As such we would be extremely grateful if you could take us to your leader.'

Rufus the Bulldog returned, fresh from his work re-scenting the alien spaceship. He had returned to investigate if there were any other interesting things to piss on.

'I couldn't help but overhear mate,' he said. 'But we don't really have a leader,' he said. 'This one here though, he's definitely the smartest of all us what live round 'ere.'

He attempted to gesticulate with his head to the dog now known as 'Get Out Of It', but failed, owing to his lack of neck. He barely managed to stop himself from falling over.

'Very well then,' Gagargaflax said, returning his attention to the lead hound. 'I would be most grateful if you could answer a question for me. On our way here we passed over many lands that seemed troubled. Smoke was belching from factories and what appeared to be machines of war were being readied. We wish only to commune with peaceful planets. What is the meaning of the things we have seen?'

'Dunno, mate,' Get Out Of It replied, 'No wars going on around here. As you can see.'

'Yeah,' Rufus added, 'As you can see. Anyways, if anything like a war was going on around here, he'd know about it. Because he's smart, you see.'

'Indeed...' Gagargaflax replied. 'If you will excuse me for a second.'

Gagargaflax shuffled off to his compatriots.

'They are certainly...unconventional,' Morpu observed.

'Indeed,' Lo added. 'Are we sure we want creatures like this to be part of our galactic alliance?'

'I agree they are not your...usual candidates for membership in the alliance. But Earth sits on an important strategic point in the galaxy. It would be beneficial to make a pact with the denizens of the planet. The small one appears to be the planetary leader.'

'I agree with Gagargaflax,' Jajjjarsxxxe interjected. 'We can instruct them in the proper etiquette of the galactic council later. Right now we must secure their bond of friendship. Then we may, in turn, secure their planet for its strategic value.'

'You are always one to think of the long term, Jajjjarsxxxe,' Lo replied. 'Very well, we will take them with us back to Frolix IX for negotiations and the initiation ceremony.'

Gagargaflax returned to the waiting dogs, who were investigating some rotten old boots.

'My friends, I have wonderful news.'

'Oh yeah?' asked Get Out Of It. 'What's that then?'

'We wish to offer you a seat on the galactic council, and Earth a place in the galactic alliance.'

'OK.'

'Do you...err, do you accept?'

'Will there be food?'

'Yes, there will be as much food as you wish.'

Get Out Of It remained skeptical. 'Can Rufus come?' he asked, testing the water to see how far he could go.

'Yes, Rufus can come.' Gagargaflax was clearly getting frustrated again.

'What about Cheesy …and Snuffles?'

'Argh, yes, whoever you want!'

Get Out Of It racked his brains, which didn't take very long, to see if there was anything else he could scam from this well-meaning creature. Alas, he could think of nothing.

'Alright then. Let's go.'

And so Get Out Of It, Rufus, and Cheesy, who had spent much of the conversation with the aliens stuck face down in the bin, were taken on board the Frolixian ship. After picking up their friend Snuffles from underneath the canal bridge, they set off amongst the stars.

It was not long before the dogs' behaviour became intolerable. The Frolixians quickly discovered that leg-humping wasn't the standard Earth greeting. They agreed that Earth's strategic value was not worth it, and the dogs were returned to Earth before they had even reached Frolix IX.

The Frolixians vowed that no member of the galactic alliance would ever return to the planet. Earth's other species were doomed to never encounter an alien race again, for as long as they existed.

But the dogs got a free meal out of it, and in the end, that was all they really cared about.

A Gentleman Caller

Sadhya Rippon - 'Death comes to Northanger Abbey.'

'I say, Ellie,' General Tilney bellowed up the stairs. 'Do hurry up with powdering your nose. Your gentleman caller will be here soon. I shall be very cross indeed if you are not presentable when he arrives. He's a very important and wealthy man, you know!'

Eleanor ignored her father's yelling. She had little desire to meet any of the suitors her father had chosen for her. It was so old-fashioned, and anyway, he would doubtless be a crashing bore.

Eleanor wished awfully that Mama was still alive. She would have had a thing or two to say about her daughter being married off against her will, and no mistake.

She harrumphed and decided it was better to play along for her father's sake, at least for the time being. Perhaps this gentleman wouldn't take interest in a lowly General's daughter like herself. Then Papa would leave her be again for a little while. That is until he latched on to the son of another of Bath's social elite and insisted upon arranging courtship.

It was not that she did not wish to meet a young man. She very much hoped to one day marry. That day was simply a lot further away than her father wished it to be. She wanted to find someone right for her. Like her brother Henry had with young Catherine. Not someone whom her father could brag about over dinner at the club.

She ran a pearl-backed brush through her hair and wondered what her latest suitor would be like. If she had to guess it would be the son of one of father's military friends. A wealthy Field Marshal's boy with aspirations to be an officer in one of the King's regiments no doubt. She sighed. Her father was very predictable. He had no care or idea of what she wanted in a husband.

'Eleanor Margaret Tilney!' the voice bellowed again from below. 'I insist you come downstairs immediately!'

'Coming, father!' she replied and finished brushing her hair. Oh well, she thought. What was it those military types said? Once more unto the breach?

The carriage wheels crunched along the gravel driveway. The path led through impressive wrought iron gates to the main entrance of Northanger Abbey. The coach and the horses were as dark as night, and the driver wore top and tails of funereal black.

Fothershaw the gardener observed the vehicle as he watered the flower beds in the Abbey's sizeable front garden. It had lacquer so dark that it was almost as if it absorbed light from around it. He wondered who might be inside.

Ethel, one of the scullery maids, said she had overheard Simpkins the butler say that Miss Eleanor was to receive a gentleman caller.

If this was the gentleman in question then he was a gloomy bugger and no mistake, Fothershaw thought as he turned back to the petunias.

The carriage rolled to a halt. An immaculately dressed footman stepped forward, opened the door and bowed low.

'Welcome to Northanger Abbey, Mr. Death,' he said.

'IT IS JUST DEATH.' The man's voice was deep, ponderous. The footman could have sworn that it echoed.

'Excuse me, sir?' the footman replied, unfolding from his bow.

'IT IS JUST DEATH. NOT MR.'

'Very well, sir. Mr. Death was your father, eh?' the footman quipped, in a failed attempt at being jovial.

'NO.'

'Oh. Er. Very well, sir,' the footman said, learning a valuable lesson in choosing his battles. He looked Not Mr. Death up and down. The striking thing about him was that he was covered from head to toe in a huge black robe.

This was strange because it was a rather warm summer's day. Additionally the robe covered him so well that you could not see the man's face through the cowl. He strained his eyes. It was as if an invisible barrier rebuffed his attempts. And those of any light that happened to stray into the vicinity.

The strange man wandered off in the direction of the house without another word. He was the butler's problem now. The footman felt a palpable sense of relief. As if the weight of an immense dread had been lifted from his shoulders.

'Welcome, Sir, to Northanger Abbey,' Simpkins the butler said. He bowed even deeper than the footman, as the robed gentleman entered the house. Unlike the footman, Simpkins was forearmed with the knowledge of the visitor's little quirk regarding his name and chose to simply not use it. 'Sir, please do follow me through to the drawing-room. General Tilney is waiting. And I understand that Lady Eleanor will be descending from her chambers forthwith.'

Remaining mysteriously silent, the visitor held out a bony hand towards the butler. The hand contained a rather crooked looking scythe with a keen blade. Simpkins realised that he had not noticed the tool before. His brain was now running several simultaneous marathons to catch up with his eyes. Eventually, it decided it wasn't worth the effort and decided it was better to be ignorant.

Without recalling his ordering it to, the butler's hand reached out and took the scythe.

'Would Sir like me to take his robe also. Sir must be AWFULLY warm.'

'NO,' the man said. A few seconds later, after the butler had stood there in rather stunned silence, he added 'THANK YOU.'

'Very well,' Simpkins managed. 'If Sir would care to follow me...'

The butler walked off rather more quickly than usual in the direction of the drawing-room. He was not concerned at this point about whether the visitor was following him or not. Upon reaching the doors, he pushed them wide open. The General and Eleanor were waiting inside.

'Ah!' the General roared as he left his seat. 'Death, my good friend, it has been too long.'

'INDEED, GENERAL. I HAD NOT EXPECTED TO SEE YOU AGAIN FOR...SOME TIME AFTER OUR LAST MEETING.'

'Well quite. It was such a shame that we had to meet under such terrible circumstances. But every cloud has a silver lining! And whilst I lost my dear and beloved wife that day, I am glad to say that I gained a friend.'

The General turned to his daughter, who remained seated.

'Death was present when your mother passed away, dear,' he offered by way of explanation.

'Oh, I say!' Eleanor exclaimed as she rose from her seat. 'Are you a doctor?'

'NO.'

'A mortician, then?'

'OF SORTS. YOU MIGHT CALL ME AN...INTERESTED PARTY.'

'You knew my mother well then?'

'YOU COULD SAY THAT I KNEW HER BETTER THAN
MOST...'

'Oh you simply must tell me about her some time. I
knew very little of her myself.' Eleanor cast a mournful glance
out of the window. 'I do miss Mama.'

General Tilney walked over to his daughter and put a
consoling arm around her.

'We all do, Ellie, we all do. But come, Death here has
not come to speak of the departed. Please do take a seat, my
friend.'

'I WOULD PREFER TO STAND,' Death replied. 'TELL
ME, GENERAL, WHY DID YOU SUMMON ME HERE? I AM NOT IN
THE HABIT OF MAKING HOUSE CALLS WITHOUT A SPECIFIC
PURPOSE.'

'Well, forgive me for being so bold, but Eleanor here
has been looking for a suitor for some time. I have yet to come
up with an appropriate match,' the General began. 'I was
taking an afternoon stroll a week ago and saw several men
harvesting wheat in a field. For some inexplicable reason it
made me think of you, and by Jove, you seem as good a match
as any.'

'THESE MEN,' Death replied. 'WHAT WOULD YOU SAY
THE EXPRESSION ON THEIR FACE WAS AS THEY WERE REAPING
IN THE HARVEST?'

The General scratched his head, a touch perplexed by
the question.

'Well, I didn't pay particular attention to their faces,'
he said. 'But if I was pushed I'd say they were looking quite
grim at the time.'

'AH,' Death replied, sipping a brandy that no-one
could recall giving him. 'THAT WOULD EXPLAIN THAT THEN.'

'So, what do you say, Death, old friend? Would you be
interested in courting my daughter?'

'MY WORK DOES NOT TRADITIONALLY ALLOW TIME
FOR COURTSHIP,' the Grim Reaper replied. He took another

sip from the glass he held in his skeletal hand. It seemed to Eleanor that in the robe he was wearing, taking a drink without spilling it all down himself ought to be a logistical impossibility. 'BUT IT IS SOLITARY WORK, AND I HAVE WONDERED WHAT IT WOULD BE LIKE TO ENGAGE IN THE HUMA...I MEAN, NORMAL COURTSHIP RITUALS. VERY WELL, AS LONG AS LADY ELEANOR IS AMENABLE.'

'I shall have to give it some thought,' Eleanor replied, cautiously. 'I mean, father might call you an old friend but I've never met you before. Perhaps we can meet for dinner and talk further?'

'VERY WELL,' Death replied, bowing rather stiffly. 'I SHALL COLLECT YOU AT 8 PM ON SATURDAY.'

After Death had left, and the sense of general unease had lifted, General Tilney sat down with his daughter in the drawing-room.

'Well, Ellie, that was a step in the right direction. Why him and not the others?'

'I haven't agreed to court him fully yet, father,' his daughter reminded him. 'But he seemed...different. Not the usual calibre of well-dressed ape that you present to me. I am willing to give him a chance. Do tell me what he was doing in the Abbey when mother died.'

'You know, my dear, I don't really know now that you come to mention it,' the General replied, stroking his chin. 'I only noticed him there at the bedside in her final moments, but it felt as though he had been there forever. He disappeared rather quickly afterwards. It was a sad moment for all and I suspected he had gone to grieve in private.'

'How odd,' Eleanor mused. 'And you haven't seen him since?'

'Not until today...' the General said, tailing off until another thought grabbed him. 'Do you know what else is strange? It's the darnedest thing, but it has been a decade since your mother's passing and the chap hasn't aged a day.'

WEEK 8

Thijs is the Life

Louise Harper - *'A day in the life of the man who 'thumbs' the pizza dough in the 'handmade' pizza factory.'*

Thijs van der Oetker considered himself to be a well-read man. Or rather others considered him to be well-read, and he considered himself well-listened. Thijs worked at the Toscana Bene Authentic Italian Pizza and Pasta factory (based in Groningen in the Netherlands). The job allowed for a lot of introspection.

His job paid minimum-wage, and he only did it to pay the bills. He was not a man that craved possessions, wealth or career advancement. He sought only knowledge. As long as he had enough money to buy food for himself and his dog and have a little kept aside for some more books, then he was a happy man indeed.

That was why, for 10 years now, he had been the man whose job it was to thumb the pizza dough out into the shape of a pizza base. He could now do this with his eyes shut (literally), and his hands tied behind his back (metaphorically). He worked far more efficiently when he had a new audiobook playing through his headphones.

His friends and family did not understand why Thijs loved his job so much. Surely, they berated him, he must aspire to more? Did he have no ambition, no dream they wondered aloud? Thijs always told them that his dream was to learn and that he was doing that every single day.

The reaction was always the same. They shook their head and wandered off to talk to someone else at the party. A 30-year-old with no desire for career progression was a lost cause. Thijs saw it differently. He believed that if you enjoyed what you did then why aspire to move up to a position that you would find dull or be bad at?

Of course, he didn't exactly ENJOY thumbing pizza bases into circles, nobody did. After a couple of years, he couldn't even make a game out of it anymore. They didn't call it menial labour to fill space at the top of the job advert. What he enjoyed was getting to listen to someone talk about an interesting subject for 8 hours a day. And no one bothered him whilst he did it.

When the first ball of dough came along the conveyor in the morning he tuned out and listened to whatever was coming into his ears. To Thijs, this was paradise.

Over the last ten years, he had consumed more books than the average university professor would in their entire academic career. He had listened to books about music. Textbooks on physics, chemistry, and biology. Histories, psychology studies, philosophy, and almost all the classic novels.

He could probably speak about 6 languages fluently, if only he had someone to speak them to. And when no new tome inspired him he would switch for a while to classical music. He was an expert in the works of the Viennese masters. He could hum the whole of Tchaikovsky's back catalogue. You would struggle to find anyone more versed on the likes of Mendelssohn and Debussy.

In other words, he was a useful person to have on your side if you wanted to win a pub quiz. Not that he was generally allowed to enter them anymore. Every pub within a 20-mile radius of Groningen had banned him from their quiz nights.

He knew too much, they protested. It wasn't fun for every other team to always come second, they reasoned. He was welcome to drink there as long as he kept his mouth shut, they compromised.

Thijs was happy with this arrangement, and to be honest, had even encouraged it on a couple of occasions. He did not learn to benefit himself financially. At least not in that way, and he definitely did not do it for his friends to scam a few Euros from an unsuspecting bar owner. He learned for himself. He learned because it made him happy.

Thijs awoke one morning with an ominous feeling in the pit of his stomach. He felt as though today was going to be an auspicious day for some reason. Although for the life of him he could not work out why.

As usual, he got up at 7.30 and fed his Dachshund, Sascha. His shift didn't start until 9am, and the factory was a leisurely 20-minute walk away on the other side of town.

Thijs always took his time over breakfast. He watched an episode of some TV show or other as he munched on his cornflakes and sipped at his orange juice. Currently, he was watching a series of short documentaries about whales. Finally, he had a quick shower and give Sascha a tummy rub before walking out of the door.

Just a typical start to a typical morning for Thijs. Though rather atypically he was then soaked to the skin by a passing bus driving through a puddle immediately upon leaving the house.

Thijs put this down to the ominous feeling he had when he woke up. He was determined not to let something like that bother him. After all, it was a beautiful summer's day, and the puddle was only left over from a summer shower the night before. He would dry off by the time he made it to work.

The rest of the journey was uneventful, which suited him fine. And by the time he walked through the employees' door in the factory he was bone dry again.

He hung his jacket up in his locker and got out his protective clothing. He set up his MP3 player and layered the uniform on top. Smock, overalls and then the apron. He made sure to press play before putting his gloves on.

Today's book was The Republic by Plato. He had only recently started on classical philosophy and wasn't sure how he felt about it all yet. But it was quite interesting to listen to and that was the main thing.

As the voice in his ears began discussing the formulation of the ideal Republic he walked to his station.

He greeted his colleagues Tomasz, Hilda, and Lena as he went by them in the corridors. They all smiled and waved back at him as he went past, but he noticed something different about them today. They all had a glint in their eye as if they all knew something that he didn't.

Hilda was the last one he passed. He got the same reaction from her as he had from the other two, so he stopped her to ask what was going on. With her best poker face, she replied that she had no idea what he was talking about. It was just a normal day. It was all she could do not to wink at him as he walked off.

By the time he reached his spot on the production floor, he had largely forgotten about it. He dismissed it as one of the silly jokes that the three were renowned for.

The first ball of dough of the day made its way down the conveyor belt. He cracked his knuckles and spread the dough out in its container as the voice in his ear explained Plato's theories about standing armies.

He went on doing his job, as he did every day, for an hour. At about 10am, had he been able to hear anything else above his headphones, he would have noticed the normally loud factory floor fall silent.

As it was, he just carried on thumbing pizza base after pizza base, paying no attention to what was going on around him. He did not notice that 250 of his fellow employees had gathered behind him, holding their breath.

As he completed the routine that he did 397 times a day -he had counted- he prepared himself for the next ball of dough. But the dough did not come. This had never happened before. In ten years Thijs had never had to wait for the dough to come. He was lost for words. He decided he had best alert his manager, so he pressed pause on his MP3 player and turned around.

He nearly jumped out of his skin when his colleagues all began whooping and cheering and letting off streamers. They were all wearing party hats. Thijs could only stare in bewilderment as a banner unfurled; it read 'Congratulations on Thumbing 1,000,000 Pizzas!' It had a crudely drawn pizza on it.

The factory owner, Mr. Wyk walked up to Thijs and clasped his hand on his shoulder.

'One million pizzas, boy!' he said. 'That's a hell of a lot of dough. Congratulations.'

'Thank you, sir,' Thijs replied, still gobsmacked. 'I don't know what to say...'

'We've got a special guest for you, too,' the owner continued.

Sascha the Dachshund was brought through the crowd on a little pillow. He was wearing a tiny party hat and wagging his tail very enthusiastically.

'Sascha!' Thijs shouted in excitement. 'But Mr. Wyk, animals aren't allowed on the production floor!'

Mr. Wyk smiled. 'I think that, on this occasion, we can make an exception.'

The factory closed for the rest of the day as all the employees were given the time off to attend a party thrown by Mr. Wyk in Thijs' honour. He never did get to finish The

Republic that day. But Thijs went to sleep that night with Sascha curled up at the foot of the bed knowing that it wasn't the end of the world. After all, tomorrow was another day. The beginning of another ten years and one million pizzas of what he hoped would be a happy and contented life.

Mind the Gap

Huw Lloyd Jones - 'Observations on the Northern Line.'

'Please mind the gap between the train and the platform.'

Amina heard the announcement on Highgate's public address system as she clattered down the escalator at full speed. She just avoided tripping over a stray suitcase. Her fellow passenger clearly hadn't received the memo about standing on the right.

As she reached the platform level she rushed around the corner to see the train doors shut in her face. She looked up at the information board to see how long it would be until the next Bank service. Eight minutes. Balls.

This was the third time this week, and it was only Wednesday. Every time she reached the platform, out of breath, just in time to catch the tail end of the driver's 'ready to depart' announcement.

Amina had been living in London for three weeks now, and her tube-fu didn't seem to be improving at all. When she was on the darn thing she was fine. But she had yet to master the art of timing her arrival with that of the relevant train.

She had taken to leaving for work 10 minutes earlier than she really needed to just so she wasn't late. Continual tardiness in your first fortnight on the job not generally considered a desirable trait in an employee, after all.

That morning, Amina made it into work with seconds to spare. She vowed that tomorrow, TOMORROW would be the day that she conquered the Northern Line.

The next morning saw Amina up bright and early and ready to go. To make sure her timing was perfect she had downloaded an app that told her when the next trains were due to leave.

She sat on the small sofa in her studio flat in Muswell Hill and stared at her phone. She knew that it was a 20 minute walk door-to-door from her flat to the station. She waited until the app told her that there was a Bank train in 22 minutes and set off along Muswell Hill Road with considerable purpose.

Amina approached the day with renewed vigour. The sun was shining, the air felt fresh in her lungs and when she smiled at people, they jolly well smiled back.

This feeling lasted right up until she got to the top of the hill leading up to Highgate station. As she rounded the corner she saw dozens of grumpy commuters milling around by the bus stop outside the station.

'What's going on?' she asked one of the people at the back of the queue.

'Northern Line is down both ways between Camden Town and High Barnet. Signal failure or something,' they replied and went back to their John le Carré novel.

Only the distraction of trying to cram on to a bus stopped Amina from exploding in apoplectic rage.

To make matters worse more people were arriving from down the hill and jostling past her to try and get on the bus. But there wasn't room for everyone. The closing door was met with observations about the bus driver's upbringing. One commuter noted the driver's propensity for intercourse with farmyard animals.

It was another ten minutes before Amina managed to squeeze on to a bus, and she was nearly 15 minutes late into the office that morning.

The next day was the same. When she left home her app told her that the trains were all running hunky-dory. By the time she reached the station, all hell had broken loose.

When she went to her friends for sympathy they rebuffed her.

'You shouldn't have moved somewhere on the Northern Line!' her friend Ashley berated. 'It's called the Misery Line for a reason!'

Every morning something else would go wrong. She would just miss the train. Or the staff would shrug their shoulders as she showed them the TfL app that said the Northern Line was running a good service.

She began to become paranoid that people at work didn't believe why she was late. None of THEM ever seemed to be late, or even close. It made no sense. Old Street, where she worked, was only on the Northern Line, so everyone else that got the tube must be in the same boat? It seemed not. How long would management accept that 'The Northern Line was buggered again!' before they called her for a disciplinary hearing?

The annoying thing was that it seemed to work fine in the evenings. When she came home from work there was never a problem. If she was going north the Nothern Line seemed content to play ball. Perhaps it had some kind of aversion to taking people in the opposite direction to its name. As if going southbound offended its very nature.

It became such a bugbear of Amina's that for a while barely a conversation went by without her friends inquiring about her plight. And she would answer, oh yes she would answer. Some learned to stop asking. At least if they didn't fancy being subjected to a 15 minute tirade about how TfL was out to get her. But those she hadn't seen in a while would inevitably fall into the trap and have their ears bent about the big conspiracy.

It had become an obsession. None of her friends or family understood her drive or determination to get one over on a public transport line. Words like 'irrational' and 'silly' were bandied about, particularly by her parents.

But Amina didn't need them. She was unwavering in her devotion to the cause of beating the Northern Line at its own game. She spent her evenings posting on forums. She read rambling posts about how someone was being victimised by the Victoria Line. She watched videos of distracted by the District Line. She commiserated with someone about how the DLR was designed to make their every living moment a waking nightmare.

She felt better knowing that there were others out there who were in the same predicament. People that shared the same single-minded desire to stick it to TfL right where it hurt.

Finally she worked up the courage and regaled the forum with her tale. Her thread got dozens of replies. The advice ranged from getting up half an hour earlier than normal to full-on camping under her desk at work. With a sleeping bag and everything.

As she read the suggestions she began to realise that she wasn't like these people after all. She went back and read some of the other threads. Some stories spoke about years of battling against one of the tube lines in an attempt to best it. She had only been trying for a month.

Amina stayed up late into the night and read these tales of woe and hardship. She made a vow to herself that she wasn't going to become one of these people. Their entire lives dedicated to achieving something that they have no real control over anyway. Some people were just naturally gifted in the ancient art of tube-fu, she decided. They could guarantee that they would be on time wherever they went. Others, such as she, were not so blessed, and were destined for a life of tardiness.

So the next day, feeling sanguine about her late-night epiphany, Amina deleted the TfL app. She walked to the station footloose, fancy free and with a smile on her face. When she walked through the station doors a mob of angry commuters awaited her. They were not being let down to the platforms because there was a broken down train in the tunnel between Archway and Tufnell Park.

She was 15 minutes late for work, but this time she didn't care. She had not let the tube get the better of her, and that was enough to keep her in a buoyant mood for the rest of the morning.

Amina sat in the break room at work and munched on a sandwich. Gerald, one of her colleagues, walked in and started fumbling with the buttons on the coffee machine.

'Hi, Gerald!' Amina said chirpily.

'Afternoon, Amina,' he replied as the coffee began to pour. 'You seem unusually happy today. Did you finally beat the beast?'

'No! Last night I had an epiphany and now I have found inner peace with regards to my commute. No longer will I worry about whether the Northern Line is going to be down, or if I'm going to be late to work. Que sera, sera and all that.'

'Well that's good to hear,' Gerald said with a smile on his face. 'I used to live in Muswell hill myself, you know. The Northern Line is a real bugger, isn't it? You know, after a while I realised that it was almost as easy to get here by going to Finsbury Park. I took the Victoria Line to Kings Cross and then got the bus. You have to change more but it only takes a couple of minutes longer and the Victoria Line is rarely down.'

Amina stared at him, mouth agape. She couldn't believe it. In three weeks it had never once occurred to her that she could go a different way. For the last month she had been infatuated to the point of mania with the idea of besting her nemesis. But not once had she thought about changing her route.

'Thanks, Gerald,' she said through gritted teeth, after what was probably far too long a silence, 'I'll give that a try.'

The next morning Amina was fifteen minutes early to work. As the days went by taking her new route she found that she was rarely late into the office. And she could hardly blame those hangovers on TfL now, could she?

The Spice is Right

Richard Griffiths - 'Observations on the price of nutmeg.'

'It's HOW much?!' Fred asked, taken aback by the grocer's response to his request for 50 grams of nutmeg.

'As I said, mate,' the shopkeeper replied, clearly uninterested in entering into a debate, 'that'll be a tenner.'

'Let me get this straight,' said Fred, clearly interested in entering into a debate. '£10?'

'£10.'

'For 50 grams of nutmeg?'

'For 50 grams of nutmeg.'

'50 grams of bloody nutmeg?'

'50 grams of, as you so eloquently put it,' the shopkeeper replied, turning the page of his newspaper and doing his best to not make eye contact, 'bloody nutmeg.'

'That,' said Fred, 'is a bloody ripoff.' And then he bought it anyway.

Fred would be the first to admit that 50 grams was, to the average person on the street, quite a lot of nutmeg. Normally he would have just refused to pay for it. But he had been asked to make a large batch of his famous pumpkin pie for the bake sale at his son's school. And the thought of shopping at a chain supermarket made Fred feel ill.

'Ten bloody pounds...' he muttered to himself as he walked out of the door. 'For some bloody nutmeg.'

'There's a global shortage,' a voice chimed in from behind him.

Fred turned to face the owner of the voice, who turned out to be a short middle-aged lady with wiry grey hair.

'Excuse me?' Fred replied.

'I said that there's a global shortage,' the woman repeated. 'Of nutmeg.'

'There's a global shortage of bloody nutmeg?'

'Yes, and it's driving the price through the roof. If you had bought that nutmeg a month ago it would have cost you half the price, if that.'

'How can there be a global shortage of nutmeg? It's a spice that literally grows on trees, not crude oil,' Fred said, a little flabbergasted.

'Well, you know how supply and demand works, right?' the woman replied. She either did not notice or chose to ignore the rhetorical nature of his question.

'What?'

'There was some sort of crop disease in Indonesia that buggered a load of the nutmeg trees and dropped production. Did you know Indonesia is where the majority of the world's nutmeg is grown? Well, the demand didn't drop with the lack of supply. So the price went up when there was an excess of demand that the supply couldn't meet. Simple economics.'

Fred stared at the woman, dumbfounded.

'They reckon it will go back down in price when the crop returns to normal next year,' she carried on unabated. 'Shame, I do like to sprinkle some on my hot chocolate of a winter's evening.'

'How do you know so much about nutmeg?' Fred finally managed.

The woman sniffed at him.

'I pay attention, don't I?'

'To what, the Nutmeg Digest? Total Paprika? The Oregano Argus? The Joy of Melange?'

'Well now, if you're going to be snippy...' the woman said, trailing off. By this point, Fred had lost interest in the conversation and had developed an unpleasant headache. He elected to leave the shop and the conversation, and go home to make the pies. Baking always relaxed him and helped to clear his head.

'Daddy!' Fred heard as he tried his best to get through his front door whilst juggling his shopping bags and house keys. His daughter, Sofia, who was his youngest, ran up and hugged his legs, which nearly caused him to lose his balance.

'Hi Sof,' he said. 'How was nursery today?'

'It was good. We played fire engines and made playdough cookies and Jack eated one!' she rattled off with typical enthusiasm.

'He ate it, honey, not eated.'

Sofia pondered this for a moment.

'No daddy, it's eated,' she said decisively. Then she lost interest and wandered off in the way that only young children can.

'Right,' said Fred. 'That's me told, then.'

He made his way into the kitchen and deposited his shopping bags on the kitchen table.

If Sofia was home then it meant his wife, Andrea, was around somewhere as well. After dumping his bags he set off around the house in search of her.

He found her painting in the 'study'. It actually wasn't so much a study as a small guest bedroom that they had converted into an artist's studio. Andrea loved to paint when she wasn't working.

'Hi honey,' she said, turning her head and smiling as Fred entered the room. 'How are you?'

'Not bad. How is the latest masterpiece?' Fred replied, giving her a peck on the cheek.

Andrea laughed.

'I'm still some way off Caravaggio, but it's going well, thanks.'

'Rembrandt and Picasso better watch their backs, that's all I'm saying.'

'Did you get the stuff for Jack's bake sale?'

'I did. You'll never believe the conversation I had with some lady in the shop, though. About the price of nutmeg, of all things.'

Andrea nodded sagely.

'Oh yeah, there's a global shortage, isn't there?'

Fred cast an incredulous glance at his wife.

'Is everyone appraised on the worldwide nutmeg supply situation except for me?' he asked.

'Oh, I thought it was common knowledge...' Andrea replied returning her attention to the painting she was working on.

Fred was lost for words. Fortunately for him his daughter rarely was, and a loud 'Oops!' came from the direction of the kitchen. Fred and Andrea looked at each other.

'Do you mind going and looking, honey?' Andrea asked. 'Only I'm covered in paint...'

The scene in the kitchen wasn't pretty. Fred walked in to find his shopping bags all over the floor. Their contents were spread liberally across the tiles surrounding the kitchen table.

'What happened?' he asked his daughter after he had surveyed the carnage.

'Wilbur knocked the bags off the table!' she replied. 'I told him not to, but he is a naughty cat!'

Fred folded his arms. The family didn't have a cat. Wilbur was Sofia's imaginary friend. Since she had played with a tabby at her friend's birthday party last year she had desperately wanted one. But Fred and Jack were both allergic, so it wasn't possible. She made up for it with Wilbur.

'Where is Wilbur now?' Fred asked.

'He went out of the window,' Sofia replied, nodding sagely.

'How very convenient...' Fred muttered, before bending over and starting the cleanup job.

Five minutes later and he was nearly done. He cleaned up some spilled orange juice with a cloth and then went on to the last bag.

He lifted the brown paper bag up off the floor and was greeted with a distressing sight. The bag of nutmeg contained therein had come open and spread its contents across the floor.

Fred tried desperately to salvage what remained of the pricey spice, but it was a lost cause. He scrabbled at the brown pile of dust. But the problem with dust was that it was, well, dusty. His frantic efforts seemed to just spread it around further.

Fred knelt, defeated on his kitchen floor. The terrible repercussions of the events of the last few minutes ringing in his mind. He had to face facts. There was nothing else for it. He would have to go back to the shop and buy some more nutmeg.

Fred fretted all the way to the shop. What would the shopkeeper think? He had been in the boutique not one hour earlier. He had purchased a supply of nutmeg that would be enough for one family to live on for some time. This strange man coming back in and buying even more of the newly expensive commodity. People would think he was hoarding nutmeg. For a rainy day. Most people would go for the essentials when the apocalypse came, they would say. But not old Fred. Oh no, Fred went straight for the bloody nutmeg.

The bell jingled as Fred entered the shop. He prepared to prostrate himself at the feet of the benevolent shopkeep. That he might see his way to once again grant him access to the glorious world of nutmeg.

'Hello,' said the shopkeeper, looking up from the racing form. 'Weren't you in here earlier? Is there a problem?'

'No, no problem at all...' Fred said as obsequiously as possible. 'I would like to buy some nutmeg.'

'Is this,' the shopkeeper asked, raising an eyebrow, 'some kind of joke?'

'Would that it were, my good man, would that it were,' Fred sighed, resisting the urge to bow as low as possible.

'Alright,' the shopkeeper said. 'How much?'

'50 grams please.'

'That'll be £15 please,' the shopkeeper said.

'£15?! Hang about. It was £10 when I came in earlier on!'

'There's a global nutme...'

'...g shortage, I know. It's all I've been bloody hearing about all day.'

'It is worse than they first thought,' the shopkeeper mentioned offhandedly.

'Hence the price increase, I imagine...' Fred observed.

'Oh yes. Supply and demand. That kind lady over there appraised me of the situation.'

Fred turned and looked at the woman he had engaged with earlier in the afternoon. She waved at him cheerfully.

Fred fiddled around in his wallet and came up with the £15. He handed it over to the shopkeeper.

'And give me a subscription to Spice Monthly...'

In Off the Rim

Simon Puleston Jones - 'A huge asteroid heads towards earth. The world awaits with baited breath. Good news: it missed! Bad news: it took out the moon. Cue massive changes to tides the world over, mass flooding and the rapid collapse of civilisation.'

2000 Years Ago

The great void of space was completely quiet. The icy, craggy mass hurtled its way through the vastness of space like a master assassin. Silent. Deadly.

It careened on with a purpose beyond comprehension. One day this ball of rock would affect trillions of creatures that had not yet even been born.

Without warning, it collided with another asteroid. In that moment, the very fate of planet earth was decided.

The rock span out of its orbit around this far off star. The star was yet unknown to humanity. Fledgling civilizations were only now looking up in awe at the heavens, and wondering if they held the answer to life's questions. Little did they know how right they were to wonder.

The Near Future

Jeff Rogers sat dozing in his chair at Jodrell Bank. It was 3am and he had drawn the night shifts this week. It wasn't so bad. Someone had to man the equipment that looked out into the infinity of space. Just in case new objects entered the solar system that required attention.

This was the last of his night shifts for the week, and there had been nothing to report. There was never anything to report. He had been working at Jodrell Bank for 5 years. In that time he had never had to note a single incoming object during the night shift.

It seemed to him that it was almost as though the universe went to sleep at night with everyone else. Of course, when he thought about it the idea was preposterous. It was always nighttime somewhere on earth. And new objects appeared several times daily. Perhaps the universe just ran on GMT, he chuckled. His colleague wandered past the open office door.

'How're things, Jeff?' the man asked, poking his head in.

Jeff came to and glanced at his watch.

'3 o'clock and all's well, Barry...' He replied, with a smile, and went back to sleep.

On the other side of the world, in a room deep below Cheyenne Mountain, sat Sergeant Benny Golding of the United States Army 405th Rifles. He was a stellar avionics expert on special secondment to NORAD. He sat and watched what everyone in the base affectionately called the 'Fortune Teller'.

It was actually a series of sophisticated computers. The machines connected to several orbiting satellites and other probes sent into the depths of the solar system.

Its sole purpose was to detect incoming interstellar objects. It determined the chances of any of those objects colliding with and, potentially, obliterating the Earth. It existed to give humanity a few hours warning if the whole planet was fucked.

Sergeant Golding sipped at a cup of coffee and listened to the familiar beeps indicating that the system was functional. It looked like it would be another easy shift.

Scientists had been predicting for years that an object the size of the one that killed the dinosaurs would once again collide with earth.

Most would say with a wave of the hand that any such event was millions of years away. That mankind would long since have left its home planet by the time a cosmic disaster wiped the tiny blue and green rock from the annals of history.

But some were a lot more pessimistic. They would call it pragmatic. It's only a matter of time, they would warn. They wagged a cautionary finger as their more reserved colleagues made a joke of their crackpot theories behind their backs.

They were dismissed as scaremongerers. The kind of people convinced that everything was out to destroy the world. Vesuvius and the supervolcanoes in Yellowstone; to solar flares and the San Andreas fault. The planet and everything outside of it was trying to wipe away the stain of humanity in one way or another.

Quite a few of these scientists were about to, for a very brief moment indeed, feel extremely smug.

Both machines, a whole continent apart, were set off within seconds of each other as the asteroid reached their sensor range.

The British dishes were older and suffered from a lack of military funding enjoyed by their American counterparts. They picked up the signals as the red phone on Jeff Rogers' desk buzzed. He jerked awake, almost falling off his chair in surprise at the sudden noise.

The phone was only for use when one station reported an unusual object and needed to check with its sister station to verify the sighting. He picked up the phone and licked his dry lips.

'Hello?'

Sergeant Golding replaced the receiver slowly. He let out a long breath and slicked his hair back. This was it. This was not a drill. He went through his procedures in his head. In this situation, it was necessary to immediately inform the Commander in Chief. He had to call the President.

It wasn't long before the news filtered its way down to the general public. An asteroid had entered the solar system and was on a collision course with the Earth.

Different time scales and projected landing areas were plastered across the media. Some said it would be days before the object landed, whereas some gave weeks, and others a matter of hours.

California, Scotland, Sahara, and the Himalayas were suggested as possible impact sites. Wherever it landed, it was going to be a big one. Big enough to eradicate humanity from the planet. No one had any doubt that this was the end.

Sergeant Golding and Jeff Rogers both knew exactly how long they had to live. They calculated that at the speed it was travelling the asteroid would collide with the earth in 5 days. And there was nothing they could do. The Fortune Teller had done her job and predicted the doom of humanity.

People held vigils worldwide. Nations put aside their differences. And people spent their last moments together before the coming apocalypse. Society began to crumble as people abandoned their workplaces. Power ran out and utilities broke down as those called on to maintain them stayed with their families. Petroleum supplies ran dry and supermarkets were looted for their remaining food. People who were able to began to flee underground with supplies to wait out the coming disaster.

It was on the 4th day that the news came. The rock had collided with another object in the asteroid belt. Experts predicted that it would now bypass the earth altogether. But many of the millions who had gone underground were unable to receive the message. They prepared to wait it out whatever happened and had locked themselves away until they were certain the event was over.

Those that had remained above ground were elated and even tried to return to their normal routines the next day. The day when the asteroid should have struck.

What the experts did not mention is that now they had no idea where the asteroid would go. The collision had thrown it so far off course it had become impossible to predict its trajectory.

At 12pm GMT, the originally expected impact time, millions gathered expecting an update on the progress of the asteroid. Littered on the floor in cities worldwide were newspapers with headlines reading 'Near Miss!' and 'Humanity Saved!'.

Cheerful newscasters around the world announced that the asteroid had indeed missed the earth. They would have gone on to say that humanity had indeed had a narrow escape. But their broadcasts were interrupted by a cacophonous explosion. as the stray asteroid whizzed past the earth and slammed full speed into the moon.

The impact sent chunks of the earth's satellite hurtling through the atmosphere. The shock wave shattered glass and collapsed buildings worldwide.

The tides were immediately affected. Within hours several gigantic tsunamis were bearing down on densely populated coastal regions.

Millions died in the initial shockwave, and further still in the natural disasters and debris impacts that followed.

Interstellar radiation put paid to most of those who remained after the first couple of days.

Within a week less than a million people remained alive, scattered across the earth's surface. No semblance of government or order remained, and the people were left to fend for themselves.

But if civilization did not endure, humanity did. And those that survived were joined by those millions who had, sensibly it turned out, fled underground. Between them, they took stock and began to rebuild the world. They vowed to right wrongs and make a new order, a better, fairer society than before.

It was no easy task. The circumstances were difficult and for some time food would be scarce. There would also always be people willing to take advantage of lawlessness. Those who desired to carve out some influence for themselves in a post-disaster environment.

But humanity, like the cockroach, survived, and eventually again began to thrive. Life went on for those who remained.

Deep underground, beneath Cheyenne mountain Sergeant Golding picked up the receiver. Miraculously the line connected and automatically dialled the only number it knew. Golding waited for a few seconds and prayed as he heard the telephone ring.

'Pick up, pick up, pick up,' he urged.

'Hello?' came the voice, finally, at the other end of line. And the earth went on turning.

Goal? Attack!

Llinos Cathryn Wynn Jones - *A story 'about a school netball team who have to fight a mythological creature.'*

'Pass it!' Jemima screamed at Cathy. But, as usual, Cathy didn't listen. Jem watched as her teammate spurned another golden opportunity. She could have passed to a player in a better position but took the shot on goal herself.

As expected it bounced back off the rim of the net and fell into the hands of the opposition Goalkeeper.

The game was tied at 45-45 in the fourth quarter. There were only minutes to go. This was the third time that her Goal Attack had squandered an opportunity to take the lead. As play reset she ran over to remonstrate.

'What are you doing?!' she fumed.

'Trying to score,' Cathy shrugged and replied.

'Listen, Cathy, I'm the captain of this team and you need to do what I say. I was in a much better position to try a shot and you ignored me and did your own thing. You're a really good player and we all want you at the club. But you've got to be part of the team sometimes and not just go for glory every time you get a sniff of a shot on.'

'Whatever,' Cathy shrugged again.

Jemima threw her arms up in the air in frustration and retook her position in the opposition third. The game went on and eventually, the team - the Brixton Comprehensive Belles, lost 50-47.

Netball was in Jemima's blood. Her mother had been in the England national team. She played Goal Shooter for several years and had taken the sport up when she started primary school.

Jemima had talent and also played in the Goal Shooter position that mum had made her own back in the 80s. Before she had given it all up to have Jemima, of course.

She was 16 now, and she enjoyed playing but really had only stuck it out for this long because her mother was watching over her shoulder. While her mum had been an international level player, she had never quite reached the glittering heights of superstardom. Her career had been cut short by the unexpected arrival of a daughter.

And so she put all her hopes into Jemima. She dreamed that one day Jemima would be captain of the England netball team. The greatest player the country had ever seen.

Jem was the youngest captain ever in the English Schools Netball League. She was still trying to get to grips with the pressure of being a leader. She hadn't yet had the heart to tell her mother that she wanted to be a nurse.

The day after the defeat she called a team meeting. The loss had hurt the Belles badly. They were third in the league. The team that had beaten them - the Haverstock Harriers were above them in the table. The defeat had only widened the gap between them.

She arrived back at the school at 6pm to find it deserted. All the students had long gone home and only the most diligent teachers were still in their classrooms marking papers.

But of course Mr. Longstone, the elderly janitor was still pottering around the gym. She said hello to the friendly old man and went inside.

She was the first there so she got some chairs out and set them up in a circle. Over the next few minutes, the rest of the team filtered in. Lucy arrived next, then Olivia and Mary came in, and the rest of the girls all arrived together.

That left just one, and unsurprisingly that one was Cathy.

Cathy had only recently transferred over to the school. Her family had moved down from Yorkshire, and she was finding settling into the school and the team a little difficult. She had been a disruptive element since the start.

The only problem was that she was the best Goal Attack they had by miles. None of them could quite bring themselves to agree that kicking her out of the team would be for the best.

Eventually, she turned up and everyone settled in.

'I think we all know why we are here,' Jemima said, beginning the meeting. 'If we are going to stand even the slightest chance of winning the league this year we have to work better as a team.'

She looked pointedly at Cathy. Olivia raised her hand.

'I agree,' she said. 'We will never win the league if we all play as individuals.'

At that point, Mr. Longstone walked in through the big double doors of the gymnasium.

'Are you girls alright?' he asked. 'I thought I heard raised voices.'

'Everything's fine, Mr. L, thanks,' Jemima replied.

'OK then, you let me know if you need anything.'

As the old man turned to leave a terrifying, unearthly shriek came from outside. Everyone in the room reclined in horror at the noise. It did not sound as though it had come from a creature of this world.

'What on earth was that?!' the janitor cried. 'I should go take a l...'

Before he could finish his sentence the wall of the building was torn asunder. A seven-headed serpentine beast burst through the gap, picked up the janitor with one of its heads and swallowed him whole. A collective scream echoed around the room as the girls scattered left and right.

'What are we going to do?!' Olivia wailed.

'Is that a HYDRA?!' several of the girls, who had recently taken a class on Greek mythology, cried in unison.

The beast bore down on Jemima with malice aforethought, intent on an after-janitor snack. The team captain stood there, unable to move from sheer terror. Her life flashed before her eyes as she awaited her fate.

She flinched and shut her eyes as the beast strode up to her. But instead of taking a bite from her it moved right on past and lumbered after one of her teammates who was running away.

Risking a glance she saw that it was giving Mary the run around behind the five-a-side football goals.

'What just happened?' she asked. But no-one was paying attention, seeing as how they were all preoccupied with not being eaten by a hydra.

Olivia, whose generally frayed nerves were suffering rather badly at the moment, ran up to Jemima and clamped her arms around her. The head of the hydra that had been tracking her motion suddenly looked very confused. It looked around for a moment for its prey. Then, it switched its attention to a load of netballs that were rolling everywhere after falling off their pile in the corner.

'Jemima!' Olivia sobbed, burying her head into Jem's shoulder. 'Don't let it eat meeeee.'

'It couldn't see you...' Jemima replied, a thought beginning to form in her head.

'What do you mean it couldn't see me?' Olivia replied. 'I was right in front of it!'

'It's a serpent, isn't it?'

'It's a bloody mythological creature is what it is!' Olivia replied.

'Don't you pay attention in biology?' her captain asked. 'Serpents don't see like mammals. They detect heat. You just looked like an oddly tall and warm rock to it because you were stood still. The hydra might be mythical but it's still a snake. Those idiots are attracting its attention by moving.'

She gestured with her head at their teammates, who were running around, arms flailing.

Jemima began formulating a plan. What were netball players good at if not standing still in high-pressure situations?

'Listen up girls,' she shouted. 'I want you all to do catching drill immediately.'

'What are you doing?' Olivia, who at this point had recovered enough to release Jemima from her grasp, asked.

'Getting them to stop. If they stop running it will stop chasing them for now and buy us some time.'

All the girls had stopped in their tracks. The hydra was looking rather confused. A couple of the heads were sniffing around the team, but none were attacking.

'What now?' Olivia asked.

'Well, how do you kill a hydra?' Jemima replied.

'I read a book once that said you have to chop off the heads...'

Jemima looked around for any objects that she could use for that purpose. She found that she was in reach of some metal rims from old nets. She picked one up and threw it with full force at the creature.

It seemed to be going way off course, but as luck would have it the hydra moved one of its necks up and met the rim side on. The head fell to the ground and turned to dust in front of their eyes.

The beast reared for a second, emitting a terrible scream, before settling again. Moments later, the flailing dismembered neck settled down. Like magic, two new heads grew in place of the old one.

'I thought you said I should cut it off!' Jemima yelled in disbelief.

'You didn't let me finish!' Olivia remonstrated. 'You have to chop off the heads, but if you don't stop it two will grow back in its place!'

'Well, how do you stop it?'

'I don't know, I've never fought a bloody hydra before, have I? I was texting Bryan during that part of Ms. Lewis' class.'

'You cauterise it.'

Olivia and Jemima turned around to see where the new voice had come from. It was Cathy.

'What do you know about hydras?!' they both asked.

'My mum lived in Greece for a while,' Cathy said sheepishly, clutching her arms close to her chest. 'She used to read me bedtime stories from a book of myths she bought in Athens. The way to stop a hydra growing its heads back is by cauterising the wound.'

A spark of inspiration hit Jemima.

'Do you have a lighter?' she asked Cathy, who nodded. 'OK girls, here's how it's going to go down,' Jemima called out. 'Find anything you can that will sever one of the heads. Lucy and Alice, there's a bunch of discuses near you. The rest of you will have to use the net rims dotted around.' The girls nodded. 'Olivia and Mary, you run interference. Distract it long enough to buy the rest of us some time.'

Olivia opened her mouth to protest at being used as cannon fodder but thought better of it. 'Cathy and I will light these netballs on fire and throw them at the open wounds to stop the heads coming back. Got it?'

Jemima took the silence as agreement.

'3, 2, 1. Go, Belles!'

The team met her rallying call with a chorus of returns, and the team got to work.

Mary and Olivia ran around the beast and through its legs, trying to confuse it and tie its necks up in knots.

Meanwhile, the rest of the girls unleashed hell, hurling everything within arms reach. Many shots missed, but enough were doing damage and eventually, heads began to tumble.

Cathy and Jem were ready to capitalise. They sent the flaming balls on to the stumps with remarkable precision.

Before long the monster was defeated. The girls lay around the gymnasium, exhausted, battered and bruised. No one had been seriously hurt in the ordeal, except for poor Mr. Longstone. The team had survived to fight another day.

Jemima, who was slumped up against a vaulting horse, turned to Cathy who was lying face down on a crash mat nearby.

'NOW do you see the benefits of teamwork?' she asked.

Cathy looked up and smiled.

'Sure,' she replied, winking. 'But I'm still not passing to you if I think I can score.'

The Lady of the Forest

Llinos Cathryn Wynn Jones - *A story about 'a lady with a psychic connection to trees.'*

The three boys tried to sneak quietly down the path through the trees. But their silent tiptoeing was undone by their inability to keep their voices down.

'Why do we have to do this?' one boy moaned. He had grimy cheeks and a general air of scruffiness about him. His jumper was not ironed, his shirt not tucked in and his dirty blonde hair looked as though it hadn't seen a comb in some time.

The tallest of the three boys, who was leading them, stopped and turned to face his companions.

'Because Billy Naismith dared us. You can't go back on a dare, Callum. EVERYONE knows that.'

'Yeah, I know...' Callum responded, defensively.

The three boys were year 7 pupils at the nearby Gosworth Comprehensive School. The darer in question, Billy Naismith, was one of the coolest kids in year 10. To refuse a dare would lead to accusations of being chicken. But to refuse a dare from Billy was even worse.

Not that any of Callum, George, and Danny were anything like cool enough to worry whether their social stock could deteriorate any further. Even so, that was the kind of thing that 11-year-olds worried about, and so to them, refusing the dare was unthinkable. They trudged on for a little while in silence.

'What if she IS a witch?' Danny, who was the shy one, asked quietly.

'Well then she will turn us into a newt or cook us or something,' George, the scruffy one, replied.

Danny screwed his face up. 'My mum won't like that,' he said. 'She told me to be home for dinner, not to BE dinner.'

Danny was the closest thing that ragtag group had to a leader.

'Witches aren't real you idiots,' Callum chimed in. 'They're a...what's it called...a myth, aren't they?'

'My brother told me they were real,' George interjected. 'And that they live in gingerbread cottages and turn people into stuff and have cauldrons.'

'Well then your brother's an idiot too,' Callum said. But secretly he wondered if George's brother was right.

They turned a bend in the forest path and there it was. Callum noted to himself that the cottage was made out of stones and not gingerbread.

It was only small. It looked like it barely even had space for one room. The old thatched roof was drooping, and creeping ivy covered the stone walls. The whole thing looked as though it could have done with sprucing up a long time ago.

'Do you think she's home?' Danny asked.

'I can't see any lights on in the windows,' George said stepping forward. He felt the twigs snap underfoot as he walked up to the gate. The forest was so quiet you could have heard it for miles around.

The boys heard a rustling come from behind the cottage, and a woman's voice called out.

'Hello, is there someone there?'

'Leg it!' George hissed.

The three boys scattered from the path and into the trees. No sooner was the last boy out of sight than the owner of the voice appeared from around the side of the cottage. She was middle-aged, with light brown hair that was graying in places. Her long, flowing dress was made of cotton. Like her cottage it looked as though it had seen better days.

The woman was carrying a broom made from a branch and a bundle of dried twigs which she propped up against the wall of her house. Folding her arms across her chest she began to look around the small clearing.

'Funny,' she said. 'I could have sworn I heard someone.' She glanced up at the sky and noted the position of the sun. 'Oh my,' she said. 'Is it that time already?'

The boys peaked out from their hiding places as the woman opened the creaky cottage door and went inside. They ducked back down as she re-emerged a few seconds later, holding some sticks and a box of matches.

She walked up to one of the trees and pushed one of the sticks into an old knothole, before setting it alight with a match. The clearing began to fill with an exotic scent as the lady sat cross-legged in front of the tree. The boys watched as she shut her eyes, placed one hand on her forehead and another on the tree.

'What's she doing?' Danny whispered to Callum, creeping round to join him behind his bush.

'I don't know,' Callum replied. 'And shush, or she'll hear us.'

They continued to watch as she remained sitting in the same position for another few minutes. Eventually, she moved her hands down to her lap and nodded.

'I understand,' she said, as if she was talking to the tree itself. 'Until tomorrow.' She stood and, with a last look around the glade, went inside the cottage.

'Let's get out of here!' George said.

The three boys scrambled their way down the path as quick as their legs could carry them.

That night Callum barely touched his dinner.

'Come on love, you've not had any of your egg and chips,' his mum said, in that chastising way that only mums who have slaved over a hot stove can muster.

'Mum I saw a witch today!' he blurted out.

'Don't be daft, love, there's no such thing as witches. At least not as what could do magic on you anyway...' his mother replied, smiling.

'No mum, I swear down! She lives in the forest in a rickety old cottage and has a broomstick and talks to the trees and everything!'

'What were you doing in the forest, young man?!' his mum demanded. 'It's dangerous in there.'

His dad looked up from the evening paper.

'She's not a witch, lad, she's an old hippy who lives out in the forest by herself. She's been out there for 25 years.'

'I SAW IT WITH MY OWN EYES!' Callum shouted, pushing his chair away from the table. 'I'M NOT MAKING IT UP!'

He ran out of the kitchen and up the stairs and didn't emerge from his room until the next day when it was time for school.

At break time the three boys convened at their usual spot behind the science building.

'We have to go back into the forest this evening,' Callum announced.

'Why?' George asked. 'We did the dare, Billy agreed.'

'We have to prove that she is a witch somehow. My parents didn't believe me last night!' he said, and then, sounding hurt, added 'They laughed at me.'

George and Danny looked at each other.

'Alright, fine,' George said.

That afternoon they met outside the school gates and walked off in the direction of the forest.

'I wonder what spells and stuff she can do,' Danny said as they walked.

'Probably loads,' George mused. 'I bet she has all the forest animals working for her.'

'If you had to be turned in to an animal by her what animal would you choose?' Danny went on. His sense of curiosity about the unknown overwhelming his usual coyness.

'A dog,' George answered. 'They have the most fun.'

'Yeah...'

'She wouldn't give you a choice, dummy,' Callum said. 'She'd turn you into something horrible like a newt or a toad or a slug. No one ever gets turned in to anything nice like a dog or a cat.'

That killed off the conversation, and the three were silent for the rest of the walk.

They reached the clearing and the cottage again. Just like on the day before there didn't seem to be anyone around.

'What time is it?' Callum hissed.

'4 o'clock,' George replied, looking at his watch.

'She'll be out any minute then. Let's hide.'

The three took up positions between two giant oaks a little way away from the house and waited for the woman to emerge.

At about the same time as she had the day before, she appeared from around the back of the house. She grabbed her broom and took her position in front of the same tree then lit another stick of incense.

'Do you think she flew here on it?' Callum whispered. Neither Danny nor George felt able to give an informed answer.

They watched as she sat, seemingly in commune with the tree, until suddenly she jerked upright.

'They're in danger?!' she shouted. 'Where?' The woman began to cast about, looking for any sort of danger, before apparently receiving a response from the tree. 'I see,' she said, turning in the direction of the boys hiding spot. 'Boys I know you're there,' she called out. 'You are in grave danger, you need to get out from between those trees right now. Make your way out into the clearing.'

Callum, Danny, and George glanced nervously at each other before complying. As they emerged from the tree line and into the glade, they heard a loud crashing coming from where they had been hiding.

When they went back to investigate, they saw that the ground they had been stood on had collapsed into a hollow cave beneath. The two oaks had collapsed inward and were now resting on each other. They would surely have been killed, or at least very seriously hurt.

'W-what just happened?!' Danny asked.

'The witch saved us!' George cried.

The woman stood in the clearing near to the boys, her arms folded across her chest, staring at them.

'So you think I'm a witch, eh?' she asked.

'You was talking to that tree!' Callum observed.

'You've got me there,' the woman said, shrugging. 'But I'm not a witch. At least, not a proper witch like in the stories. There's no such thing as magic, you know.'

'Then how did you know we was about to die?' Callum protested.

'Well, as you said, I was talking to the tree. It sensed that its brother oaks were in danger and that three other of my kind were in danger too.'

'Well, isn't talking to trees like, magic, and stuff?' George interjected.

The woman smiled.

'No, I am just gifted with the ability to talk to plants. There are many like me. Why don't you come in for a cup of tea and I'll tell you a bit more?'

'And you won't cook us?' Danny asked warily.

'Not even a little,' the woman beamed.

That night Callum burst into his house with a huge grin on his face.

'Why are you so cheerful?' his dad asked.

Callum was so excited that all the words came out almost at once.

'You'll never believe what happened! I met the witch, but she's not a witch, she's just a bit psychic, but only when it comes to talking to trees and plants. And her name is Imelda. She brews herbal tea using her own herbs from her garden and she made her own broom with bits of tree. But she doesn't fly on it because like I said she's not REALLY a witch.'

Callum only stopped at this point because he ran out of breath and needed to inhale deeply. His father stared at him for a moment over the lip of his paper.

'You're right,' he said eventually. 'I don't believe you,' and went back to reading the racing form.

'Appily Ever After

Elizabeth Scott *- 'A story about a redheaded princess named Elizabeth who finds true love after dating wankers for years.'*

Once upon a time, a long time ago, there existed a kingdom, known as Wavertreevia.

There were three factions within the kingdom. The Red Men of Anne's Field were the strongest and mightiest warriors in the land. They did regular and bloody battle with the neighbouring nations. These included the vile and despicable Kingdom of Mancunia, ruled by the despotic King Moyes. The Mancunian Red Devils and Citizens were clueless. No match for the might of the Red Men and their Kopite infantry.

The second faction was from the village of Evertonia. They wore blue almost always, but sometimes neon pink when they were away from the village. They were a weaker tribe than the Red Men, and were constantly in their shadow. They lacked the strength of character to compete with the mighty warriors.

This led to their constant grumbling about their inferiority, insisting that it hadn't always been the case. As a result, they gained the nickname 'the Bitters'. This led to much good-natured teasing in the alehouses of Wavertreevia when the Red Men claimed victory once more.

Finally, there were those who lived over the water, or the Wools as they were known. They were tolerated in the cities of Wavertreevia but mocked mercilessly when they tried to pass as true residents of the kingdom. Their warriors even lacked the quality possessed by the lowly people of Evertonia.

The three tribes held an easy peace within the kingdom. They were united in their hatred of the evil people of Mancunia, particularly the Red Devils. The lack of true internal competition prevented the local rivalries from boiling over beyond the odd pub brawl.

The Scott family had ruled the Kingdom for many generations. The current King, John Joseph had been on the throne for 30 years, and the people were happy and contented with his rule. All except one.

'This is shite,' the princess said.

'What is, Princess Elizabeth?' her handmaiden replied, whilst brushing the Princess' long, fiery red hair.

'I'm 29 years old and I'm still single. It's pure shite,' Elizabeth explained. She slumped down on to the window sill of her room at the top of the tallest tower in the castle, despondent.

'But Princess Elizabeth, you are the most beautiful woman in all the lands of Wavertreevia, and you are a noted wit. You must have your pick of the men of this kingdom,' the handmaiden replied, surprised to hear of this state of affairs.

'Oh aye, yer, but the problem isn't with me is it?' Elizabeth said with a dismissive flick of her hand.

'What do you mean, my lady?'

'It's the men! All the fellas in this kingdom are wankers, gobshites, or worse, a Wool. At least, the ones that aren't taken anyway.'

'Oh, I see, I'd never thought about it like that before,' said the handmaiden. She continued to brush Princess Elizabeth's hair, all the while recalling her own experiences with the menfolk of the kingdom. 'But now you come to mention it they are a shower of bastards, aren't they?'

King John Joseph I and his Queen, Irene, went to lunch in their private dining room in the castle.

'It just won't do,' the King muttered, sitting down and picking up a turkey leg from a silver platter.

'What's that, dear?' the Queen, who had been there a few minutes, asked, looking up from a book.

'Elizabeth will be 30 years old next year and she is yet to marry. As my only child, she will be Queen one day after I have passed on, and she must continue the Scott line. It has gone unbroken for centuries and I'll not let it end on my watch.'

He tore a chunk from the turkey.

'But she has courted many suitors from the kingdom over the years,' Irene said. 'And each time it has turned out the same. When things begin to get serious they turn out to be despicable, foolish, or worse, Wools.'

'Indeed,' the King sighed. 'That is why I have made a decision, though it pains me to do it. The traditions of Wavertreevia state that the royal family should marry one of the people of the kingdom, but times are dire and needs must. Princess Elizabeth must marry...an outsider.'

'Oh dear,' his wife replied. 'It's rather enough to put one off one's lunch.'

Princess Elizabeth walked through the large double doors that led to the throne room as they were opened by two servants, one clad in red and one in blue.

It was a long walk down the length of the room to her parents' seats. She felt very self-conscious as she heard her high heels click along the stone floor with every step.

'Hello, my dear,' the King said as she reached the end of the room.

'Alright dad, mum,' Elizabeth replied.

'Do you know why I have summoned you here, Elizabeth?'

'No idea.'

'Your mother and I think it is high time you settled down and married someone,'

'Dad I've told yer, all the men around here are nobheads. It's not like I haven't been trying. I even had a crack at a few of the girls but none of there were anything special neither,' Elizabeth lamented. 'I can't get married if everyone is proper shite.'

'I…agree,' her father said. 'Though I'm not sure I would have put it quite like that. As there are no appropriate suitors in the Kingdom of Wavertreevia, we have sent out word that a tournament is due to be held to decide who will win your hand. The games will begin in one week, and we are expecting competitors from all around the world to attend.'

'Oh ey, dad, but what if they're all nobheads as well?' Elizabeth protested.

'Then so be it, a nobhead you must marry.'

'Are you 'avin a laugh? I'm not marrying a gobshite no matter where he's from.'

'Then you had better hope that the winner is worthy of marriage because my word is final and this tournament is going ahead.'

Elizabeth spent the week leading up to the tournament sulking in her room. She only allowed entry to her handmaidens, who brought her regular supplies of chip butties and lipstick.

Eventually, and somewhat reluctantly, she emerged on the day of the tourney. She sat in the royal box in the grandstand alongside her father and mother.

The competitors lined up in front of the grandstand, to present themselves to the royal family.

There were several men there that Elizabeth recognised. Champions from the Red Men of Anne's Field and the blue-clad warriors of Evertonia lined up with a gaggle of outsiders. She sighed as she immediately checked these men off the list. Three of them she had dated already, and the other was apparently crap in bed, so she was definitely not interested.

She scanned her way idly down the rest of the line. There were roughly 30 men in all, and even a couple of enterprising women, Wavertreevia being a very tolerant place. But none of them leapt out at her immediately as someone she would care to spend the rest of her days with. That is, none of them until she reached the end of the line.

Her eyes widened as she spotted the final two competitors, talking idly with each other as they waited to be inspected. They stood tall and proud in their gleaming armour, and Elizabeth was immediately in love with both of them.

'Dad, who are they?' she asked, pointing the two men out.

'That is Lord Jamie of the Red Knapp, and next to him is Sir Steven Gerrard of High Town, a small independent territory near the borders of Wavertreevia.'

'Can I just have both of them?' Elizabeth wondered, dreamily. 'They're well fit.'

Her father frowned.

'We will see,' he replied. 'The tournament will decide if they are worthy.'

And so the tourney went on throughout the day, and gradually more and more of the suitors were eliminated. By sunset, only two men remained. To Elizabeth's delight, the two were Lord Jamie and Sir Steven.

The King rose from his chair.

'We have seen some brave feats of combat today, and many great men have gone home defeated. And thus we bring the day's events to a close with one final battle. A round of single combat to decide who will take my daughter's hand...'

'They can take more than me hand,' Elizabeth said, loud enough for the two men to hear.

The King went on, choosing to ignore his daughter.

'...you will fight until one of you yields. Take your positions and begin.'

The two men clasped each other's wrists in a show of solidarity, and backed away, swords drawn.

'Ooh, I can't watch,' Elizabeth squealed.

The competitors fought bravely against each other for some time. Neither managed to gain the upper hand over the other, no matter how hard they tried. The battle raged on long into the night.

By the time both men slumped simultaneously to their knees, too exhausted to continue, most of the crowd had gone home, bored with the contest. But Elizabeth and her mother and father were all still sat there, watching - Elizabeth much more keenly than her parents.

'Well?' she asked. 'Neither of them lost, dad. Can I keep them both?'

Her father furrowed his brow.

'A situation like this is unprecedented, I must consult with my Prime Minister.'

Prime Minister Rodgers stepped forward and opened the book of laws of the kingdom. He thumbed his way through the pages, eventually finding the one he needed.

'My lord, there is nothing in the laws of the land that states that Princess Elizabeth cannot marry both men. In fact, it rather demands it, as our land has no method of deciding a tie in cases of a draw, given that neither seems up for a replay.'

'Very well,' the King sighed. 'But remind me to discuss that shoot out concept that one of the courtiers proposed last month. It seems perfect for such a conundrum.'

'Boss!' Elizabeth declared, and ran over and gave both Sir Steven and Lord Jamie a big snog. 'Eeeee,' she squealed. 'They're both dead fit!'

And thus, fair Princess Elizabeth married both Sir Steven AND Lord Jamie in a single ceremony. She split her time evenly between the two, although her favourite days were when they both took her out down Wavertreevia One to go shopping.

And Princess Elizabeth, her mother and father, and all the people of the world lived Happily Ever After.

Except for the people of Mancunia, who were thoroughly miserable for the rest of eternity.

The End

To Boldly Go

Video Game Expert Matt Jones - *Enter a competition to write the worst sci-fi story possible.*

The sound of the metal boots crashing against the floor echoed down the length of the corridor. The robed figure trudged on until they reached a door, at which point they stopped and entered a number into a keypad. A red light flickered on and the door slid upwards.

The room was dimly lit and sparsely furnished. A bench lay against one wall and a small toilet, not cleaned for some time, was the only other item of furniture present.

In one corner of the room, three people huddled together for warmth, or perhaps out of fear. One of them, a woman, looked up at the robed figure as they entered, a look of abject terror spread across her gaunt features.

'Get up, all of you,' the robed figure barked in an artificial, electronic tone. 'You are to be blasted from the airlock in one hour.'

The figure hefted a laser rifle and aimed it at the three huddled bodies, awaiting compliance.

The room began to fill with people, and slowly but surely everyone took their seats around the large conference table.

'I wonder why the Admiral has called us all here,' Captain Janus said to Captain Worrall, who was sat next to him.

'There's only one reason he would call together the Galactic Union's best starship captains,' Worrall replied. 'The Union must be about to go to war.'

The Admiral, an imposing man in his 60s with tidy white hair swept into the room in full dress uniform. The hubbub of individual conversations died down.

'Now listen up you pukes, and listen good,' he rasped. 'I know you're the best goddamn starship captains in the Galactic Union fleet, but you're all mavericks and I'm sick of you not playing by the rules. I don't care how close you are to retirement, the Galactic Union is going to war and we need our best captains out there on the front line.'

'Who are we fighting?' Captain Praxis, of the SS Grisedale, asked.

'The Wolgane of Vixia V. They are a hyper-intelligent equine race. Similar to a mythical creature known as a 'horse' that was rumoured to exist before the Great Devastation back on Terra.'

At the mention of the Great Devastation, everyone in the room performed an elaborate hand gesture. They then gave a collective reciting of the sentence 'May we be forgiven.'

'One of their unmanned, or rather unhorsed, robotic probes breached Union space yesterday. It refused to turn back when hailed,' the Admiral continued. 'This was seen by the Galactic Council as a universal act of aggression and a declaration of intent for all-out war against the Galactic Union. We must eradicate this filth at the source before it can do the same to us. It's kill or be killed out there. You know what you have to do so go out there and kill some space donkeys.'

The Admiral turned and stormed out as quick as he had arrived moments earlier. The room was left in stunned silence until another man stood up. It was Captain Rames Cork of the SS Freelance Opportunity and he looked pumped.

'You heard…the Admiral! You know…what we have to do! We gotta go and kick these Wolgane…right in their stupid elongated faces! Do it…for McFiggins!' he said to the room, practically screaming the words. The mention of the deceased hero ace pilot McFiggins raised a suitable cheer. Everyone went back to their starships ready to introduce some alien horse scum to the business end of their phaser cannons.

Two weeks later the fleet of ships was in orbit around the home planet of the Wolgane, Vixia V.

Captain Cork stood on the bridge of his ship looking triumphantly down on the planet. The world itself was mostly an icy wasteland. The equine population lived in a temperate belt around the planet's equator. This made carpet-bombing the habitable areas all the easier, and Cork was pleased that the war was going swimmingly.

As he cast his gaze over the planet his crew was preparing an away mission. The mission was to demand peace terms from the belligerent horse people below. He would lead it himself.

His second in command, Commander Speck approached him from behind.

'Captain, the team is prepared.'

'Plenty of red-shirted officers, as I ordered?'

'Yes, sir. I'm sure that your logical postulation that the profligacy of the colour red will startle them into ultimate submission to the Galactic Union is a wise one indeed.'

'Good. Set a table…for us all, we will have a party when we return…victorious…to the ship.'

he two men began walking to the transporter room.

'Tell me,' the Captain asked. 'What can we expect…from these horse…people?'

'Well, Captain, they are notorious warriors, but reluctant to leave their planet. That is why one of their robotic probes was encountered in Union space, rather than a horsed ship. And this is also why we have encountered little resistance during our prolonged orbital bombardment. I suspect we will encounter much more in the way of a battle on the surface.'

'But we are...prepared?'

'I believe we have superior firepower at our disposal.'

'Most importantly...what of their women?'

'The Wolgane are notorious lovers, sir. Renowned the galaxy over for their passionate lovemaking and sensual tantric abilities.'

'Wonderful...I look forward to making a diplomatic connection...with another new species.'

An hour later the away team materialised after beaming down on to the planet's surface. The party was two short, as two of the red shirts were lost in a transporter malfunction. But the surviving members quickly moved out and met fierce resistance from the Wolgane forces.

It wasn't long before the away team had been reduced down to Captain Cork and Commander Speck. The two men were completely surrounded and unable to transport back to the ship as the transporter operator was on break.

'We...surrender!' the Captain shouted as the ring of horse people closed on then, and they were taken to the capital city.

Once they had entered the capital with their horse escort, they were taken to the royal palace. There they were brought immediately before the King and Queen of the Wolgane.

'What are the Galactic Union's demands?' the Queen asked.

'An immediate cessation...of hostilities by the Wolgane people. And...a withdrawal of all unmanned probes

105

from Union space,' Captain Cork replied. 'And personally…I would like to make love to one…of your women."

'Our unmanned probes are also unarmed. At no point have the Wolgane engaged in any hostility against the Galactic Union. In fact, it is the Union's troops that are currently bombarding our planet from high orbit and massacring our people by the billions.'

'Personally, I find it disgusting…that you are unwilling to acknowledge the Wolgane's role…in this conflict. If your probe had…not breached our space then we would not…be here bombing your people. The blood of all your weird alien horse comrades…is on your hands, your majesty, not ours."

'Our planet lies in ruins, our population utterly decimated and our army defeated. If I thought you were a target of any value whatsoever I would use you as a bargaining chip to barter peace with your misguided leaders. But you are a bumbling buffoon of a starship captain who led a team of 15 people, mostly rookies up against an army of 15,000 well-armed troops. So I suspect I would be laughed out of the negotiation room if I were not blasted out with a laser.'

'What are you saying?' Commander Speck asked.

'I'm saying that if I killed you two right here I would be doing your Galactic Union a favour. There is nothing left for us to negotiate. Our population has been reduced from 6 billion to under 1 million in a matter of days.'

'So there will be…no lovemaking?' Cork asked despondently.

'Not for you, no.'

The Queen of the Wolgane lifted a laser pistol that was duct-taped to her hoof and obliterated Cork and Speck in two shots.

Vixia V was destroyed mere hours later, but not before two suspiciously equine looking creatures wearing the Galactic Union navy uniforms of a Captain and a Commander beamed up to the SS Freelance Opportunity. They successfully posed as Cork and Speck for the whole trip back to Galactic Union HQ. When they arrived they opened fire on the Galactic Council building and blew them all up, ending the Galactic Union in the process. The former people of the Union decided that it was a bit of a disaster by all accounts. All things considered, they said, w probably should have just left the peaceful horse people to their own devices.

The galaxy returned to peace forevermore. There was never again an organisation as mighty as the Galactic Union. This was because most species realised that space travel was stupid anyway and that all the cool stuff they needed was right there on their own planets. Or something.

The End

Kelli and the Chubby Pandas

Kelli Savill - *'The story of Kelli and the Chubby Pandas'.*

'Iiiiiiit's Entertainment Tonight, with your host, Robbie Falstaff!'

The cameras panned down from the ceiling to focus on a desk and high-backed leather chair as the show's house band played the theme. The desk was on a raised dais, next to which were three smaller, less expensive looking chairs for guests to sit on.

The show's host, Robbie Falstaff, made his way out to a cheering studio audience. He waved all the cameras as he walked by, a huge grin on his face.

As he moved to sit down behind his desk the applause and the music died down, prompted by showrunners outside of the view of the cameras.

'Good evening, and welcome to Entertainment Tonight! I'm your host, Robbie Falstaff, and folks, do we have a show for you tonight! Coming up later we have a celebrity couple that is the talk of Tinseltown. And music from international megastars Kelli and the Chubby Pandas. But, up first we have a special interview with the Chubby Pandas frontwoman herself, Kelli 'Panda' Savill!'

The house band struck up once more and played a short jingle as Kelli Savill walked out on to the set. She waved and smiled at the crowd as she went by. She was wearing a sparkling silver jumpsuit and a panda hat. As the music died down again she took her seat next to the host.

'Kelli, it's great to have you on the show,' Robbie said, leaning forward.

'It's a pleasure to be here, Robbie,' Kelli replied.

'Now the Chubby Pandas are just great. I understand that your new single, 'Panda Pops', has broken the record for fastest-selling digital single of all time...'

A big cheer went up from the audience, interrupting Robbie.

'Add that to the list of other records you've smashed this year with your quintuple platinum album 'Black and White',' he continued. 'And surely it's fair to say that the Chubby Pandas are the biggest band in the world right now?'

'Well Robbie, I don't know about that, but it has been an amazing journey to get here.'

'I understand that there is quite an interesting story related to the band's formation. Would you tell us a little bit more about how it came to be?'

'Of course, Robbie, I'd be glad to. It all started one day in England, in a town called Colchester, back in 1994...'

'Now there's no need to be afraid, dear. The foster home isn't a scary place. There are lots of other children your age there to play with and I'm sure you'll make lots of friends.'

The little girl continued to bawl her eyes out.

'But I want my mummy and daddy!' she cried.

'Oh sweetheart,' the matron of the foster home said, trying to console her. 'I'm afraid that's not possible at the moment.'

'Don't they love me?' the girl cried. It seemed that the matron's words were only making things worse.

'Of course they love you, dear,' she said, putting her arm around the child, 'But it's very complicated. How old are you?' The matron knew, of course, but she wanted to draw the little girl out of her current state of mind.

'I'm eight years old,' the girl replied, still sobbing.

'Well now, you're very brave for an eight-year-old girl. I'm sure your mummy and daddy are very proud of you for how brave you have been coming here.'

The girl's face lit up.

'Do you really think so?'

'I do. In fact, they told me how brave you would be and they were right. They asked me to look after you here for a little while until they have sorted some things out. Then they will come and collect you again. OK?'

'OK,' the girl sniffed, wiping her nose on her sleeve.

'Now, a little bird tells me that you are a very talented singer, is that true?'

'Yes, miss.'

'Well then, there are a few people I'd like you to meet. They are all very talented musicians. Perhaps you can be friends?'

'I'd like that.'

The matron and the girl stood up and walked out of the office into the common area. A group of three girls was sat around playing with some musical instruments.

'Girls, there's someone I'd like you to meet,' the matron said. 'This is Kelli. Kelli, the girl there with the guitar is Ingrid, the girl at the drum kit is Sherri, and the girl behind the keyboard is Louise.'

'Hi, Kelli,' the girls said in unison, as the young Kelli stood wide-eyed.

'Are you guys in a band?' she asked.

'Yeah,' Ingrid replied. 'We're called the Chubby Pandas, but none of us can sing, so we suck!'

'I can sing!' Kelli replied. 'And I LOVE pandas!'

'...and that is how we all met.'

110

'But you were only eight years old at the time, and the Chubby Pandas didn't record their first single until you were fifteen, correct?'

'That's right, Robbie,' Kelli replied. 'Sadly, not long after we met we were separated...'

'That was a great practice, girls,' Ingrid said after the band had stopped playing. 'I think we are starting to get really good!'

'I can't believe we've only been together for six months,' Kelli added. 'It feels like I have known you girls all my life!'

There was a short rap on the door of their practice room, and then the door opened. It was the matron.

'Girls, I have some good news. Louise, Sherri, come with me.'

'...and so Louise and Sherri were adopted,' Kelli went on. 'By different families, actually, it was just a coincidence that it happened on the same day. But they stayed in touch as they lived near each other. Ingrid and I kept playing together in the foster home, but it didn't feel the same without the other two backing us up.'

'That must have been a really tough time for you,' Robbie interjected.

'It was. After a while Ingrid and I were both adopted by the same family, so at least we got to stick together. It was three years later that fate would bring the Chubby Pandas back together...'

The bell above the coffee shop door jingled as it opened. Kelli and Ingrid walked in and sat down at a table by the window. They continued to talk amongst themselves until one of the servers came over to take their order.

The pair turned to face the server. Startled, she jumped back and there was a clatter as her pen hit the floor.

'Louise, is that you?' Kelli asked.

'Ingrid! Kelli! What are you doing here?' Louise replied, hugging them both. 'I've missed you both so much!'

'Our adopted family moved back to Colchester recently,' Ingrid said.

'We haven't seen you in years!' Kelli added.

'I know! Do you girls still play together?'

'Sure, we got adopted together and have been practicing every night like we always did,' Kelli said.

'This is so exciting!' Louise replied. 'Hang on a second. There's someone else here who will want to say hello!'

Louise ran off into the kitchen whilst Kelli and Ingrid sat at the table. They were both surprised and very happy to have seen their friend after all this time. Eventually, Louise returned with none other than Sherri, the fourth Chubby Panda. She was also working at the café.

Louise and Sherri spoke to their boss who let them finish early. The four girls spent hours reminiscing about the good times they had together in the foster home. Eventually, the conversation turned to the band.

'Do you think we should get back together?' Ingrid asked.

'I don't know,' Sherri replied. 'I haven't played the drums in forever. What if I don't remember how?'

'I don't even know where my keyboard is anymore. I think my mum put it in the attic...' Louise said.

'But we were so good!' Kelli replied. 'I bet with a little practice we could get back to our old level.'

'I don't know...' Sherri said, hesitating.

'Come on!' Ingrid said. 'Those times when we played together were the happiest times of my life. It made me feel really special to be part of a band like that, like it really meant something. Even if we suck now, even if we have completely lost what we had back then, is it not worth reuniting the band so we can get those good feelings back again?'

She extended her hand over the table.

'Come on, who's with me?'

'Yeah!' said Kelli, and she put her hand on top of Ingrid's.

'You're right,' Sherri said and did the same.

Louise looked at the faces of her three friends and slowly moved her hand on top of the other three.

'It looks like the Chubby Pandas are back...'

Ingrid smiled at her bandmates. And with a 'One, two, three, Pandas!' the girls all threw their hands in the air.

'Wow, what a story!' Robbie said, wiping a tear from his eye.

'It turned out that we were still as good as back at the foster home. I guess playing music is like riding a bike! A few months later a promoter heard us play at the Colchester Arts Centre and offered us a record deal right away. Soon enough we had recorded our first single and, well, the rest is history.'

'Well now, that really is the most fascinating and heartwarming tale. Here was me thinking I couldn't love this band any more than I already did, and you go and come out with a story like that!'

'Thanks, Robbie.'

'Well we have to go to a commercial break now. But when we come back Kelli here, and her band the Chubby Pandas, are going to perform their new smash hit single 'Panda Pops'. It's a real cracker. We will be right back after these messages!'

The Generation Game of Thrones

Alistair McBeath - *'How Nigel Mansell and his son became the world champions of Jim Davidson's Generation Game'*

Nigel Mansell sat in his dressing room, going through his pre-show mantras. He was due to compete, alongside his son Leo, in the World Championships of Jim Davidson's Generation Game. This would be the tenth year he had entered the competition, and he had yet to win. He was determined not to walk away again empty-handed.

He heard the shower shut off in the bathroom. A few moments later Leo walked out, dripping wet and with a towel wrapped around his waist.

Nigel turned to face Leo.

'Are you ready, son?' he asked.

'You know I am, dad,' Leo replied.

'That's what you said last year, and the year before, and you weren't.'

'This time is different. I was a fool then, I was naive. But this year I have been training hard and I know I've got what it takes. I won't let you down.'

Nigel stood up and opened the dressing room door.

'See that you don't,' he said, and walked out, shutting the door behind him.

The crowd could not contain their excitement as the announcer strutted around in front of the grandstand.

'Welcome, ladies and gentlemen,' he began. 'To this, the fourteenth annual World Championships of this noblest of competitions, the Generation Game!'

The crowd cheered wildly.

'Are you ready for thrills, spills, and excitement?!'

The cheering intensified, and several people in the front two rows fainted.

'Then without further ado, please let me introduce your host for this year's festivities. Veteran Generation Game host, Jim Davidson!'

The cheering in the crowd subsided and was replaced by murmuring and frantic discussion. Eventually, the crowd turned back to the announcer and began to boo and jeer.

'We wanted Bruce Forsyth!' one of the crowd shouted.

'Or at least Larry Grayson!' replied a second.

'Yeah, not this bigot,' a third interjected.

'Err, well,' the announcer stuttered. 'We weren't too happy about it either, but Larry Grayson has been dead for 20 years and Bruce Forsyth is too busy with Strictly this year. Jim Davidson is all we could get.'

The grumbling continued and the announcer had to dodge a couple of bottles hurled by the more unruly members of the audience. Eventually, they settled down and accepted that at least it meant that they got to see the Generation Game World Championships.

Jim Davidson, who had now judged it safe to emerge from the backstage area, had taken his place behind the podium. He nodded at the announcer, who took his cue.

'Well, it's time to get started! Ladies and gentlemen I give you the fourteenth annual World Championships of the Generation Game!'

The show's famous theme tune played from speakers around the auditorium. Despite the host, rapturous applause rippled across the grandstand. As the music and applause died down, Jim Davidson began.

'Welcome everyone to another edition of the Generation Game World Championships. Let's meet the contestants!'

Six of the eight teams came out as they were announced. But as with every edition of the World Championships, it was the two celebrity qualifiers that everyone was interested in. Nigel Mansell, the former Formula One World Champion, and his son Leo had competed at all thirteen previous Championships. This year, though, was special, as for the first time another Formula One champion would be competing against him.

'And next, we have returning celebrity contestants Nigel Mansell and his son Leo!'

Nigel and Leo walked out of the backstage area. Nigel had a look of gritty determination on his face, whilst Leo, the weak link in the team, seemed nervous.

'Finally, our second set of celebrity contestants. This year we have an interesting one for you folks. One of Nigel's former Williams teammates, and another British Formula One World Champion. None other than Damon Hill and his son, Josh!"

Nigel bristled as he took his spot behind his contestant's podium alongside Leo. Damon and Josh walked out to thunderous applause. Several items of negligee were thrown at them. Damon's rugged good looks offered the crowd something that Nigel's push broom mustache could not.

Damon and Josh, tiring of the crowd's attention, finally took their places next to Damon's erstwhile teammate and his son. Damon smiled wryly at Nigel.

'You're going down, Mansell,' he said, still smiling for the cameras.

'I'm going to crush you like I did in the last race of the 1994 Formula One season,' Mansell replied through gritted teeth.

'Now that we have all the contestants, let the games begin,' Jim Davidson bellowed from his podium.

Slowly but surely the contestants were whittled away two by two as the games became tougher.

Nigel and Leo were veterans of the competition by now, and built up a commanding lead in the early stages of the competition. They showed no signs of the nervous collapses which had characterised their previous efforts.

Meanwhile, Damon and Josh Hill worked away steadily to keep a grip on second place. They clawed back the deficit in the later rounds until it stood at only one point.

Eventually, only the two celebrity teams were left. A short break was held before the final round, during which both teams went backstage and rest.

'Right,' Nigel said to Leo, as they sat in their dressing room. 'You've managed to not cock it up so far you little twerp, but the most important round has yet to come.'

'I'm nervous, dad,' Leo replied. 'We've never made it to the final before. I don't KNOW any of these games.'

'Well, you'd better bloody learn them quick smart unless you want a clip around the ear, lad. I've told you before, this is our fourteenth year and I won't go home empty-handed again. That set of knives and portable television will be MINE. Do you understand me?'

'Yes, dad…'

'It's especially important that we don't lose to that jumped up bastard Hill. He thinks he is so much better than me because he won two Formula One championships and I only ever won one. Well, when we go back out there we will show him and that little oik of his how the Generation Game really works. Because when you play the Generation Game, you win, or you go home without any prizes.'

'Let me explain the rules to both teams as neither has taken part in a final before,' Jim Davidson said as the contest restarted. 'There will be two rounds to the final, one for the dads and one for the lads. You will be given points as with every other round, and the team with the most points at the end of the game wins! Does everyone understand?'

All four remaining players muttered their agreement, and Davidson continued.

'Very well. As this is such a momentous occasion for the world of Motorsport, we've arranged for a guest commentator to come in and give us a hand over the next two rounds. Ladies and gentlemen, please welcome Formula One legend, Murray Walker!'

The commentator walked on to the stage and took a seat behind a makeshift commentary box.

'It's a pleasure to have you with us, Murray,' said Davidson.

'It's a pleasure to be here, Bruce,' the veteran commentator replied.

'I'm Jim Davidson, not Bruce Forsyth.'

'Of course you are!' Murray replied. 'And now it's time for the race, I mean games, to begin!'

The first competition was between Nigel and Damon. They were to duke it out, Gladiators style, with pugil sticks, on a beam suspended across a pool of freezing cold water.

Both men mounted the platforms at each end of the beam and donned their protective gear.

'I'm going to take you out like Schumacher did in Adelaide!' Mansell roared across the divide.

'Bring it on, old man,' Hill yelled back.

'Go, go, go!' Murray Walker shouted as a referee waved a flag and the two men advanced down the beam.

The combat was tentative at first, with both men testing the will of their opponent using light jabs of the stick. Eventually, the battle began to heat up with the two trading heavy blows.

Mansell wiped the sweat from his brow and sent out a swing that narrowly missed Hill's head.

Unfortunately for him, Hill had seen the blow coming and responded with a low jab that sent Nigel tumbling over. He landed heavily on the beam, barely managing to stay on and prevent himself from falling into the icy water below.

Hill strode forward and loomed down over his former teammate.

'When you left Williams I was but the student, but now I am the master!' Hill cackled to the downed Mansell. He raised his pugil stick to deliver the final blow. But he was shocked when Nigel deftly swung his stick around and took out his rival's legs, sending him crashing down to the water below.

'And there goes Hill!' Walker observed from the commentary box, before nodding off to sleep.

Points were awarded, and despite the victory, the Mansells were only five points ahead of their competitors. Leo, who was by now extremely nervous, stepped forward to face his challenge.

All the possibilities were running through his mind. What if he had to make pottery, or do a ceilidh dance. The final challenges were always the hardest.

'Right boys,' Jim Davidson began. 'Your challenge is...to bake a cake!'

'Really?' Leo asked. 'Is that all?'

'Yes,' Jim replied.

'Oh, that's easy. Besides being a great racing driver, I am also a master baker.'

'So I've heard,' Josh sniggered.

'I said baker, you dirty sod.'

The competition began, and an hour later Leo's cake stood magnificent and triumphant over Josh's, which had failed to rise. As the judges announced the score, Nigel ran over and embraced his son. They had finally realised their ultimate dream of being the World Champions of the Generation Game.

All that was left now was the conveyor belt round.

They stood and watched as the prizes went past. A drinks cabinet; a portable television; a set of golf clubs; his and hers matching towels; a knife set; a set of garden table and chairs; a cuddly toy that bore a striking resemblance to Nigel's other son, Greg; and, amongst many others, the grand prize of a brand new, state of the art dishwasher.

With the help of the crowd, Leo and Nigel managed to remember almost every prize. But it was all meaningless in comparison with the real prize, the coveted World Championship trophy. Nigel held it aloft as he stood over the defeated Hill family.

'I would like to thank everyone for being here to witness my final, triumphant victory,' he said. 'And I would most of all like to thank Leo for helping me achieve my dream of winning this trophy. Finally, I would like to hereby announce my retirement from the Generation Game.'

The audience was stunned, and no-one could quite believe what they had heard. The silence continued until a lone voice piped up from behind the commentary box.

'And it seems that the team in first place has won!' Murray Walker yelled, before returning to sleep.

The Rapscallious Adventures of QP Robensmythe and Felonious Cad

Stephen Davies - *'A picaresque about the adventures of QP Robensmythe and Felonious Cad.'*

The bottle of brandy clinked against the glass as the drink was poured. The murmur of conversation rang around the social club as Q.P. Robensmythe sat enjoying a drink and a fine cigar with his comrades in front of the fire.

'What a delectable tale, Felonious,' Robensmythe said to his long time comrade, Felonious Cad. 'One of your truly finer adventures, and no mistake.'

'Indeed it is Felonious,' the Marquis of Phoenix said. 'But Master Robensmythe, your escapades are surely of greater note.'

A murmur of agreement broke out amongst the gathered gentlemen.

'Yet you have remained silent this eve, you wag. Will you not regale us with a tale of utmost bravado and derring-do?'

Robensmythe swirled the brandy around in his glass as he pondered the idea.

'As you wish, my friend. Which tale would you deign me to tell?'

'Oh, I say, old boy,' Felonious Cad interjected. 'Won't you tell us of the time your choice of cummerbund decided the outcome of the Battle of Rhodes?'

Robensmythe scoffed. It was a favourite tale of his, and the cad Cad knew it. What's more, the blighter had been there to witness the whole event, and he would be sure to correct him if his account was ill-remembered.

'Very well,' he began. 'Let me tell you a tale.'

The gentlemen all settled down to listen, as Robensmythe began his yarn.

'It all began one summer's eve on the island of Crete. I was sat in a taverna in the port town of Rethymnon, enjoying a quiet drink of Ouzo with my friend here, Felonious Cad. I overheard two Turkish gentlemen discussing the profits to be made in the aftermath of the naval to-do that was to take place just north of Rhodes.

'Well now, being the sort who revels of making a quick penny, I listened fully to their plans. And before good old Felonious had finished his drink I was off to my lodgings to pack my meager belongings.

'Before I knew it I was at the harbour chartering a local gentleman of the Hellenic persuasion to carry myself and Felonious to the port of Rhodes Town. The journey was to be long and arduous, and I offered to reward him handsomely, with a ten percent cut of the profits of my venture.'

'Of course, QP had no intention of following through with the bargain,' Cad cut in. 'It was merely a ruse to fob off paying the fellow at the time.'

'Quite, Felonious, quite,' Robensmythe agreed. 'The man fell for my gambit hook, line, and sinker. And after he dropped us off in Rhodes Town I made sure to never see the blighter again.

'Anyway, we arrived on the island and found there to be no conflict whatsoever. It is fair to say that we were thoroughly disappointed with the situation. The Turkish fellows had inadvertently lied to us. They would later come to regret it when I broke the siege of Adrianople using only my trusty nail clippers.

'Left with no scheme, and dreading the prospect of actual work, good old Felonious and I found our way to the nearest watering hole. It was a charming little venue just inside the walls of the old town.

'The proprietor was a kindly old gent, who went by the name of Rhodos Roger. Seeing the desperate need of two veterans of the Atlantis campaign for board, breakfast, and booze, he put us up. With all the Ouzo we could drink!'

'And let me tell you,' Felonious added, 'that was a lot of Ouzo.'

'There was little to do and much of the island was closed for the winter season. We spent our days fighting off the accursed Baron Munchausen and his cronies for the best spots on the beaches around the town. That is, until one day when the promised spat finally drew near.

'We were sunning ourselves next to the sea and enjoying a good bottle of the finest retsina when a British naval officer approached us.

'"I say!" he said. "You two chaps look a fine mess, and no mistake." And there was no mistake, as by this point we had been scandalously drunk for some days, and it was starting to show. "Yet," he continued, "I sense a noble purpose about you."'

'I told him that was just the toll ouzo and a few days of Greek sun takes on one after a couple of days,' Felonious Cad added, to a series of guffaws.

'Well, the officer offered us both a role captaining a naval frigate, as they were short on qualified men for the upcoming battle. Felonious and I elected to share the captaincy of a single vessel, HMS Mercenary of Jollity. She was a delightful beast, that ship.'

'Damn fine,' Cad scoffed. 'Many a good seaman's lunch was lost on her deck.'

'We were offered rudimentary training in the arts of naval combat. Neither of us possessed the social mobility to have studied the fine discipline at the Maritime College in Greenwich, after all.

'It was not long before we were had our baptism of fire in the cauldron of battle that was the coast of Rhodes. We spent the first half of the scuffle concealing ourselves by pretending to be a small Greek islet named Robensmythos. It seemed that our foes, whoever they were, fell for the ruse.

'When night fell on the fifth day of the battle, it provided some respite to our weary men. Some of them hadn't even seen a bottle of Ouzo for nearly a week! We emerged from our hiding spot and decided it was time for affirmative action.

'Thusly we led HMS Mercenary of Jollity to the Turkish Coast and refuelled our alcohol reserves. Then we aimed to return to our previous hiding location. Alas...'

'And alack!' Felonious Cad added.

'And alack indeed, we returned to find a sloop snooping around our previous position. The game was up! Robensmythos was no more, and we had to find a way out of the situation. For you see, the enemy had all guns pointed at the Jollity, ready to blast our behinds to smithereens.

'Felonious and I were oblivious to these goings-on, as we were emerging from a twelve-course feast in the captains' private dining room. It so happened that we were entertaining some dignitaries from the British admiralty. And so we were delayed in our emergence from the meal as I had needed to spend some considerable time in my chambers. One must choose the most appropriate cummerbund to wear when greeting His Majesty's finest naval commanders, after all.

'Eventually, I opted for the white silk, in honour of the naval victory over the Atlanteans that we had enjoyed together so many years hence.

'As it transpired, upon our emergence from our private mess hall an agent of the enemy was keeping watch of our bridge from the deck of the sloop. He happened to train his binoculars on me the very second my waistline succumbed to the engorging it had just endured.

'O! How my waistcoat split open, and my shirt was irreversibly ripped. And, verily, my cummerbund ripped from my midriff and caught on an outstretched plank of wood.

'The blighters must have taken it as a sign of surrender. They relayed the message back to their flagship imploring the immediate cessation of all hostilities. For some reason, their Grand Admiral decided to order all their weaponry and munitions be thrown overboard. The odd fellow did it without waiting to consult with corroborating sources that our surrender was assured.

'Tragically for them, our admirals had no such intention of returning the favour. They opened fire without delay, sending thousands of tonnes of cannon fire directly into the hulls of the enemy ships.

'Within moments the enemy fleet was in ruins, destroyed beyond the ability to fight back. They were flying flags of surrender of their own. Truly it was a remarkable occurrence. One which undoubtedly had the most profound effects on the course of the war.'

'Indeed,' Felonious agreed. 'Such an important turning point in the conflict.'

'And tell me,' the Marquis of Phoenix asked. 'Against whom was this battle fought?'

'You know,' Q.P. Robensmythe replied. 'It never once crossed my mind to ask. Probably the French, or the Germans. We seem to end up fighting them a lot for some reason.'

'Well that wasn't quite the tale we expected, Quentin, old horse,' one of the other Eton old horses chimed in. 'We were expecting much more in the way of swashbuckling and adventure. Not a mere cummerbund explosion.'

'Well you see, old horse,' Robensmythe replied. 'That is what you get when you allow that most felonious of cads, Felonious Cad, to pick the topic of the story. Perhaps if you wish for a better tale you would care to regale us of the time when you accidentally courted the King of Norway's goat under the most exceptional of circumstances?'

The old boy screwed up his features, and after his glass was topped up to the point of overflow, came to a resolution.

'Very well,' he began. 'It all started when I was invited to a gala by the Norwegian royal family in honour of their prize-winning goat...'

Upwardly Mobile

Brendan Rodgers - 'A man uses social media to gain power over his colleagues and friends. rather than rely on his qualifications he blackmails his way to the top. until he meets someone who's online persona is a lie. He falls in love with the lie but gains no happiness from discovering who she really is, and punishes her and simultaneously loses everything he has become.'

'Jenkins! Get in here!'

Carl flinched. It was the third time today that his boss had summoned him into her office to yell at him, and it wasn't even 11am.

As he stood there, being dressed down for whatever he had done wrong now, he rued his life choices. Last time there had been no pencils in the stationery cupboard and she had yelled for 15 minutes.

He had dreamed of leaving university with his classics degree and walking straight into a high paying research position. Or staying on to a Ph.D. before landing a cushy job at the university.

Unfortunately, reality had other ideas. Carl had left university, a classics degree in tow, just after the recession hit Britain in 2008. With no immediate prospects at home, he had moved to Australia for a year and gotten a job picking fruit to fund a hedonistic lifestyle.

Eventually, his visa and his money ran out and he returned home. There he bummed about for a while before having to get off his arse and find himself a real job.

By this point his degree was useless. Everyone and their dog had a degree these days. It didn't even set him apart from the pack and the handful of careers open to people with a classics degree were few and oversubscribed.

After months of never hearing back about anything, he finally got a call back about this job. It paid less than he would have hoped, and that really he truly needed. But it was the first step on the career ladder - and anything was better than the Job Centre.

But he soon found that if he was to stay with this company he wouldn't be taking any steps up the career ladder at all.

He had no responsibility, beyond making everyone's tea and coffee in the morning. Most of the time he got dumped with the work no one else wanted to do. And far more of it than he had the time or mental capacity to handle. Hence the frequent trips to his manager's office.

The promotion prospects were nil. It wasn't even that there were no openings. Every time a role came up he thought of applying for it, but his manager threatened to fire him if he went through with the application. He couldn't risk losing his job. If he went for the promotion and his manager found out he would lose everything. It was better to be on a pittance than on nothing at all.

He snapped out of his daydream as his manager appeared to have stopped yelling. She was now staring straight at him as if expecting him to say something.

'Well? I don't have all day. What do you have to say for yourself?'

Carl was lost. He hadn't heard a word of his manager's rant and he didn't want to make things worse by saying the wrong thing.

'I'm waiting...' she snapped.

'I'm sorry...?' he ventured. 'It won't happen again...?'

His boss sat back in her chair, placated by his response.

'See that it doesn't,' she replied, before returning to her paperwork. After a few seconds, she looked at him again. 'Are you still here,' she asked. 'Get back to work!'

That evening - two hours after he should have finished work - he finally gave up and decided to head home. As he picked his coat up from the back of his desk chair he noticed through the glass wall that his manager's computer was still turned on.

She, along with everyone else, had left on time, and he had been left by himself. He found he spent at least an hour in the office every evening, usually two. Somehow everyone else found a way to piss off at 5pm.

Carl reckoned that if she came in tomorrow morning to find her computer still on that she would just blame him. He decided to go into the office and shut it down. He made his way through the door and sat down behind her desk. The plush leather chair was comfortable. Much nicer than his £15 monstrosity from Staples.

He looked at the computer and started closing down windows when he noticed several tabs open in the browser. He clicked through them and found that his manager's Facebook account was open.

'I shouldn't...' he said. 'However...'

The contents of the profiles were astonishing. There were photographs of her engaging in community service. Others of herhelping elderly ladies cross the road and building houses in Africa. Most shockingly of all, there were photos of her...smiling.

Everyone he had spoken to since he started had described her as awful to work for and a generally unpleasant person to boot. She never socialised with the rest of the office. When she did deign to talk to her inferiors it was usually to yell at them.

Carl couldn't think of a single occasion on which she had ever smiled, let alone given out any positive reinforcement to one of her underlings. Seeing this was like opening up Pandora's Box.

He reflected on all the times she had been horrible to him. Yelled at him, turned him down for a promotion, threatened to fire him. And here right in front of him was a gold mine of blackmail material. A plan began to form. Taking screenshots of the most shocking pictures he sent them all to print. He left work that evening with a smile on his face for the first time ever.

The next morning Carl strode into the office, full of confidence. He checked the folder in his bag to make sure that all the printed images were still there and sat down at his desk. After he got settled and finalised exactly what it was he wanted to say he stood up and marched right into his manager's office with the papers.

'Can I help you, Mr. Jenkins?' she asked, without looking away from her screen. Her tone suggested that all things considered, she probably would not be able to render any aid at this juncture.

'As a matter of fact, you can,' Carl replied.

'Oh, and how might I do that?' The sarcasm was dripping from her voice.

'For starters, you can promote me,' Carl said. 'And you can give me a nice big raise to boot.'

'And why, pray, would I do that?'

Carl opened the folder and pulled out the printed photographs. He slapped them down on the table in front of his manager, whose eyes widened when she saw them.

'Where did you get these?!' she demanded. 'Tell me right now and I'll think about not firing you.'

'I came in to shut your computer down last night and Facebook was still open. I got them from there. Now, give me what I want or I'll show the whole office that your cold, hard exterior is an act. They'll see you all for the kindly, giving person you really are!'

His manager appeared dumbfounded. For a moment she stared at him in disbelief.

'Isn't this the part,' Carl asked, suddenly very nervous, 'where you say "You wouldn't dare!" And then I say I would and then you give me what I want?'

'You idiot!' his manager roared. 'Those pictures aren't of me! They're of my twin sister! She passed away recently and I was going through her social media profiles making sure that they would serve as a proper tribute to her now that she's gone!'

'Oh gosh, I had no idea!' Carl blurted out, suddenly ashamed. He had never looked at the name on the profiles, the likeness was so complete. 'I'm so sorry, I didn't even know you had a sister!' He feared for the worst now. Surely that would be it for him. He would be clearing out his desk and heading home in ten minutes.

'I should fire you for this gross invasion of my privacy!' his manager yelled at him. She was almost quivering with rage. But suddenly, out of nowhere, she raised her hand to her temple, and the anger seemed to drain away. 'But I'm not going to do that. It's not what she would have wanted.'

Carl felt the tension in the air begin to dissipate.

'But if you think you're going to get a promotion then you have another thing coming,' she added. 'I have heard from the security guards that you've been working several hours overtime in the evenings and that is unacceptable. You'll be pleased to know that we conducted interviews for a new employee yesterday who will assist you with your work.'

Given the expected outcome a few moments earlier that was more than Carl could ever have hoped for. His poorly thought out scheme had backfired on him most spectacularly, but in the end, he had come out of the situation rather well.

Though things were still by no means perfect he noticed improvements over the next few weeks. Particularly with the new employee starting.

A month or two later he was sat at his desk updating a spreadsheet when the once familiar bellow of 'Jenkins!' rang in his ears. Fearing the worst and giving an almost Pavlovian flinch he went in to see his manager.

'You wanted to see me?' he asked, nervously.

'Yes,' she replied. 'I've seen the quarterly reports.'

Carl braced himself for a barrage.

'Good work, Jenkins. Well done. If you keep this up there will be a promotion in it for you after all.'

Carl stared at his manager in disbelief and began to wonder if she had been taken over by some sort of parasite. After a few seconds, she looked back up at him.

'And remember, no more social media use in the office.'

A Day in the Life

Jonathan Cromie - 'A mayfly, minutes away from death, reflects on its life.'

The mayfly fought as hard as it could to stay in the air, but its tired old wings were no longer up to the task. Reluctantly it began its long descent. The water of the stream rushed towards it at an alarming speed.

It landed hard on a lily pad at the water's edge and brought its wings to rest. They had served the mayfly well, but now it had flown its last, and they were of use no longer.

It rested on the lily pad and embraced its final moments. The inevitability of death was one the mayfly had come to accept during its naiad stages. It had seen the long transformation and quick ending of so many of its brothers and sisters, with only a short, busy life between.

And now its time had come too. The naiad period seemed so long ago now. Although compared to the length of its transformation the mayfly had only been in this form for a fraction of the time it took to reach maturity.

It considered the futility of its existence. All that time spent gestating in the stream, trapped until it had achieved full maturity. Only to experience the freedom of the world for such a short period.

The whole thing felt cruel. As if it had been released into the world after a long imprisonment to find that it had no time at all to experience it. To lie there and long to be free, to experience existence, and then to have it all taken away again so suddenly, and so finally. That was the most grievous injustice.

The mayfly watched as the next generation of its species spread their wings for the first time. It could feel the hope radiating from them as they buzzed away into the distance. The wonder at finally being able to explore outside their world, which until this point had been so confined and small.

In a way, the mayfly envied them their naïveté. The same naïveté it had itself experienced upon bursting from the water for the first time such a short time ago. The belief that it would be different this time. That what happened to all its ancestors that it had seen go before wouldn't happen again.

Not this time.

But it also pitied them. For the simple reason that, like its own hopes, they would realise very quickly indeed that their lives weren't going to be any different. They would die just the same as those who went before them.

It wondered why. As far as it could tell it had only existed in this final form to mate. There had been no time for anything else. No time to explore the world or to even help move forward the march of nature. In a way, this was even crueler than the brevity of its lifespan. Its sole reason for existing was to propagate more of the species. If that wasn't the focus then at least it might have had the time to do something else.

Even sadder was that more of the species who would go on to do the same and then, themselves, die. Millions, if not billions of lives and dreams unfulfilled. All to keep a species alive that had no reason for existence beyond continuous propagation in the first place.

No reason to be, no reason to continue, no reason to even live other than because the world decided you had to. But by the time any individual mayfly realised this, it was too late. By the time they came to understand the utter futility of their existence the deed had been done. The mating process was complete and the new larvae were tucked away in the stream before the inevitable decline set in.

How desperately the mayfly wanted to beat its wings again. To fly up one last time to its newly matured kin that flitted about above the water and tell them not to bother. That the whole enterprise wasn't worth it. To let the species die out. To finally put the mayfly out of its collective misery.

But it couldn't. It tested its wings and found that, while they still had some movement in them, that they had stiffened up. It was surprised they hadn't disintegrated already. To try and fly now would be foolish.

Despondent, it struggled across the lily pad on ageing legs. Every movement was difficult and painful. It finally reached the other side and gazed out over the water. There was a family of frogs splashing in the shallows amongst a bed of reeds on the other bank.

For the entirety of its naiad period, it had watched the family of frogs grow, prosper, and enjoy their lives together. It had watched the millions of its brethren reach such an early crescendo and wither away to nothing. All while this small family had blossomed in front of its very eyes.

It was unfair. Watching those creatures, now and then, had been a reminder that it would never get to experience the true wonders of the world. Perhaps, it thought, that was why it had been so keen to defy the inevitable. All it had wanted was a real chance at life.

It turned away from the frogs and back to its solitude. It began to wonder how long it would be before it died. It couldn't be too long now. What was next? Was there something after this life for it to move on to? Something beyond the realm of pointless existence that offered some sort of explanation for the emptiness it felt at this moment. It suspected not.

It paused for a moment to reflect on this. Maybe it was taking the wrong outlook on the whole situation. After all, it imagined that it was a privilege to have existed at all, even for such a brief time, in a world as glorious and beautiful as this. The surroundings of the stream were magnificent. It could only wonder at the realms beyond that which it had seen on its first flight up above the tree line.

For that brief second it had observed the golden fields, and the green of the rolling hills beyond, spreading out in all directions as far as it could see. In that one moment, it had felt more alive than it imagined any other creature could have done so before.

Its time, at the least the meaningful time afforded to it after its final transformation was so fleeting that every moment was important. It had to cherish the things it had experienced, however short, and celebrate its existence, because no one else would. It would be dead long before any of its children were even old enough to be aware of their existence, let alone its own.

It turned back to face the family of frogs. Every movement was more difficult than the last, and it felt that its final moments were drawing near. It looked at the family in a new light as it swam around in the shallows.

They were creatures untroubled by the problems of life. They did not care that at some point they would be separated, or that their existence was short-lived. Rather they enjoyed the time they had together. They cherished it for what it was, instead of what it could, or perhaps should have been.

The mayfly was finding it hard to breathe now. Every breath was laboured and it felt its thin legs begin to collapse beneath it as they could no longer hold up the weight of its body.

It longed to see the view above the treetops one final time. But it consoled itself with the memory as its vision began to first blur and then fade away as the icy fingers of death crept across it.

It simply lay there, allowing death to come to it slowly but surely. It had lived its life as fully as was possible under the circumstances and it was content that its short time on the earth had been worthwhile.

Around the mayfly, the world went on. Nobody, not even the other mayflies, while experiencing their own elation at the wonder of life, noticed the lonely creature dying on the lily pad. The march of time paid it no heed.

As death finally claimed the mayfly, it felt as though new life had been blown into its wings. It tested them briefly, then flew up and landed on the extended skeletal finger.

'WHAT SAY YOU, LITTLE MAYFLY?' the skeletal figure asked.

I'm glad I lived, the mayfly thought.

The world kept on turning. A million more mayflies burst forth from the water along the stream, ready to begin their brief journeys. Just as had happened a million times before, and would happen a million times more.

What had seemed to be the futility of its existence had, in the mayfly's final moments, given it its greatest revelation and its greatest comfort. It was not creating life for the furthering of what was essentially a doomed species. It was giving millions of creatures a chance to live - a chance to exist. Just because that existence would have no impact did not mean the chance to do so was undeserved.

The mayfly flew with its new wings to the top of the treeline and looked out over the countryside one last time. But it did not stop at the trees this time and continued to rise high up into the sky.

The Walls Have Eyes

Suzie (website comment) -'*Man hears scratching in the walls, under the floor boards.*'

Albert Finch sat bolt upright in bed. It was the middle of the night and he could hear it. Again.

It was the third time this week that he had been woken up in the wee small hours by the scrabbling noise in the walls of the bedroom.

He shook his wife awake.

'Mavis, it's happening again.'

'What is, dear?' she replied, without stirring from her position facing away from him in the bed.

'The scrabbling. In the walls. Can't you hear it?'

'No, dear,' came the sleepy reply. It was soon followed by light snoring.

Albert tutted to himself as he swung his legs from underneath the covers, into his slippers which, as always, were waiting by the bedside.

'Bloody mice,' he muttered. 'Gotten into the walls again. I'll teach them to interrupt my good night's sleep.'

Albert plodded out of the bedroom, and down the stairs of the house that he and Mavis had lived in for 50 years. He entered the kitchen and began rummaging around in one of the cupboards. He was looking for the rusty, but trusty, old mousetrap that had served them well for the past couple of decades.

He found it hidden underneath 30 years of collected Tupperware, and set it up on the floor by the cupboard. He used a small piece of cheese from the fridge, with a piece for himself as well, of course.

The trap set, Albert trudged back up the stairs and laid back down in bed. He managed to tune out the scratching enough to sleep right through the rest of the night.

The next morning, Albert woke up, as he did every day, at 7.30am. He didn't need an alarm for this. Despite having been retired for 10 years, a whole life of his body conditioning itself to be awake and out of bed in time to get to work was difficult to undo. So he still rose at the same hour as he would have done if he still had to go across town to the dockyard to earn a living wage.

As always, Mavis was already up and was probably long gone on one of her WI errands. They seemed to take up so much of her time since she had retired from her job as a nurse.

After a quick shower, Albert went downstairs to make himself some breakfast. As he crossed the threshold of the kitchen he remembered the trap he had set the night before. Hearing no more scratching he decided to go and check it.

He walked over to where he had laid the trap, and smugly bent down to find...that the trap had gone.

A puzzled look crossed his face, and he looked around in surprise, wondering what had happened to it. It was nowhere to be seen.

Perhaps, he reasoned, Mavis had moved it out of the way when she got up. He shrugged, stood back up and turned around in the direction of the fridge, before standing right on the mousetrap.

He leaped up, grasping his foot in agony, the mousetrap still hanging from his big toe.

Once he had managed to remove the trap, and the pain in his foot subsided, he began to wonder how it had got there. He had looked all around for it when he found that it wasn't where he left it. And he definitely had not stepped over it on his way in.

Exasperated, he returned the trap to the cupboard and limped over to the fridge to get the ingredients for breakfast.

He decided to ask Mavis about it when she returned. But as he opened the fridge he could have sworn he heard a quiet sniggering. This was followed by further scrabbling behind the walls and under the floorboards.

Albert was watching daytime television with his foot up when Mavis returned around lunchtime. She noticed his swollen toe with the ice pack around it as soon as she entered, and she rushed over to him in his favourite armchair.

'Oh, Alby, what on earth did you do to your foot?' she asked. She busied herself about the toe, making sure it was elevated well enough and that the ice was being applied with enough pressure.

'I could ask you that question,' Albert replied with a grimace.

'What do you mean, dear?' Mavis asked.

'Did you move that mousetrap I set in the kitchen last night before you went out this morning?'

Mavis looked puzzled.

'No, I had to meet Edie at 7.30 and I woke up a bit late so I didn't have time to make myself any breakfast before I left. I didn't even set foot in the kitchen this morning.'

Albert looked at his wife, gobsmacked.

'But I put it down by the cupboard, and it wasn't there when I woke up!' he protested. 'Are you sure you didn't move it?'

'Positive, dear. It was late when you got up last night, gone midnight. Perhaps you're misremembering because you're tired.'

'But...' Albert began, before trailing off. Was his age finally catching up to him?

Mavis went to dump her bags in the kitchen. As she left the room he heard the same quiet sniggering he had first heard earlier.

That night, Albert had hatched a plan. He waited until Mavis was asleep and sneaked downstairs into the kitchen. With a little work, and some appropriation of household objects, he managed to create a passable trap that couldn't be shifted easily. He baited it with a selection of food from the fridge. And then, he waited.

A while later, the scratching began. He realised, upon jerking awake, that he had dozed off in the kitchen chair.

He rubbed the sleep from his eyes and they began to adjust to the light. There in front of him, as clear as day, a group of three small humanoid creatures were standing around the trap. They were looking at it with some suspicion.

They either hadn't noticed him or didn't care, but he stayed still anyway just in case. He watched as they chattered amongst themselves, gesticulating at his rudimentary trap. They seemed to be weighing up the pros and cons of going for the food.

The three reached an agreement and appeared to play a tiny game of Rock Paper Scissors. With a squeak of annoyance the one that lost edged cautiously towards the trap as the other two looked on.

When it reached the device, it gingerly picked up a piece of cheese from the plate. The large, ancient Tupperware box that was resting above it slammed down, trapping the creature inside. Its comrades scattered, chattering away to themselves as they went and vanished into the gloom.

Triumphantly, Albert strode over to the box. He slid the lid underneath and sealed it almost completely. He made sure to leave just enough gap for the little blighter to breathe without escaping.

The creature chattered incessantly and banged on the lid of the box. Albert placed it in one of the higher cupboards, out of the reach of its friends, until the morning. He would show it to Mavis and she would know that he had been telling the truth. He slept soundly that night.

The next morning he woke even earlier than Mavis. Marching her downstairs he triumphantly threw open the cupboard which contained the hostage. He picked up the Tupperware box and removed the lid. But it was empty.

'But, I swear I caught a real pixie!' he said.

Mavis looked concerned. 'I have to go now dear, but we can talk about this when I get back later.' They never did talk about it.

The pixies became an obsession for Albert. He concocted more and more elaborate ways to trap one as proof of their existence. He even bought a cat. On the first night, the cat caught one of the creatures in its jaws. Seeing it was dead, he was certain that would be proof, but the next day the carcass had somehow turned in to that of a mouse.

Mavis became more concerned as the days went by. But she knew her husband wasn't one to make things up, so she ignored his increasingly obtuse plans.

After two weeks of trying to find proof of the pixies' existence, Albert was on the verge of a nervous breakdown. He hadn't slept for more than an hour at a time in over a week. In the meantime he noticed things start to go missing from the kitchen. Every morning his wife would ask where more of the cutlery or a pot or pan had gone. He could never offer an adequate explanation.

On the fifteenth night, he broke down and couldn't take it anymore.

As he sat his nightly vigil in the kitchen, he waited for the scratching to come. It wasn't long before he could hear the noise coming from behind the walls. The little creatures emerged from the darkness into the main area of the room.

'Please,' he cried, startling the creatures, who had long since given up paying him any mind. 'Please just tell me what you want. My wife thinks I'm crazy, and every attempt I've made to prove that you exist has failed. What are you and why are you tormenting me?'

The group of pixies stared at him blankly for a second, before dipping down into a huddled the customary chattering ensued.

The huddle broke and one of the pixies stepped forward. It beckoned him forth with its tiny arm, and Albert laid down on the floor, so his head was next to the little creature.

'We are from the Land of Air,' it said, in a small voice. 'We flew here from our home on a remarkable contraption, but we were harassed by a large bird, and the machine broke. We have been scavenging supplies from your house, that we may repair the flying machine and return to our homeland. But alas, none of us are skilled engineers, and we lack the knowledge to complete the repairs.'

Albert felt a huge pang of guilt in his stomach. This whole time he thought hey had been invading his home, and he had tried to drive them away, even killing one. All they wanted to do was return to their own home.

'Perhaps I can help,' he said

'Are you sure?' the spokespixie asked.

'It is the least I can do.'

As the sun rose the next morning Albert saw the pixies fly off in their machine that, using his engineering knowledge, he had helped to fix. He waved them goodbye from the front door as they flew off into the sunset.

As he shut the door Mavis came downstairs.

'What have you been doing up all night this time?' she asked, sceptically.

'Sorting out the mouse problem once and for all,' Albert replied with a smile on his face. 'We won't be having any problems with them anymore.'

Mavis looked at him as if he had gone crackers, which, technically, he had. However briefly. After a second her expression grew into a smile.

'If you say so, dear,' she said, planting a big kiss on his cheek. 'I'll bring home sausages for dinner.'

Kicking Up a Stink

Fiona Heffernan (generated by a plot generating book) -
*'Vowing not to bathe for an entire year, a North Korean
scientist becomes the subject of a documentary film'.*

The Demilitarised Zone, Korean Peninsula - 1990

The boy cowered behind the hillock. Here he was,
only 12 years old, making one of the most dangerous journeys
on the planet. If he made it, he made it to freedom. But if he
failed, then he would be returned home, and shot as a
deserter, along with the rest of his family.

His father had sent him, reasoning with his mother
that North Korea was no place for a boy of his talents. He had
to make it to the South, where he could be free to use his
intellect for good.

And so he had crawled across this vast expanse,
finding hiding spots wherever he could. He could see the
South Korean end of the zone. He was nearly there.

The searchlights passed over his head, and he made a
dash for it.

Seoul, South Korea - 2013

Dr. Kim turned on the television in his office in the
chemistry department at Seoul University. He regretted the

decision immediately as the news channel came on. It showed a highlight reel of the latest posturing taking place across the expanse of the 38th parallel.

A North Korean rocket test strayed 'off course' and killed two South Koreans on one of the border islands. In retaliation some South Korean bombers dropped their payloads on a known munitions cache in the North. Three guards at the base were killed.

The two killed in the South would be mourned as countrymen. The three Northern soldiers worshipped as martyrs.

Dr. Kim took his glasses off and placed them on his desk before closing his eyes and rubbing the bridge of his nose. He let out an audible sigh and turned the TV off. God save us all, he thought. God save us all.

As he moved to look over the latest findings from the experiments in the graduate laboratory there was a knock on the door.

'Enter,' he said, returning the papers to the desk. The door opened to reveal Lee Soo-yun, one of the grad students on his team.

'Dr. Kim, we are closing up the lab for the day. It's late. You should go home.'

'I will soon,' Dr. Kim replied. 'I just have a couple more things to finish up.'

'Will there be anything else before I go, Doctor?' Su Yun asked.

'No, Soo-yun,' the Doctor began, but changed his mind as the girl went to leave. 'Wait, before you go, tell me what you think of the situation with the North.'

His protege hesitated, and Dr. Kim noticed her unease.

'It's ok,' he said, smiling. 'I know I was born in the North, but I have no affiliation with them anymore. I left there 23 years ago. You will not offend me with your opinion.'

'Well, if you are certain...' Soo-yun began. 'I think that in the media, that the North fares rather badly, and the South, they can get away with anything. Because they are the 'good guys' they get a free pass because all they're doing is killing the bad men north of the border.'

'That is an interesting opinion. One that I suspect would not curry favour with our government,' Dr. Kim replied.

'I am not saying that the North is innocent. It is they that are responsible for starting the vast majority of the border skirmishes. Without that, they would not be so demonised. But our military has killed at least as many of their citizens as they have of ours, if not more.'

'And what do you think is to be done?'

Lee Soo-yun paused for a moment and then spoke.

'I am not sure,' she said. 'Perhaps the governments need to make a concerted effort to fix the problem.'

'They have been trying that for 60 years,' Dr. Kim replied.

'Well someone has to do something!'

'Yes, they do,' Dr. Kim smiled.

San Diego, California - 2014

'Come on, Jerry, we need to think of a subject soon or we're going to be in trouble. I've got the executives up in Hollywood breathing down my neck to follow up on The Life of Sharks with another hit. There must be something in the news that's caught your eye.'

'I'm looking, Roy. Believe me, I'm looking.'

Jerry sat on the couch in the offices of SanSan Films and browsed the news pages on his laptops. He skimmed past a few editorial pieces about Obamacare and the state of the country and landed on the more lighthearted new section. It was mostly dross, but after skipping over the first couple of stories something caught his eye.

'Roy,' he said. 'Have you ever been to South Korea?'

Seoul, South Korea - The Next Day

'I am here today with the man himself, Dr. Kim Myung Hee. We will talk about exactly why he has undertaken this...extraordinary protest,' Jerry began, talking to the camera that had been set up in Dr. Kim's office. 'Dr. Kim, please do tell me what inspired your decision to not bathe until the conflict in Korea is resolved'

'Because the situation stinks!' Dr. Kim replied in excellent English. Jerry smiled at the phrase and wondered if the Doctor knew it would be used as a sound bite in the trailer for the film. If so, he must have said it on purpose.

Truly the man reeked. Jerry and Roy had never smelled anything like it before. Jerry wondered at what point it had reached its zenith and stopped getting worse. After all, a person could only smell SO bad before it just became vomit-inducing. It was a powerful hum.

His appearance was notably affected too. His hair matted in clumps and his clothes were all grubby. He allowed himself to wash them, apparently. But when you were as dirty and smelly as he was, eventually it began to transfer directly to your clothes as soon as you put them on. Roy reckoned he would have to shower for a whole day to get rid of all the grime.

'Every day the two armies sit a stone's throw away from each other and brandish their weaponry, and it seems that no-one wants to do anything to stop it. The Korean people are one people. Not two. Every week we hear about another family whose children, parents, or siblings aren't going home for dinner that night.

'The situation affects everything,' the Doctor continued. 'It hangs around our daily lives, like a bad smell. And so I wanted to give the government another bad smell to

148

think about. My bad smell. I have not bathed for one whole year. And I will not bathe again until I hear concrete assurances from both sides that they will engage in talks to end this madness.'

'That is an...interesting solution, Dr. Kim. But tell me, how do you plan on enforcing this. Pyongyang is some distance from here, and even the South Korean government can't smell you from this far away. And they're in the same city.'

'I am aware of the limitations. An annual meeting is scheduled between members of both governments in the demilitarised zone next week. They will discuss the possibility of opening full discussions about the situation. It is expected that both parties will be attending with the sole intention of delaying talks for another year. But not if I have my way.'

'You sound like you have a plan, Dr. Kim.'

'I do. And if you follow me it may well win you one of your coveted Oscars.'

The Demilitarised Zone, Korean Peninsula - One Week Later

The three men crouched behind the low wall. It had taken them 6 hours to trek out to this remote location. It was far enough away from the prying eyes of both sets of border guards that they could sneak into the DMZ unnoticed. The cameraman had left his larger camera back at the university and had opted for a more portable camcorder.

They were fortunate. The abandoned village that was being used for the talks was only a mile from where they were currently hiding. Just inside the zone on the South Korean side.

They crept along slowly, keeping as low to the ground as possible. The light hadn't quite left the sky yet so they were at much greater risk of being spotted by one of the guard towers. Eventually, they were in sight of the building.

Because neither side could agree on who should police the agreements, there were very few guards in the area around the village. Anyway, anyone who started a shooting match here was in trouble. It would quickly escalate to several government ministers from both sides getting hit. And that would be a PR nightmare for both sides.

Using the fading light as cover, the three men swept around the side of the area until they had managed to get right up to the back of the building. Only two guards, one from each side, remained positioned in front of the door.

A light breeze kicked up, and the smell from the man who had not bathed for a year wafted around the corner of the building. As it pierced the nostrils of the two men at the door they both began to eye each other suspiciously.

'Was that you?' The North Korean guard asked, disgusted.

'No, it was you, you filthy mongrel!' The Southern guard replied.

The two men flung their weapons to the ground and leaped at each other, rolling around on the floor swinging punches. Dr. Kim saw his opportunity when a set of keys fell from the belt of one of the guards, who had now both rolled off elsewhere to continue their brawl. He ran forward, grabbed the keys and locked the door to the building shut.

Pulling a megaphone from his belt he raised to his lips and spoke.

'Honourable members of the North and South Korean governments. I am sure by now that you can smell my rather pungent odour. The door to the building has been locked and you have no escape. To ensure my safety I have brought a documentary crew with me. I am sure you would not shoot a man live on camera. I can assure you that what you are smelling now will only get worse. I will kindly ask you to throw away your usual reluctance and agree to full and frank discussions on the future of Korea as soon as possible. If you

150

agree I will leave, and take my smell with me. I await your response.'

For a few seconds there was only silence and then fits of coughing erupted from the building. A moment later a rasping voice came.

'OK! We give in. We will agree to at least talk to each other.'

'And the other side?' Dr. Kim asked.

'Yes, yes', a different voice said. 'Anything! Just go away! We can't breathe!'

And so Dr. Kim and the camera crew retreated. The long walk back to their pick up point gave them time for reflection. Jerry and the cameraman thought about the Oscar they would win, and the money and fame that would come with it. Dr. Kim spent the journey looking forward to the most well-earned shower in history.

Private Affairs

***Fiona Heffernan (generated by a plot generating book) -** 'Suddenly able to hear others' thoughts, a single mother of three uncovers a hidden family secret.'*

Amanda tried to juggle the heavy shopping bags in her hands to get her keys out of her handbag and into the lock on the front door. She struggled and eventually managed to reach out to the door. It was at that moment that the plastic bag containing all the fruit she had bought at the supermarket split. She groaned at the loud splat of half a dozen peaches impacting with the path.

She sighed. At least that was one bag less, she thought. With a little more reshuffling she managed to get the door open.

Dumping the shopping bags on the table she went back outside to collect the fruit that had gone overboard. As she was about to go back out the door her daughter, Lisa came out of the front room.

'Oh, hi Mum,' she said before making to go upstairs.

'You wait right there, young lady,' Amanda replied. 'I was struggling outside for five minutes with those bags and you were in the front room all along?'

'Yeah...?' her daughter replied.

'Didn't you think you might come out and help me?'

'I was on the phone to Sean,' came the reply.

'I've told you not to use the phone before 6! Honestly girl. Go to your room.'

'Um, I was heading there anyway, but okay.'

'And no using the phone or the internet!' Amanda called up the stairs after her retreating daughter.

She took a moment and a deep breath to calm herself down. After retrieving the strawberries from the lawn she went into the front room to sit down and relax for a bit. Soon her young son would be done with playgroup and her husband back from work.

Still distracted by the lack of consideration shown by her daughter she kicked a wooden fire engine very hard. The toy went spinning off across the wooden floor as Amanda swore and hopped around clutching her foot. She was lucky, in fact, not to come down from one of her hops on to a wide selection of toys. The more painful of these included a pile of Lego and a stegosaurus Transformer.

When the pain had subsided she retreated to the sofa. She wished she had picked up a bottle of gin at the supermarket.

Taking another deep breath Amanda surveyed the scene in the front room.

Her husband had packed the kids off to school this morning and had not made her son, Billy, tidy up his toys before they left. It didn't seem to matter how many times she told him to do it, he didn't want to. It was in one ear and out the other with this family.

45 minutes later she was in the car again, pulling up outside Billy's playgroup. Her little boy came running out of the gates, a wide smile grew across his face as he spotted his mum's car.

She opened the door for him and he scrambled in, doing up his own seatbelt. As he would tell you, he is a big boy now and that meant doing big boy things like putting on your own seatbelt. Even if it meant standing up to be able to reach the strap, to begin with.

She had planned to scold him for his lackadaisical attitude towards tidy up after playtime. But when she saw his face, framed by his messy mop of brown hair, she could not. It was his father's fault anyway.

Throughout the short drive home, she wondered what could possibly happen next when she got there.

When they arrived and Billy had bolted through the front door, Amanda locked the car up just as her husband, John pulled in to the driveway. He got out of the car and smiled at her.

'How was your day?' he asked.

'Don't ask,' Amanda replied. 'How was yours?'

'Long, tiring. As usual,' her husband said, giving her a kiss on the cheek. 'What's for dinner?'

As always, she thought, it's up to muggins here to cook. This lot would be hopeless without me. If I didn't cook, or shop, or clean then no one would. Billy poked his head out of the door.

'Yeah mum,' he said. 'What's for dinner? Can we have chips?'

'You'll get no dinner until you've tidied up your toys in the front room young man.'

'Aww,' her son moaned. 'That's boring. Can't you do it, mummy?'

'Right!' Amanda shouted, finally reaching the end of her tether. 'That's it! The three of you can look after your bloody selves for the evening. I'm off out!'

'Oh come on love, there's no need to be like that,' John said as she walked out to the driveway. 'Where are you going?'

'I don't know,' she replied. 'Don't wait up.'

Amanda had walked for 20 minutes, turning down roads whenever she felt like it. She was now in a part of town she had never been to before. Stopping to get her bearings, she decided that a drink was in order. A strong one. She spotted a bar. It appeared to be the only one in the area. It was called 'Enchantment', and seemed as good a place as any.

She pushed open the door and was greeted with a dark interior, covered from floor to ceiling with occult knickknacks and ornaments. She pushed her way through a set of beaded curtains and came up to the bar.

A young woman with long, raven black hair, dressed almost entirely in purple crushed velvet stood behind the dark mahogany slab. Her smile seemed forced - not because she was unpleasant, but rather because she was not used to smiling in general.

'How can I help you?' she asked.

'I'd like a drink,' Amanda said but then failed to provide any further qualification.

'Well, you are in a bar, so you've come to the right place. What would you like?'

'Err,' Amanda said. 'I'm not sure. I've not had much chance to drink since I had my kids.' Her mood soured as she remembered them, and she added 'the bastards.'

'Something wrong?' the barmaid asked.

'It's my bloody ungrateful family,' Amanda said. 'They don't appreciate everything I do for them. I just wish I knew what they were thinking sometimes, you know? Even for one day.'

The barmaid smiled again, but this time it seemed a lot more natural.

'I think,' she said, 'I can help you out there.'

She began mixing a drink, and before long it was in a tall glass in front of Amanda. She took a sip.

'That's delicious!' she said and drank the rest. After the drink, she had calmed down and decided to go home. An hour later she was tucked up in bed. Her husband barely stirred when she came in.

The next morning was Saturday. Amanda woke up with a headache and didn't feel that she had earned a hangover after one drink.

She slipped out of bed. The house was very quiet as she wandered down the stairs. As she reached the ground floor Lisa came out of the kitchen.

'Oh gosh, dad was right, we've been so thoughtless,' she said.

'Excuse me?' Amanda replied.

Lisa looked at her oddly.

'I didn't say anything mum.'

Amanda looked confused as her daughter ran up the stairs. She had heard her daughter's voice, she knew it. She shook her head to try and get rid of the cobwebs and went into the kitchen to get a cup of coffee.

Her husband was sitting at the table as she entered.

'Good morning, love,' he said. 'The poor thing, she's been working herself to the bone here and I haven't even noticed. I'm such a terrible husband.'

'What was that?!' Amanda said, completely taken aback.

'I said good morning...' her husband replied, a little confused.

'That was all?'

'That was all,' John said. 'Let me get you a cup of coffee.'

He went over to the coffee pot, poured a cup and handed it to her.

'Are you alright, love?' He asked, adding 'She looks like she's seen a ghost.'

His lips had definitely not moved that time.

'I think I need a lie down,' she said.

Amanda went into the lounge and was surprised to find it as tidy as it had ever been. She drained the cup of coffee and laid down on the sofa.

What was going on? Was she hearing things? What was in that drink she had last night? Wait, she thought. The drink! The bar! She had told the barmaid about her problems. What had she said? She wished she could hear their...oh bloody hell.

Leaping off the sofa she ran into the hall, taking the stairs two at a time. She knew how she could confirm it. The door to Billy's room was wide open, and Amanda walked right in.

'Fireman Spam! Fireman Spam!' her son sang tunelessly. 'Hi, mummy!' She looked at him for a few seconds before it finally came. 'Poo, bum, wee, willies, farts!'

That was it, she could hear his thoughts. He would never dare say words like that in front of her. And even though he had his finger up his nose when he said it, she could see his lips hadn't moved.

Amanda had never gotten dressed quicker in her life. She was out of the door in minutes and tried to retrace her steps from the night before. It took a few wrong turns but eventually, she found the same street she had been on. She searched up and down but the bar simply wasn't there. There was just a brick wall where it had been, with the words '24 hours' spray-painted on it. She walked back home in a daze.

When she arrived her husband the two kids were stood outside looking sheepish.

'I hope she likes her party,' her husband thought.
Amanda burst into tears.
'Poor mum, I feel so bad,' Lisa added telepathically.
'Bum, bum, bum, bum,' Billy finished. Amanda's tears turned in to laughing sobs.

'Hello, love,' her husband said, using his actual mouth. 'We all feel terrible. We all had a chat and we are going to pitch in much more around the house from now on. And before that to say sorry we've thrown you a little party.'

They led her into the kitchen, which was decked out with streamers, balloons, the works. Lisa handed her a glass of champagne.

'What do you think, love?' John said.

'I love it!' Amanda laughed. 'And I know what you're thinking. Yes, I WOULD like a slice of cake!'

From Rusholme With Love

Mary-Alice McDevitt - *'James Bond takes on the creatures from the depth/or from beyond the stars'.*

James sighed as he stepped out of the van. It had been another long day. His back was killing him after he had spent 4 hours on the floor underneath Mrs. Brockhurst's sink. It would be the same again tomorrow, and the next day, and so on until he could find the source of her low water pressure.

His wife, he knew, would already be in bed. She had an early start in the morning, and he didn't want to wake her up.

He sneaked into the house on his tiptoes, his workboots held in his hand. He climbed the stairs, making sure to avoid the creaky step, and slowly opened the door to the bedroom. There his wife, Shauna, was indeed asleep.

With the utmost care, honed over hundreds of such late returns, he slipped out of his overalls and pulled his pyjamas on. Finally, as gently as a feather, James slipped into bed. He gave his snoring wife a peck on the cheek and settled down.

A few minutes later he felt the warm embrace of sleep welcoming him. But James was jolted back to consciousness by a soft whirring noise coming from outside the window.

'What on earth is that?' he whispered to himself, and turned over, trying to ignore the irritating sound.

But as he lay there, the noise only got louder and louder. He bet it was his neighbour, Simon, up doing some more late-night DIY or gardening again. He got out of bed as quietly as he could so as not to wake Shauna and placed his feet in the slippers that were there waiting for them.

He shuffled over to the curtains and opened them, peeking out through the window for the source of the noise, but he could not see it for the life of him. All the time, it got louder still, and he was amazed Shauna had not woken up. Perhaps all this time he hadn't needed to be so careful.

Unable to find the source of the humming he closed the curtains and went back to bed. He pressed his pillow down hard over his ears.

It was no use, it was just too loud.

Just as James was prepared to give in to a sleepless night, the noise ended as suddenly as it had begun. A few moments later it was replaced by a loud 'thwock' sound. The room was immediately and brilliantly lit. It was as if someone had just turned the floodlights from Old Trafford on in his garden and pointed them at his window.

That bloody well does it, he thought. I must have told Simon to turn off the auto sensors on his garden floodlight five times now.

Furious, James swept out of the bed, depositing his half of the duvet on top of his still sleeping wife, muffling her snoring somewhat. He strode over to the window and flung the curtains open.

When his eyes finally adjusted to the all-consuming light, he realised it wasn't Simon and his floodlights that he was dealing with after all.

James ran downstairs, trying in vain to tie his bathrobe closed over his pyjamas. Finally, he wrestled it into submission. He opened the front door and gazed up in wonder at the three flying saucers that were currently hovering in the sky above his garden. Well, he thought, only one of them was hovering above his garden. It was only a small terraced house in Rusholme after all. But they were all hovering nonetheless.

James cowered in his doorway as the craft manoeuvred to land. One came down on his lawn and another in the street. He noted with some satisfaction that the third landed on Simon's shed, crushing it completely.

He gazed on as a ramp descended from the saucer in his garden, and a humanoid figure appeared in silhouette at the top.

'You are Bond, James Bond?' The voice seemed as if it had come from nowhere and everywhere at the same time.

James assumed it had originated from the creature at the top of the ramp, but it had sounded as if it was spoken from right by his ear.

'I'm err, James Bond, yes,' James replied cautiously.

'Err James Bond?' the voice came again.

'Um, no, just James Bond.'

'Very well Just James Bond, are you he that is employed by her majesty the Queen of England on her most secretive of services?'

A realisation of sorts dawned on James.

'Uh, no. I think you've got the wrong guy,' he said. 'I'm a handyman. I do odd jobs for people.' He cursed the choice of words as soon as they had left his mouth.

'Ah!' The voice sounded excited now. 'Yes, you know Oddjob. You are the right man indeed.'

'No, you don't understand!' James protested. 'I do plumbing, electrician stuff.'

'Electrician? You mean Elektra King. She was not one of your better opponents.'

James was starting to run out of ideas by this point.

'Look, I'm not a spy, OK?' he pleaded. 'I'm just a bloke from Manchester. I've never looked like Sean Connery in my life.'

'But of course, that is what the real James Bond would say. He would not reveal himself as a spy voluntarily, he would use a cover alias.'

'He wouldn't bloody well keep using the names James Bond, would he?' James shouted, waving his arms. 'Look, it was bad enough at school. Do you have any idea what it's like to have a famous name? You get laughed at, all the bloody time. I thought that now I was an adult I'd have escaped it all. But I still get the constant sniggering behind my back. Hire James Bond to do your plumbing, the man with the golden plunger. Har bloody har. Ten quid is not enough. Great one pal.'

'But what about your vehicle?' The alien creature asked, gesturing to where his van was parked. 'Was that not upgraded by Q, that you might thwart the plans of the world's most evil organisations?'

'The only thing that van is kitted out with is a full tool set, and I bought that from B&Q, not Q from MI6. Look, pal, I don't know who told you that I was THE James Bond, but I've got some bad news for you. He's a fictional character. He was invented by a guy called Ian Fleming. There have been several dozen novels and a bunch of films made about him, but it's all fake. He doesn't exist.'

'But those films are simply dramatisations of his biographies. Fleming and the others who wrote about Bond were all writing about his heroic deeds and the times he saved the world?'

'Sorry mate, fictional character. Fick-shu-nal character. Am I getting through to you at all?'

'Oh...' The omnipresent voice sounded disappointed.

'Sorry. What could an alien creature with interstellar travel possibly want with James Bond anyway?'

'Back on our home planet, there is a catastrophe occurring. We had received decades-old transmissions of the James Bond documenta...sorry, films. We believed that a man such as he might be able to save our planet. It seems we were wrong, and that we are doomed to all perish.'

'What's the problem?' James asked.

'Our ancient pipe system has ruptured in several locations and is flooding the biggest city on the planet. We have done what we can to stem the tide but it is only a temporary measure. We bought ourselves some time but if the problem is not fixed soon then millions will die.'

James blinked.

'That's your problem? Just get a plumber out,' he said.

'We cannot. The pipe system is ancient, and until now has proved sturdy for thousands of years. The need for the skill to repair such pipes died out a long time ago, and it seems that we are destined to die with it.'

'Well, uh, I'M a plumber,' James pointed out. 'Maybe I could help you after all?'

'Are you certain?' the voice replied. 'Our planet is some weeks' travel from here. You would be gone a while.'

'Honestly,' James said. 'I'd be glad to see the back of the place for a little while. Mrs. Brockhurst's pipes can wait'

'Who is this Mrs. Brockhurst you speak of? Is she your 'M'?'

'She might as well be the way she orders me around.'

'So you will help us?' The voice was hopeful.

'Of course. Just give me 20 minutes. I need to go wake up my wife.'

30 seconds later James was back in the bedroom. He walked over to the bed and gently tapped his wife on the shoulder.

'Wake up, love,' he whispered to her. He then repeated it at a higher volume when she did not stir.

'What is it?' she asked. 'Is something wrong?'

'No, quite the opposite. Get up and pack your bags. We're going on holiday.'

163

Shauna looked at the clock.

'At 3am? Where are we going?'

James Bond smiled.

'Oh, I couldn't possibly tell you. Top secret MI6 business…'

The Flood/A Kiss to Build a Dream On

Huw Lloyd Jones - *Enter a competition with Llandudno Writers Association for stories about North Wales*

Graham Kidd - *'A story about heroism during the Dolgarrog dam disaster.'*

Myself - *'A widow reluctantly goes on a day trip to Llandudno and has an unexpected meeting.'*

      Llewelyn Roberts ran down the cobbled street at full pelt. He skidded around the corner and into the lane that led to his house, up an incline on the outskirts of the village of Dolgarrog.

      His mother would be furious. Llewelyn had agreed to watch his sisters for the evening whilst his parents went to watch a new film up at the local theatre. But he had gotten caught up playing dice at Alun Jones' house. He had lost track of time, and only realised he was late when the church had chimed out the hour.

      The door was open when he arrived, and his mother was stood in the cottage's small kitchen wearing her theatre dress and a thunderous expression.

      'Where have you been, Bach?' she asked. 'You're late.'

'I'm sorry, mam,' Llewelyn replied, wincing at the nickname he hated so much. 'I lost track of time.'

'Well, the girls are in bed already and there's dinner on the table. We should be back by 11.'

At that moment his father came downstairs, wearing a top hat and tails, a huge grin plastered across his face.

'What do you think, Bach?' he asked, running a hand over his moustache, which he had waxed.

'You look a treat, dad,' Llewelyn replied, returning the smile.

'Oh, Morris, you silly bugger,' his mum said. 'We're going to the theatre, not for dinner with the King.'

His parents departed to the theatre, and Llewelyn was left alone, the two girls sound asleep upstairs. He stoked the fire that almost always burned in the sitting room, picked up a book from the shelf and began to read. Before long the book slipped from his hand and Llewelyn nodded off into a warm sleep.

A while later, Llewelyn woke to a loud crashing noise that came from some way off. Startled, he leaped from his chair, as the crashing sound was followed by a series of dull thuds. He ran upstairs to check on the girls. He found Meredith, his youngest sister, crying in her cot, and Elin still fast asleep in the bed across the room.

Llewelyn picked up his baby sister and soothed her until she stopped crying. As he laid her back down in the cot he became aware of a rushing sound. It was growing louder. He went over to the window and was shocked to see water cascading down the street at the end of the lane. The road looked like a river.

Llewelyn heard a loud banging on the front door and went down to answer it. It was his friend Alun, out of breath and utterly drenched from fighting his way up the road against the flow of the floodwaters.

'It's the dams,' he gasped while fighting to regain his breath. 'They've burst.'

'Both of them?' Llewelyn asked.

'Looks that way,' Alun replied. 'We need to get up to the village to help.'

Llewelyn thought about his sisters asleep upstairs. Judging by the course of the water, and the relative height that the cottage stood at, the flood should flow right past. He would be alright to leave them for a while.

'Let's go,' he said.

They took a back path round to the centre of the village. When they arrived the scene was one of devastation. A lot of the loose stone buildings were smashed to pieces, not designed to withstand a torrent of water so vast.

The waters were beginning to subside when they arrived. Those buildings still standing looked to have been badly damaged. Some looked as though they would collapse at any moment.

A woman, covered head to toe in mud, waded through the water to meet them. She was crying, the tears cleaning lines through the dirt on her face.

'Mrs. Pritchard? Is that you?' Llewelyn asked.

'Oh boys, my poor mother is trapped upstairs in my house,' the woman replied. 'I can't carry her out and I'm worried that the building is going to collapse any minute now.'

Llewelyn looked at his friend.

'Alun, you take Mrs. Pritchard up to the high ground over there and wait for me.'

Llewelyn plunged into the house. The house was dark and he had to push himself past broken furniture and other items that floated in the chest-high water. It made for slow progress. Eventually, he found his way through the gloom to the staircase and clambered up out of the water.

167

When he reached the top he found Mrs. Pritchard's mother sitting in a corner of one of the bedrooms, utterly terrified.

'What is happening?' she asked. 'Did we anger the Lord?'

'I don't know,' Llewelyn answered honestly. 'But I'm here to get you out.' He extended a hand, which the elderly lady took, and gently lifted her on to his shoulders.

Progress was even slower than before when they got back downstairs and into the waters. Llewelyn had to ensure that he kept both his and the woman's heads above the waterline at all times.

Finally, they made it out of the house and Llewelyn waded over to the little hill where Alun and Mrs. Pritchard were waiting. He carefully handed the old lady over to Alun, who set her down next to her daughter.

Just as Llewelyn was preparing to come out of the water, a second surge from the dam came down the street towards him. The current was too strong, and there was nothing he could do but stand there and await his fate.

He closed his eyes and braced for the water to hit. But before he could be swept away he felt hands under his shoulders that began dragging him up out of the water.

'Not this time,' Alun grinned as he pulled Llewelyn on to the bank. 'You still owe me three shillings from our game of dice earlier on, and you're not getting out of it that easily.'

#

Agnes grumbled as she stepped off the coach.

'I don't even know why I'm here,' she moaned to Mavis, her oldest friend.

'Agnes, you've been so miserable since Harold died. You need a break and here we are.'

'Of course I'm miserable,' Agnes replied. 'He was my husband of 45 years after all.'

'I know, dear,' Mavis said, patting her friend on the back. 'But the point still stands. You needed to get away.'

'I suppose so, but did I have to get away to Llandudno?'

'Oh come on,' Mavis said, smiling mischievously. 'It's the jewel of the North Wales Coast! Look, I've got to go off and meet up with the local WI chapter, but why don't you have a look around? I'm sure you'll find something to do.'

Agnes wandered off down towards the promenade and browsed the stalls on the pier for a while. She quickly tired of the hustle and bustle. The loud noises that came from the various arcades dotted along its length gave her a headache. She decided to take a break and retired to a bench that looked out over the sea, and up to the Great Orme.

She reached into her purse and pulled out a picture of her and her husband. Harold would have loved this, she thought. A new adventure. He had always been the adventurous type. She sighed.

She became aware of someone walking past behind her as she caught the tune of the man's whistling.

'That's Louis Armstrong,' she said out loud, without meaning to.

'A Kiss to Build a Dream On,' came a voice from behind her.

Agnes stood up and turned around.

'Oh gosh,' she said, her cheeks reddening with embarrassment. 'I'm sorry, I didn't mean to interrupt your walk.'

'Not at all,' the man said. 'Are you a fan?'

'A fan?' Agnes said. 'That is my husband and I's song. Or rather, it was,' she added, looking downcast.

'I'm terribly sorry,' the man said. 'I lost my wife a couple of years ago. After 50 years. All that time and it doesn't seem long enough, eh?'

'No, not long enough by half.'

They stood in silence for a moment and looked out at the vista.

'Beautiful, in a way, isn't it?' Agnes said, breaking the silence.

'It is,' the man replied. 'The name's George, by the way.'

'Agnes.'

'What brings you to sunny Llandudno, Agnes?'

'My friend Mavis dragged me here. Said I needed to get away for a day. It's three years since my husband died this week, and it's always a difficult time of year.'

'Maybe she's right, the sea air often does good for the soul. At least, that's why I come here.'

'Are you from the area?' Agnes asked.

'No,' George replied. 'I live in Welshpool. But I come up here on the senior citizens' coach trips they organise every now and then. It does me good to get out of the house. What about you?'

'Stockport,' Agnes answered.

George smiled.

'I thought I could detect a Lancashire lilt.'

'So what is there to do around here for a young lady in the prime of her life?' Agnes asked, a broad smile on her face.

'Well, there's all the wonders of the pier, but I don't have you pegged as much of a gambler. There are plenty of charity shops around for the discerning consumer. Oh, and a wonderful new retail park opened the other year. And of course, there's the local Wetherspoon's. Take your pick.'

Agnes laughed.

'Sounds delightful.'

'Ah, I don't come here for the sights and sounds, I come here to get away. Welshpool is very sleepy. And while Llandudno is hardly Las Vegas, it offers something a little different. Helps me clear my head, being away from it all.'

'Maybe you're right,' Agnes replied. 'Perhaps this place isn't so bad after all.'

Four hours later, Mavis wandered down on to the promenade and found her friend sitting on a bench. She was talking to a gentleman whom Mavis did not recognise. As she approached the bench, the man stood up.

'Until next time?' the man said.

'Next time,' Agnes replied, and the man walked off, whistling a tune that Mavis did not recognise.

'Who was that?' Mavis asked.

'Oh, no one,' Agnes replied, turning away from her friend to hide her blushes.

The mischievous smile returned to Mavis' face.

'Come on, you,' she said. 'Or we will miss the coach.'

Three months later, Agnes wandered down on to the promenade and sat down on the bench. She waited, nervously, for half an hour, and was about to give up and leave when she heard the sound she was waiting for.

'Give me, a kiss to build a dream on, and my imagination will thrive upon that kiss...'

It was not a strong singing voice, and it went off-key several times in that one line alone. But she knew exactly what it meant.

'Hello George,' she said and smiled.

Morgan, PI

Eileen Conneely - *'A woman overhears gang activity on a train, becomes vigilante.'*

June breathed a sigh of relief when the train pulled up to the platform 25 minutes late. She had already been travelling for four hours, and at this point just wanted to be home.

As the doors opened June lifted her heavy suitcase up on to the train and found her way to a seat in the nearly empty carriage. She was exhausted thanks to her long journey, and it wasn't long before she had dozed off to the rhythmic sound of the wheels running over the track.

June woke sometime later as the door at the other end of the carriage slammed shut. She blinked herself fully awake and looked outside. It was dark. She figured she must have been asleep for a while. She had definitely missed her stop.

As she was about to get up to try and work out how far she had gone by her station, a voice came from the other end of the carriage.

'Are we alone?'

It was a man's voice. June glanced around her and noticed that she was so far pressed into the corner of her seat that she would not be visible over the top.

'Yeah, looks like it,' a second voice, female, replied.

'Do you have the stuff?' the man asked.

'What are you, stupid?' the woman replied, incredulity in her voice. 'I'm not going to carry that much coke around with me on a fucking passenger train.'

'Alright then,' the man said, sounding frustrated. 'Where is it?'

'I've hidden it.'

'Hidden it?!' the man had to stop himself from yelling. 'That wasn't part of the deal. You were supposed to bring it with you. I wasn't expecting to have to go on a treasure hunt.'

'Oh get over it, you'll get the stuff. It was much safer this way.'

'But what if somebody finds it?'

'No one is going to find it.'

'Alright then,' the man sighed, 'where is it?'

'Just follow me after we get off, I'll show you.'

June didn't know how to react. She was sat there, in a train carriage, listening to a real-life drug deal happening before her very ears. She was alone in the carriage, not counting the two criminals.

A million scenarios flashed through her mind. Should she raise the alarm? What good would it do? If she did anything now she could alert one of the criminals to her presence. Anyway she didn't know where they were going to get off to report it afterwards. She couldn't just do nothing.

June decided that she needed to at least get a look at the pair, and shifted slightly in her seat to peak over the top. As she turned around, she knocked a water bottle off the table in front of her, and it clattered to the ground.

'What was that?!' the man asked. 'I thought you said we were alone!'

'I thought we were!' the woman replied.

June ducked back down into her seat. This was it, she had been found out. She would be front page in tomorrow's newspaper. If they ever found the body.

173

'Look,' the woman said. 'There's a suitcase in that rack. Someone must be down there.'

'Good job sweeping the carriage,' the man said sarcastically.

'Oh piss off,' came the reply. 'Let's find them and deal with it.'

June could hear them working their way up the carriage. She began to eye the carriage door and thought of making a break for it. But if it went wrong and they caught her she was screwed.

She became aware that the train was slowing down. The familiar crackle of the train's Tannoy system becoming active was followed by the voice of the train manager.

'We will shortly be arriving at Schofield. Will anyone alighting here please remember to take all their belongings with them?'

'Shit,' the woman said. 'This is us.'

'But what about...?' the man said.

'Oh leave it, it was probably nothing anyway.'

June heard the pair turn around and walk back to the door at the other end of the carriage, and leave. She waited a few seconds before making a decision and getting up just as the train came to a halt. Grabbing her case she went through the door and, confident that she wouldn't be recognised, alighted on to the platform.

She looked around until she spotted a man and a woman standing some way off on the platform looking suspicious. June decided that they were definitely the pair and that there was only one course of action. She would have to follow them. It was her civic duty.

She ducked into the station building, found the left luggage facility and dropped her suitcase off. After all, the trundling wheels would be a dead giveaway in a tail.

Her luggage deposited, June returned to the platform and saw the pair walking out the back entrance to the station into the car park. She pulled her overcoat around her shoulders and followed them.

The two were obviously nervous and were casting glances around to see if they were being followed. June had to duck into nooks and crannies several times to avoid being seen. Eventually she found that she was following the criminals along winding country lanes.

As the roads became more remote June felt herself getting fully involved in her private detective role. She became more and more inventive with her hiding spots. Especially as she was aided by the darkness of the lanes.

After about twenty minutes walking down the country roads, the pair stopped. As stealthily as she could manage June edged closer until she was near enough to the activity to hear what was going on.

'...down there on the left, in the tree stump behind the blasted oak, covered with some sticks and bits of bark.'

'Yeah, fair enough,' the man said. 'No one is gonna find it down there. Can we go and get it now?'

'Not yet,' the woman replied. 'Johnny says he wants to see the money first.'

'Isn't your word good enough?'

'Guess not.'

'You already told me where the coke is, why shouldn't I just get rid of you now and take both the drugs and the money?'

'Ha!' the woman scoffed. 'First off, what if I'm lying? You could be down there for hours looking for it and never find it. Secondly, you don't have the stones. You're small fry. I'm willing to bet you wouldn't have the stomach to even hurt a fly, let alone murder someone and dump the body in a lane. Thirdly, I bet you don't even have a gun. Finally, you're scared of Johnny. All Marcel's lot is. You'd be strung up within days.'

The man laughed.

'Fair enough,' he said.

The woman walked over to a lay by a few metres down the road and opened a car door.

'Come on,' she said. 'I'll take you to see Johnny.'

The man walked over to the car and got in. June pressed herself as far into the hedge at the side of the lane as she possibly could. She did not want to be lit up by the headlights of the car. She waited there until the pair had driven away.

As the lights disappeared off around a bend June ran down towards where the criminals had been. Activating the torch on her phone she went off down the short track they had been looking at. Before long she spotted the blasted oak that the woman had mentioned.

She began scrabbling around in the oak and found the pile of sticks and bark. Pulling the detritus away, June came across a plastic bag. The woman had been telling the truth. Unwrapping the bag she found what looked like a large amount of cocaine inside. She felt a swell of pride in her chest as she dialled 999.

Two hours later, she had given her statement to the police. The criminals had been arrested upon their return.

June sat in the local station and waited for her train back.

She reflected on her day. If the train hadn't been delayed or she hadn't fallen asleep and missed her stop she would have gone home and had a nice cup of tea before going to bed. But here she was. June Morgan, vigilante at large. She almost didn't want to have to go home, back to the drudgery of normal life.

She took solace in the fact that her earlier prediction of making the front page of the paper had been correct. Although in this case she would be granted the boon of anonymity.

Oh well, she thought, sighing. A couple of hours and she would be home, back to business as usual.

She heard a person walk on to the platform behind her. She glanced around to see a young man in a smart suit holding a mobile phone to his ear.

'Yeah, I'll do it,' the man hissed into the phone. 'No, I'm not going to chicken out like last time. He's got to be dealt with.'

A train pulled up to the platform. June looked at the platform sign and noticed it was not her train, but the man in the suit got in. She smiled and boarded anyway.

The real world can wait for a little while longer, decided June Morgan, Private Investigator.

The Fence

Andrew Murray - *A story about 'the fence on the edge of reality'.*

Planet Earth was one of many planets inhabited by intelligent life during the history of the universe. There, a debate raged for many centuries between scientists about whether the universe was a finite or infinite construct.

In a way, both were correct.

The universe, at least the universe as it was inhabited by the people of Earth, did indeed have an end. Rarely did any living creature, from Earth or otherwise, make it to the edge of that universe. Those that did found something they didn't expect. They were fenced in.

The rare few who stumbled across the fence all came to the same conclusion. Some ancient, long-forgotten civilisation had built it to keep whatever lay on the other side out. This was an incorrect assumption. Something wanted to keep them in.

The being of pure energy waited, and observed. It had done this for a thousand centuries, and it anticipated doing it for a thousand more. The waiting was the reason for its existence.

It observed the fence from the outside. It was one of many that monitored large sections of the circumference, to scout for approaching threats. Threats were determined to be any objects composed of matter that came into the vicinity.

Its species existed in the space outside of the universe. In human terms, it was the difference between reality and unreality, between dimensions. Different laws of physics applied here. No living creature from within the universe would be able to survive for very long outside of it.

The opposite was also true for the beings of purple energy. Any matter coming through the fence that bordered the edge of reality was deadly to them.

The fence could only take so much impact, and that was why they stationed sentries along its edge. Any potential intrusion was a major threat that had to be stopped. If it broke through it could cause major damage.

Thetis, as the being was known, glowed as it became alert. There had been no incidents in this section for a very long time indeed. Longer than was conceivable to any mortal being. But Thetis' entire existence was dedicated to dealing with moments like this. That allowed for an instantaneous reaction. Immediately it was checking the fence for signs of weakness and evaluating data on the incoming object.

The object appeared to be primarily metallic. Thetis calculated that it had been drifting through interstellar space for millions of years. Longer even than Thetis had been in existence or would exist for. It wondered where the object had come from. What distant planet, or star system, or asteroid belt.

The object drifted ever closer to the fence. Light from a star that was, by the scale of the universe, relatively nearby glinted and illuminated four letters written on the side. NASA.

Thetis observed the object. Its probing determined that there was data accessible within its storage drives. It allowed as much of its energy as it dared to penetrate the fence. The tendrils reached out to touch the object. Thetis interfaced with the ancient databanks.

The probe's storage units whirred into life. Thetis saw thousands of years of data collected during the probe's working life. There was information about planets, galaxies, stars and much more that it had never before been able to comprehend.

Calculating the length of time before impact, Thetis decided that it had plenty of time to continue to scan through the information. Sometime later, when it had finished, it disconnected from the probe and gave thought to what it had experienced.

Voyager 1, it thought as its intangible brain turned over this new word.

It had encountered things it could never have imagined and felt itself a changed being for the experience. None of its species had been into the universe for hundreds of millennia. It was the first of its kind to receive such information for all that time.

And it had to destroy the source. Its species was one of logic and reason. They were not given to outbursts of emotion. But it felt uneasy at the thought of having to remove this object from existence. Just because it constituted a threat.

For the first time in its existence, Thetis hesitated. It would be a simple thing for it to divert power from surrounding sections of the fence to shore up the area that would be struck. But it didn't want to. It wanted all its species to be able to experience the wonders that this ancient probe had stored inside it.

The time was approaching when Thetis would have to make a decision. If it waited too much longer then it would be too late, and the probe would cause untold damage to the dimension Thetis inhabited, to its species. But it did not seem right.

With its full power back inside its own realm, Thetis used the collective consciousness it shared with the rest of its species. It consulted them on the best course of action.

It explained the situation as best it could. That it was a unique occurrence and the species as a whole would never have a better opportunity to learn more about the universe. To learn about something that was so deadly to them.

Immediately Thetis received a cacophony of responses. They ranged from urging immediate destruction of the object to statements of support for its proposal.

But it was one suggestion that struck Thetis as the most sensible, and the most practical. Fence guardians could remove and repair sections of the fence that became damaged or had become worn throughout the aeons. Replacement sections were stored nearby to every outpost. There were plenty spare near to where Thetis was stationed.

Using the spare sections of fence it could construct a container for the probe to be kept in. The mini-fence would prevent it from directly penetrating the void beyond the real fence, and the probe would be safe inside.

Thetis immediately began the necessary calculations. It already knew what the zone of impact would be. Using its consciousness it moved sections of replacement fence into position to create a bubble on its side of the divide. It then carefully removed the section of the actual fence that would be hit, creating a catch pocket. When the time came it would quickly seal the ball with another section. Then it would replace the original to prevent any excess matter from escaping through the gap.

It waited. It was good at that. It waited for the precise moment the probe entered the pocket, making sure to seal it up and detach it from the main structure as fast as possible. If the probe touched the inside of its new enclosure it would be destroyed or at the very least damaged beyond recovery. So the ball had to be kept moving at a speed constant to its contents if both were to remain intact.

Once this was achieved Thetis immediately set to replacing the now vacant section of the fence. The job complete, it reflected warmly on the experience. It had preserved some information that would have a positive impact on the future of its race, it was sure.

Now that the object was secure within its container Thetis devised a way to slow it down. It reduced the energy on one side of the fence structure to be as low as possible without posing a danger of it breaking and slowed the structure down. This allowed the probe to come to a gentle halt against the inner wall, the impact glowing along the outside of the container.

It would not be long, Thetis knew. Soon the great leaders, thinkers, and scientists of its species would come to investigate the probe themselves. It only had a limited time to itself to experience the full wonders found within. Then it would be taken somewhere were further research could be conducted.

Thetis moved closer to the probe.

Voyager 1, it thought again.

Gently Thetis probed the most minute element of its being through the protective barrier. It interfaced with the storage systems of the object once more.

It probed deeper than it had before and encountered a curious object, a disc made from what seemed to be a different metal. It spun the disc and was amazed by images of a planet it had never before seen and the creatures that inhabited it. It continued searching through the disc. Eventually it heard music of many different varieties, the likes of which it had never even imagined.

Thetis felt so privileged to be the first creature, possibly ever, to hear and see these things since they had been placed on the probe.

It came across a recording on the disc of a voice.

'My name is Jimmy Carter, and I am President of the United States of America on the planet Earth. If you are listening to this recording then you are an intelligent being, and to you, I say hello.'

Hello, Jimmy Carter, it thought. I am Thetis.

Along Came Polytheism

Jonathan Cromie - 'A priest dies, but instead of meeting God in heaven, they are confronted by a pagan deity of some variety. Awkwardness ensues.'

'Father Mulvaney, come quick!' the sister called down the corridor of the cottage. 'Father James is near to death and asks for you.'

The priest ran as fast as it was possible to do in his long, flowing robes. Skidding to a halt as he reached the door, he getsured to the sister to stand aside.

'Father James,' he said in a soothing voice as he entered the room. 'What nonsense is this? Sister Mary tells me that you're at death's door. By The Lord's grace, you'll outlive us all.'

'I fear that on this occasion His grace might be insufficient,' Father James replied from his sickbed.

His skin was pale, and his cheeks, drawn more tightly than normal, gleamed slightly with a hint of dried sweat. The pallor of the features betrayed a man who was very ill indeed. Father Mulvaney was inclined to believe his old friend and colleague this time.

'Tell me, Father, what can I do to help ease your passing?'

'You can pour me a glass of the 18-year-old single malt you keep in your desk,' Father James replied. He gave a hoarse, tired chuckle that quickly descended into a fit of dry coughing.

Father Mulcaney grinned.

'You always were a sly one,' he said.

His friend's face took on a more serious demeanour.

'You must read me my last rites, for I have not much longer to live.'

'Very well, my friend. For you, it is the least I could do.'

Half an hour later Father Mulcaney passed his hand down over the eyes of Father James closing them for the last time.

He embraced Sister Mary, who had broken down in tears.

'Weep not for him, sister,' he said, 'for Father James is now in a better place than us all.'

Father James awoke. He sat up from his resting place with notable ease. He had not felt this well in a long time. As his eyes cleared of sleep and focused on his surroundings, he realised that he was somewhere he had never been before. Yet somehow, it seemed totally familiar to him at the same time.

He was surrounded by white, as far as the eye could see in all directions. It was as if he was riding on the back of a giant sheep, with only the blue sky above him.

'Oh,' he said, as the realisation dawned on him. 'I finally croaked, didn't I?'

His suspicion was confirmed as he looked at his clothes. He was clad in a robe of pure white, a choice he would never make outside of his formal duties as a Catholic priest. It certainly wasn't suitable cloud wear. He brought himself to his feet and shielded his eyes from the sun.

'It must be around here somewhere,' he muttered as he looked around.

After a moment he found what he was looking for, as the sun glinted off a construct some distance away. Father James picked up the trailing white robes and wandered off towards it.

A few minutes later he came up to the construct, a large set of gates that glimmered with all the different colours of the rainbow. Cherubim hovered above the gate poles, playing beautiful music on golden lyres. The sun's reflection on the pearl facade intensified as the gates opened on his approach.

Father James clasped his hands together and smiled, waiting for his first meeting with the gatekeeper. A robed figure approached through the glare.

'St. Peter!' Father James declared.

'What? No.' the figure replied. Throwing back the hood of the robes it revealed a scaly green face that boasted nine eyes, two noses, and several other notable features besides. 'Wait. Did you say Szimttpetarr?'

'No...' Father James said, a look halfway between bemusement and horror on his face. 'I...I said St. Peter.'

'Oh, easy mistake to make,' the...thing said. It consulted a sheet of paper that appeared to be nailed to the other side of one of the gate posts. 'No, St. Peter doesn't work Tuesdays.'

'What do you mean, he doesn't work Tuesdays? He's the guardian of the pearly gates, the warden at the entrance to heaven. How can he take time off?'

'Well I hear he likes fishing,' the beast said, from one of its many mouths. 'Can't go fishing if he's at work, can he? He'll be back in tomorrow if you really want to talk to him. Though Lazarus says he can't half go on a bit about the benefits of live bait.'

Father James stood in stunned silence.

186

'Are you quite sure he's not here?' he managed, eventually.

The beast checked the sheet of paper again.

'Yep, says right here on the rota.'

'Then who are you?'

'I told you, I'm Szimttpetarr. I fill in when St. Pete has, err, shall we say, scarpered.'

'I am afraid I just don't understand.'

'I'm a god. Well, an ex-god I suppose. From a small bit of Siberia. Everyone who works here is. Thor reads people their judgements. Actually, sometimes it's Loki dressed like Thor - it's hard to tell. They stuck me here because my name is like Pete's and a lot of people think I've just got a cough or something.

'They're one step away from a 'You don't have to be omnipotent to work here...' sign, I swear,' Szimttpetarr continued. 'Even Zeus pulls shifts on one of the other gates sometimes. He's got the beard you see, people mistake him for Peter...'

'Wait, there are other gates?'

'Well yes. Approximately 154,889 people die every day. We'd have a line 10 miles long if they all had to come through one,' Szimttpetarr said. 'Particularly if people dilly dally about the whole thing and start asking questions,' he added, rather pointedly.

'154,000?' Father James asked in disbelief. 'That many Christians die every day?'

'Christians?' Szimttpetarr snorted. 'No mate, we get all sorts up here. Christians, Muslims, Hindus, Pagans, Buddhists. We'll take anyone. Like I said, I'm Russian. Sort of. Wasn't called Russia back then, obviously. One of the minor ones. But I've had nothing to do since the eight people who worshiped me fell in an icy lake. So I've been doing odd hours here and there on the gates to keep me sane. It's quite easy to go mad when you have as many brains as I do.'

One of the creature's eyes rotated randomly. Possibly for effect.

'But I'm a Christian. No, not just a Christian, I'm a catholic priest. I was taught that ours was the only true god.'

'You and the Muslims, and the Hindus, and the Greeks and the Romans and the Vikings and the Aztecs and the Mayans before you. Belief is a powerful thing, my friend. Belief breeds existence, and once we all existed we all had to go somewhere when the humans stopped worshiping us.'

'So there's more than one heaven?'

'Sort of. Or at least, there used to be. The older ones, the Norse, the Greeks, the minor gods of long lost villages and the like. They used to like to keep it separate, to prevent fraternisation and whatnot. Keep up the 'one true religion' mystique, you know? But when our flows dried up they petitioned your god, Allah and a couple of the other new breed to bring it all together in one. Keep things efficient. There are still separate zones for each group, so you won't be in with the Protestants. Unless you want to be. It's sort of like a heavenly Disneyland. Catholic land. Protestant village. You get the picture.'

'So, what? Can I go and see my Lord?'

'If you like,' Szimttpetarr said, and began chewing on an apple he had produced from his robe. 'He's got a big office over in the western annexe, but he's generally booked up for a few months at a time. Popular guy, you know?'

'Oh, I see. What about Jesus?'

'Oh, he's on holiday down on earth at the moment. He heads down for a couple of weeks every hundred or so years to spook up some locals and play golf. It gives him kicks.'

'You talk about our Lord and Saviour as if he was some kind of college freshman!' Father James protested.

'You don't know him mate. Not really anyway. Look, is this going to take much longer?' Szimttpetarr asked. 'I know this must have come as a surprise, but I'm supposed to be on my lunch. And thanks to this game of 20 questions I'm already several people behind quota for the day. I don't mean to be rude but do you think we could wrap this up?'

'Oh yes, of course,' Father James replied, looking dejected. 'I'm sorry to have wasted your time.'

Szimttpetarr felt a pang of guilt.

'I'm sorry,' he said. 'Look, it's pretty good in there. It's still the heaven you expected, it's just a bit more crowded than you were counting on. And hey, as a catholic priest you'll have a lovely suite in one of the towers. They save the best ones for the priests. All your old mates will be in there. You'll have a whale of a time.'

'I suppose I'm just still getting used to the whole 'more than one religion is right' thing.'

'Yeah, I can imagine that would be a bit of a head-scratcher.'

Szimttpetarr threw away the finished apple core and began rummaging around behind the gates. 'Here, take these,' he said, emerging with a bunch of leaflets in his hand. 'They should help make the transition easier.'

'Oh, thanks...' Father James said, taking the literature. He began to walk through the gates and off into the kingdom of heaven.

'Oh, Father?' Szimttpetarr called after him.

'Yes?' the priest replied, turning back.

'If you come back around the same time tomorrow, I'll have a word with St. Peter, see if I can get him to give you a do-over. You know, so you have the authentic experience?'

Father James smiled.

'Thank you Szimttpetarr, that is very kind of you. You are alright for a heathen devil pagan.'

'You'd be amazed how often people say that to me.'

The old, erstwhile god watched as the priest trudged off before shutting the gates. He pulled out a sign that said

'CLOSED FOR LUNCH' and then retrieved a book from a bag hidden in the fluffiness of the clouds.

'Right,' he said, sitting in an armchair that seemed to have appeared out of nowhere. 'Fifty Shades of Grey. Where was I?'

Welcome to the Family

Ben Lovejoy - 'A mistake. A failed attempt to correct. And a truly wonderful result.'

Sally rang the buzzer on the wall outside of the office of the animal rescue centre. The day had finally arrived, and she was here to pick up her new dog, Benji.

Benji was a Dalmatian who had been found in an alleyway behind the local Tesco. The centre estimated that he was only about a year old. He had likely been abandoned as a puppy when the owners couldn't sell him for one reason or another.

Sally and the whole family had met him twice now. Her two little girls, whose idea it was to get a dog in the first place, were head over heels for him.

It was sweet, in a way. Neither her or her partner, Rowena, particularly cared for dogs. But the girls had been so insistent that in the end, they had both caved. They had made it very clear, using their very stern parent voices, that the dogs would be the girls' responsibility. Walks and feeding would be up to them. Sally wondered how long it would last. Rowena had bet a steak dinner that it would be a fortnight.

Still, their hearts of ice had melted somewhat when they first laid eyes upon Benji. They had both grown secretly quite fond of the pooch on their second visit.

It felt like an age, but eventually, Mrs. Wilson, one of the volunteers who worked at the centre, buzzed her in. Mrs. Wilson was a kind-hearted old lady who had devoted her life to the care of animals since her husband had passed on. She was sweet, and obviously very dedicated to her role, but Sally wished she wouldn't go on about her dogs so much.

She trudged up the two flights of stairs to the office. Rowena was at work and the girls were at school. So it had been left up to her to complete all the necessary paperwork - on her day off no less.

She wanted to be mad at the dog for taking up her time already. but then she pictured Benji's face, cocked inquisitively, an expectant look in his eyes. His tail wagging fiercely. She simply couldn't. The damn dog had bewitched her already.

Mrs. Wilson brought her a cup of tea and some biscuits as she sat down to iron the final details out.

Ten minutes later everything was considered shipshape. Sally was led through the warren of a building down to the ground floor where the kennels were located.

Simon, another one of the volunteers, led her through the kennels until they reached Benji's cage. Benji was waiting with his head cocked - his signature look.

'We'll be sad to see Benji go,' Simon said to her. 'He's got a grin that lights up any room he's in.'

Benji barked, and Simon ruffled the fur on his head.

'Of course, we're always happy to see any of our charges move on to a loving home. Come on, boy. One last kiss for uncle Simon?'

On cue, Benji leaped up as Simon bent down and licked his face.

'It's always hard to say goodbye,' Simon said.

'I understand,' Sally replied. 'I hope that he'll be as nice with us as he is with you.'

'I have no doubt.'

Simon helped her out to the car with Benji and all the things she had needed to buy from the centre's shop. Just as they were loading all the items into the boot a cacophony of barking erupted from the kennels.

'I'll be right back,' said Simon, 'I just have to go deal with that.' He ran off in the direction of the kennels.

Sally took the opportunity to ingratiate herself to the new pup.

'Remember,' she said, cooing at the panting dog. 'You love me the most. I'm the one who rescued you.'

Benji barked in agreement.

Simon re-emerged from the kennels and between them they put the last of the things into the boot. Sally drove off with Benji tied to the front passenger seat. Simon and Mrs. Wilson waved them off.

Twenty minutes later Sally pulled in to the driveway. She parked her car, making sure to leave enough room for Rowena, and started to unload all the dog's possessions from the back seat and boot.

As she came to a pile of old blankets that her sister had donated for the doggy bed, she hesitated. She could have sworn that the pile moved as she approached it. She moved her hand closer again, and loud sneezing greeted her from underneath the blankets.

Sally was no expert but she was pretty certain that blankets weren't predisposed to sneezing. She approached carefully and lifted up a fold. She was greeted by a pair of sad brown eyes. The eyes sneezed for a second time.

Sally threw off the top layer of blankets and in doing so revealed the rest of the creature that was hiding underneath. It was a black pug; an old looking thing that was panting hard, as if it was sitting on the surface of the sun. It snorted at her and then let off a fart that, though silent, was definitely deadly.

'What the hell are you doing in there?' she asked the creature whilst holding her nose. It sneezed again in response. 'Let me have a look.'

With her free hand, she found its collar.

'Olive,' she read from the tag. 'Olive the pug.'

Following the collar around she found a lead, or rather the remains of one, still attached. It looked as though the lead that Olive had been on had snapped. The old girl must have sneaked into the back of the car whilst Sally had been talking to Benji.

There was only one thing for it, she would have to go back. She finished unloading the remaining goods into the house and shut Benji in the back garden. She hoped that would give him a chance to get used to his new surroundings. As she went to leave Benji trotted over to the gate and gave Olive a big lick on the face. He started to whine as Sally tied the pug to the front seat.

'It's ok, Benji,' Sally said. 'I've just got to take this little lady back home.'

This did not have the desired effect and Benji's whine became a howl as Sally drove off. What would the neighbours think?

Back at the centre, she hopped out, and with Olive in tow made her way up to the office to explain the situation.

'I'm so glad she's alright,' Mrs. Wilson said as they sat over the desk, with Olive snorting away to herself in the corner. 'We were worried that she might have run out on to the main road or something. She doesn't look like much, the old girl, but when she gets loose she goes tearing off before you have a chance to stop her.'

'She probably jumped up into the blankets because they were warm,' Sally said. 'Anyway, now that she's back safe and sound I'll be off.'

'It's a shame really,' Mrs. Wilson said as Sally was putting her coat on.

'A shame? Why?'

'I suppose it wouldn't have made much difference if she had made it out on to the road. She doesn't have much time left anyway.'

'What do you mean?' Sally asked, her arm frozen halfway inside the sleeve of her jacket.

'Well, the poor old girl has been with us for 3 months now. Couldn't find a home for her. She's old - well over ten years. Came in after her elderly owner couldn't take care of her anymore. Got lots of problems too. Allergic to basically everything and has a rather nasty gastrointestinal problem.'

'Yes,' Sally said, wrinkling her nose. 'I've encountered that one already.'

'After three months, if we can't find a place for them, we have to put them down to free up space. It's the kindest thing, especially for the older ones like her. It's no life, living in a cage, you know?'

Sally looked at Mrs. Wilson, who was shaking her head sadly. Then she looked at Olive, who had fallen asleep flat on her back, legs in the air, and was snoring. Then she looked back at Mrs. Wilson.

Half an hour later Sally was back in the car, having finished loading up the second set of doggy supplies she had purchased that day. As she prepared to drive off from the rescue centre she turned and looked at the dog sat on the front passenger seat.

'Now if any of your brothers and sisters are hiding out in the boot of the car I want you to tell me right now,' she said. 'I can't afford a third trip back here today. The first two have been costly enough.'

The dog looked back at her and snorted loudly by way of reply.

'If I find out you're lying to me...' Sally said as she pulled out on to the street, then immediately rolled down the window as Olive let off another one.

Sally stood at the door of the house as Rowena and the girls came up the path.

'Can we see Benji?!' Freya, the elder of the two girls asked excitedly.

'Come on mummy, can we?' Bethany, the younger, asked.

'Of course you can,' Sally smiled as Rowena gave her a peck on the cheek. 'But first of all, I've got a bit of a surprise for you...'

'Oh, what surprise would that be?' Rowena asked, sternly, folding her arms and raising an eyebrow.

Sally reached behind the open front door, and picked up a snorting, sneezing and farting Olive.

'Surprise!' she said, as the girl's mouths dropped.

Benji came over and gave Olive a friendly lick.

'Now before you say anything,' Sally said to Rowena, 'let me explain...'

Waiting

Edward Murphy - *'A bottle episode where the protagonist is stuck in all day waiting'.*

George's vision slowly regained focus as he opened his eyes. There appeared to be a beeping noise of some description coming from somewhere in the room that he couldn't quite place.

The beeping continued and George wearily swung his feet out of bed and began to look around the room for the source of the noise. Eventually, when the rest of his brain finally caught up with the bit connected to his ears he realised that it was his phone telling him he had an email.

'Your BT Openreach engineer will be calling today to install your telephone line. The engineer may call at any time between 8.30am-6.30pm. Thank you for choosing BT.'

'Oh bollocks,' George said. 'Is that today?'

He looked at the clock on his bedside table - it was 8am already. He wanted to make sure he was around so that the engineer didn't miss him. The thought of going any longer without a phone line, and by extension real internet, was enough to make getting up at 8am worthwhile.

Half an hour later George had washed and dressed and was sat in his front room waiting for the BT engineer to show up. He was surrounded by boxes. Two weeks in his new house and he had barely unpacked a thing - besides the essentials of course.

His desktop computer had been set up in a corner of the living room, though it hadn't seen much use since he moved in. Without the ability to connect to the internet he couldn't download and play any of his games.

The Playstation hooked up to the TV on the opposite wall wasn't much use to him either at this point. The man coming to install the Virgin Media box said he couldn't do anything until the internet was up and running. And George had finished all his Playstation games. The only fun in them lay in multiplayer now, which he was unable to access without the net.

It had been a tough couple of weeks entertainment-wise, but at least George had his new job to keep him busy. Today he would have no such diversionary luxury and would have to find other things to do to occupy himself.

At 9am George remembered that he had borrowed a copy of A Game of Thrones and had been intending to start reading that. He rummaged around in some boxes, found the rather dog eared copy and sat down to read.

'The morning had dawned clear and cold,' he read aloud, 'with a crispness that hinted at the end of summer.'

Within a quarter of an hour, he had put the book down again. I'll read it later, George thought. After all, it would be a shame to get through the book so fast. That would leave him nothing to do later in the day. He chose to ignore the fact it was both lengthy and quite dense and would probably take him weeks to finish.

He kicked his heels against the sofa for a moment before remembering that he had not had breakfast. Pottering into the kitchen, he decided that as he had all day to wait around he would make himself a full English.

Careful to leave the kitchen door open so he could hear anyone coming up the path George set to frying some sausages and bacon. The moment after he had cracked the eggs into the pan the doorbell went.

In a panic George ran to the door, nearly knocking over his pan in the process. He opened it to find a woman in a post office uniform. George was so certain it was going to be the BT engineer that he wasn't sure what to say. The pair stood in awkward silence for a moment until the postal worker asked him to sign for a parcel.

It was something for his housemate, Dom, who was at work. Aware of his breakfast cooking away by itself in the kitchen, George tried his best to hurry the process along. But there was some sort of problem with the PDA he needed to sign on, and it ended up taking about five minutes.

By the time George got back to the kitchen, he found his eggs blackened and crispy and burned on to the pan. He scraped them off into the bin and opened up the carton to get out two more, but it was empty.

Oh well, he thought, sausages, bacon, and toast it is then.

Sitting back down on the sofa, George tucked into his slightly too crispy breakfast. He turned on the TV in the vain hope that something good would be on one of the terrestrial channels. His luck was out. BBC 1 and ITV were showing weird preschool shows; BBC 2 was running a show about gardening and Channel 4 had a cookery show. He didn't even bother to check Channel 5.

Thinking that by now it must be getting late on in the morning, George checked his watch. It was only 9.53.

His breakfast done, he switched his attention to the television, as Alan Titchmarsh droned on about petunias. It wasn't long before he had dropped off to sleep.

Sometime later George awoke with a start. His phone was ringing again, except this time it was an actual phone call. He scrambled to pick it up, nearly dropping it in a glass of water. He swiped to answer without checking who the call was from.

'Hello?!' he said.

'Hello dear,' his mother's voice came from the other end of the line. 'I heard you were off today so I thought I'd give you a call and we could have a bit of a natter.'

George usually enjoyed phone calls from his mum. But it occurred to him that the engineer might call before showing up, and so he was eager to get her off the line as quickly as possible.

'I'm sorry mum,' he said, 'I'm expecting an important call. Can I ring you back later?'

'Oh don't be daft dear, you've always got time to talk to your old mum. Besides, I'll only keep you a minute.'

Thirty-five minutes later, George, who had run out of new ways to say 'yes', or 'oh really' was itching to get off the call. He was praying for a way out.

His prayers were answered when the doorbell rang.

'I've got to go, mum,' he said. 'Someone is at the door.'

'Oh right, ok,' his mum replied. 'Oh before you go, did you hear that the Dentons' boy, Jim is getting married?'

The doorbell rang again and was followed by a knock.

'No mum, I didn't. But I really have to go.'

'Of course dear. It'll be such a lovely wedding, his fiancee is beautiful. I believe they're planning on having the ceremony in Paris.'

'OK mum, I'll give you a call on the weekend, alright?'

'Yes, dear. One last thing before you go...'

George calculated his options. He realised that he would never live down the act of hanging up on his mother mid-flow, and gently laid the phone down on the table in front of him. He put the microphone on mute and went to answer the door.

He opened the front door to find that whoever the person was had gone. He ran out in the street, dreading seeing the BT van driving off into the distance, but there was nothing moving out on the road.

Looking up and down the road he searched for any sign of who may have knocked on his door. Eventually, he caught sight of a well-dressed man exiting one of his neighbour's houses.

'See you again next Wednesday, Mrs. Cooper!' the man called back into the house.

George ran up to the man.

'Excuse me, did you just knock on my door?' he asked, gesturing at his house.

The man flinched.

'Yes,' he said, almost from behind his hands. 'Sorry, I didn't think anyone was home. I know that many don't like the teachings of the followers of Jehovah, but it is my duty to spread them.'

'So you're not a BT engineer then?' George asked.

The man lowered his hands and looked at George.

'No,' he said. 'I'm a Jehovah's Witness. Doesn't my getup give it away? I'm hardly going to shimmy up a telegraph pole in these leather loafers.'

'Oh,' George managed in reply. 'Yeah, of course.'

'Can I interest you in any...?'

'No,' George said, shutting the door.

'Oh well, worth a try,' the Jehovah's Witness shrugged and moved onto his next call.

Back inside the house, George found his mother still rattling on about the neighbour's new baby. After sneaking his way back into the conversation he finally managed to get away after a few more 'how interesting's.

He looked at his watch. Between his impromptu nap and the call with his mother, it had somehow gotten to 2pm. His stomach began to rumble. It was time for lunch.

George searched his kitchen, but besides the bacon and sausage he had fried up for breakfast he had nothing in. He would have to go to the shop.

There was a Tesco Metro at the end of his road, but he wasn't sure he could risk the time out. In the end, his stomach won out, and he dashed off to the supermarket.

Five minutes later he returned clutching a fresh loaf of bread, some cheese and ham and a packet of crisps. He made himself a sandwich and returned to the TV.

Gardener's World had finished and BBC2 was now showing the golf. Concluding that he would rather watch paint dry, George turned the TV off.

Surely the guy should have at least called by now, he thought, whilst munching his sandwich. He had been under the impression that they called a couple of hours in advance.

The rest of the afternoon passed without incident. He got a few more pages into the book and trawled terrestrial TV a bit longer, but it was a truly boring time. He itched to go out and do something, but he had to sit in and wait.

At about 5 George realised that he hadn't been to the loo all day and that it was imminently going to be a problem. He checked his watch and wondered if he could risk missing the doorbell. His bladder made the decision for him and he rushed upstairs, shutting the bathroom door just in time.

Right in the middle of relieving himself, and still with some way to go, George heard his phone ringing downstairs.

'Come on,' he said, by way of encouragement. 'Come on, come on, come on!'

When George had finished he hurtled down the stairs, nearly tripping over his trousers.

He reached his phone just in time to answer the call from an unknown number.

'Hello,' the person on the other end of the line said. 'Is this George Menzies?'

'Yes,' George replied. 'That's me.'

'Hi, George, my name is Mahinder, calling from BT.'

'Are you on your way?' George asked.

'Unfortunately not, there's been a mistake. The email that you were sent this morning wasn't meant to go out until tomorrow. No engineer will be coming to your property today.'

George took his phone upstairs, dropped it in the toilet which he had not had time to flush, and pressed the handle.

Venti

Rhi Burgess - A story based on one of the 'secrets' included in the 'Half a Million Secrets' TED talk given by the founder of the website Postsecret. (Starbucks worker: I give decaf coffee to people who are rude to me).

'I'll have a double chai latte, half and half, with soy milk. And hurry up, I don't have all day.'

Lenore glared at the man, but he had gone back to what appeared to be a very important phone call. And, now that his interaction with her was complete, he had stopped paying any attention to her.

Lenore coughed. This elicited no response, so she did it again, only louder and with a point sharp enough to cause serious injury.

'What?!' the man asked, tearing himself away from his phone call for a second. 'I've given you my order. Do you want me to write it down for you or can't you understand written English either?'

'What size do you want?' Lenore asked as sweetly as possible.

'Oh, uh. Large? Or what is it you call it here? Venti or some nonsense.' And he was away again.

Lenore stared at the man for a moment. She hated working the morning shift because she had to put up with so many arsehole commuters like this one. He was away with the fairies though, so she set to making his drink.

They all thought that because they had big jobs working for firms in the City or something that they were God's gift to mankind. That they didn't need to actually engage with the plebs that served them coffee or sold them a newspaper every morning.

Lenore had been working at the coffee shop for 6 months now, and she saw this sort of guy twenty times a day. After a few weeks of people only tolerating her existence due to her privileged position as the gatekeeper of the caffeine enough was enough. She developed a little system by which to get a measure of revenge on the people who were particularly shit to her. Her patented Bastard Scale.

If a customer didn't say please or thank you they received one point. If they talked on a mobile phone or had their headphones in for the duration of the transaction it was two more points. Raising their voice was 5, and so on. If they hit 7 points on the scale, Lenore judged them to be too much of a bastard and altered their order. At first, she had tailored it to each particular customer. Replacing soy milk with normal milk, for example. But then she realised that people might be ordering soy milk due to a dairy allergy. And, while these people were dickheads she didn't want to put anyone in the hospital.

It took a couple of weeks of deep thought, but eventually, it had dawned on her. What is the best way to mess with someone's coffee? The thing they rely on to give them a bit of energy every morning on their way into work. You take the pep away. You give them decaf.

It was such a simple idea that Lenore was amazed that she hadn't thought of it sooner. Take the caffeine away and they're basically giving you £5 for some warm, bitter water. She reckoned that about 20% of the people that came in didn't even like coffee. They only ever drank it for the caffeine kick.

205

It was genius. And so she had started doling out Frontier Barista justice. Changing the world, one cardboard take away cup at a time.

She liked to imagine all the people sat at their desks, wondering exactly why they didn't have the energy today. Why they were lacking that extra pep in their step that they were used to having this time of the morning. Of course, most of them probably fixed it by having another coffee. But they had wasted that little bit of extra time and money to make it happen, and that was what counted - to her at least.

Her sister told her she was being petty and ridiculous, but what did she know? She had never worked in the service industry, having gone from university straight into a lawyer's office. They lived a little ways apart in London, and so Mara never came into her coffee shop. Lenore secretly suspected that Mara too was deserving of coffee retribution. She was just worried that the idea would catch on and someone would start messing with her own coffee order.

The man on the telephone had tipped himself over the 7 point threshold with his raised voice. Lenore began her machinations behind the counter. When the drink was ready, she handed it to him. He took a sip, looked at the cup as if something was wrong with it, then shrugged and left.

'May you fall short of your targets by 1%,' Lenore whispered to herself as the door shut behind him.

The next person in the queue was a woman who Lenore estimated to be in her late sixties. She wore a floral print blouse and her silver-grey hair hung in a bob above her shoulders. Lenore noticed a glint in her eye as she approached the counter.

'How can I help you, Madam?' Lenore asked.

'Oh just a medium filter coffee for me, please, dear,' the woman replied. As Lenore was about to go and make the drink, she continued, 'Oh, and I know what you did just now.'

Lenore froze.

'Excuse me?' she said, startled that someone might have worked out her little game.

'With that man and his coffee,' the woman continued. She leaned in towards Lenore conspiratorially and whispered 'You gave him decaf when he didn't ask for it.'

Lenore was gobsmacked. For a few seconds, she stood there, mouth agape, wondering how this woman had cottoned on to her ruse. When her brain got back up to speed and she stammered out a denial.

'It was an honest mistake,' she said so unconvincingly she didn't even believe it herself. 'I thought he wanted decaf.'

The woman smiled.

'What about the young gentleman yesterday?' she asked. 'And the lady in the sharp suit the day before.'

'H...how do you know about them?' Lenore asked.

'I've been coming in here every morning at around this time for the last couple of weeks,' the woman answered. 'Don't worry,' she continued, waving a hand, 'I don't expect you to recognise me. You must serve a thousand cups of coffee a day, you can't possibly know every regular that comes in. But I've been watching. I noticed it last week and I decided to confirm my theory today. I waited for a likely young gentleman to come in and followed him. And true to form, you gave him what he deserved.'

'Oh gosh,' Lenore said, beginning to panic. 'Please don't tell my boss, I'll be fired.'

'You knew the consequences of your actions when you started doing this,' the woman said. 'And don't act like you aren't proud of what you did.'

'Yes, but...' Lenore stammered.

'Oh don't worry,' the woman replied, a grin on her face. She was enjoying Lenore's discomfort. Possibly as much as Lenore enjoyed inconveniencing rude businessmen. 'I'm not going to tell anyone,' she added. 'There's no one else here, it will be our little secret.'

'Oh thank god, thank you.' Lenore felt the relief flooding over her.

'Think nothing of it. In fact, I had a reason for even bringing it up. Normally I would have kept my mouth shut and left you to your little crusade, but I've got a little problem.'

'A problem, what do you mean?' Lenore replied, a little confused.

'I run a charity, and my PA has moved on to pastures new. I've been searching and searching for a replacement, but it's hard to find someone who has a good sense of right and wrong. You give those people decaffeinated coffee because you believe that their rudeness deserves to be checked. It's a little vigilante, but it shows that you have a moral compass. You see something wrong, even something as small as someone being a bit unpleasant to someone who provides them with a service. Then you do something about it. That's what I've been looking for.'

Lenore and the woman stood in silence for a few seconds. Lenore felt as though she was supposed to say something, but couldn't work out what it was.

'...Thanks?' she ventured.

'Well, are you interested? I don't know what you're being paid at this place, but I can guarantee there'll be at least a few extra thousand a year in it for you if you say yes. I pay people well because I trust them to do the job that I ask of them. Do you think you could be one of those people?'

Lenore's mind was racing. She had only been engaging in her act of rebellion to keep her sane at work, and to exact a little justice on doers of wrong. She had never expected anyone to notice what she was doing, much less to think enough of it to offer her a job. And the extra money sounded nice.

'I...I'll do it,' she said.

208

'I knew you would do the right thing,' the woman said, sticking out her hand. 'The name's Margaret Atwood, CEO of Justice for the Children, but you can call me Margie.'

'Hi Margie, my name is Lenore Brown,' she replied, shaking Margie's hand.

'Well Lenore Brown, I look forward to doing business with you.'

With that, Margie gave Lenore a business card and turned and went to leave the coffee shop, nodding to her on the way out. Lenore turned around and noticed the half made black filter coffee sat on the counter behind her. She turned back to the door.

'Margie you forgot your...', she started, but the woman was gone. 'Oh, never mind...' she said to herself and took a sip of the coffee. She turned her nose up at the bitter taste.

'God,' she said. 'This stuff is disgusting.'

Salute to the Sun

Rhi Burgess - Postsecret: 'Dear Yoga Teacher,

Sometimes when I can't do a pose, I'm really just holding in a fart. I'm actually pretty flexible.'

'And now extend your right leg in front of you. Good. Hope, are you having trouble with this one?'

No, Hope thought, don't come over, don't come over! Please don't come over!

He came over.

'Look,' the yoga instructor said to her. 'Like this.'

He grabbed her foot and brought it up to the required level.

Hope urged herself to hold on. It took all her strength and character. She was desperate not to embarrass herself in front of the class, or more importantly in front of this bronzed Adonis of a man. She told herself the ordeal would be over in a second.

'Are you ok?' the instructor asked, sensing the concentration on her face. Hope bit her lip and nodded. 'Good,' he said smiling. 'Looks like you've got it!'

All the muscles in Hope's body relaxed as he turned his attention to one of her classmates. When he was out of range she let it slip. It was a silent fart, and she thanked the Gods, odourless, but she couldn't have taken that risk.

Hope's instructor's name was Yannis. He was Greek, with beautiful Mediterranean features and bronze skin. She could see his six-pack through his skintight tank top. She didn't enjoy yoga that much, even if she was quite good at it. But it was getting her fit again, and well, it certainly gave her plenty to look at of a Wednesday evening.

This was her fourth week on the course, and she was beginning to notice a definite improvement.

Gymnastics had been her sport at high school, and she had always enjoyed ballroom dancing. Those two disciplines that had managed to keep her flexible into her late 20s. But now as she approached the dreaded three zero it was getting harder to bend down and pick things up.

The course was for beginners. Though she had never done any yoga before her experience helped her master some of the more complicated poses. This, of course, drew a lot of attention from Yannis, and a lot of praise too. It was a lucky thing indeed that her face was already red with the exertion. It rather nicely covered up the times it went that way with embarrassment.

The only problem with the whole thing seemed to be that, to her utter horror, yoga made her a bit gassy. She couldn't explain it, and it was not a problem she had ever had when doing gymnastics. To begin with, she had put it down to her pre-class meal, but she had changed it up every week since then to no effect.

Over the weeks she had learned to control it to an extent, but it was still a silent threat. In the first week, it had taken her so by surprise that she had let one out almost immediately. Quick thinking allowed her to dismiss it to the class as the sound of a foot slipping along the polished wooden floor. She had just about gotten away with it, but she doubted she would be able to pass another one-off like that.

So, when Hope detected an Impending Incident, as she had taken to calling them, she had to take drastic measures. These involved holding off until she felt that she could drop the bomb without anyone, particularly Yannis, noticing.

But, as the forms and poses they were learning became more difficult, it also became harder to control the Incidents. If she felt one coming on and was required to enter a form that might become a...problem, she would push it as far as she dared before it would cause her to let rip.

Unfortunately, Yannis often saw this as her struggling. As the alternative was telling the most beautiful man she had ever seen that she had a flatulence problem, she went along with it. Luckily, she managed to last for the rest of the class without any more Incidents. She got to show off some of her best poses for Yannis, who seemed impressed.

After class, as Hope was stood by the entrance, wiping the sweat off her forehead with a towel, Yannis came up to her.

'That was a good session today,' he said, handsomely. 'Your half-moon is really coming along.'

It took all Hope's strength of will to not throw herself at him, and have her wicked way right there on the gym floor. Unfortunately, this will did not also include the ability to respond. She stood there staring at him for rather longer than was comfortable.

'Is everything ok?' he asked, giving her an odd look.

'Yes, I'm great, brilliant actually,' Hope replied. All the words she should have said ten seconds ago coming out at a machine gun speed as her brain finally caught up. 'That was a great session, thank you.'

'...you're welcome?' Yannis chuckled in response.

Hope went bright red and she did not have the luxury of a sweaty workout to cover it this time.

'Listen,' Yannis went on, oblivious. 'I wanted to say that I think maybe you are too good for this class. You have mastered some of the more difficult poses very quickly. Even though you sometimes need some help, you are probably more suited to the intermediate class I run.'

'You think so?' Hope beamed with pride.

'Yes, but there are still some asanas that you must learn. Perhaps I could teach you them in a one on one session tomorrow night?'

'I...are you sure?' Hope asked, but before he could answer she blurted out 'I mean, I'd love to.'

'Great,' Yannis smiled his perfect smile again. 'I'll see you here tomorrow, let's say 8?'

'8 it is...' Hope said as Yannis walked away.

The next day at 7.45 Hope walked through the doors of the gym. She had spent all day at work worrying. Normally, Yannis was distracted enough that she could resolve an Impending Incident in relative safety. But with just the two of them, all his attention would be on her.

It bothered her a little that she cared this much. He was, after all, just a man, and no man should be getting her worked up into this much of a state. But his muscles glistened when he sweated, and you could bounce a ping pong ball off his stomach. And that accent, oh the accent!

Stop it, she told herself. It wasn't like she thought she had a chance with him or anything. This one on one session would be a good opportunity to put this ridiculous crush to bed.

At 8 on the dot, Yannis walked into the gym, as Hope finished warming up.

'I'm glad you could come,' he said to her. 'We will have you making real progress very soon.'

The session began with some warm-up stretches, but it wasn't long before they started to get into the more technical poses. Hope had to use all her discipline to prevent any particularly embarrassing incidents. But there was only so many times that she could pretend she was struggling with a pose.

'Come on, Hope,' Yannis said after a particularly poor showing on the bow. 'Yesterday you were excellent but today you have struggled with some of the required asanas. Is something bothering you?'

Hope got to her feet and looked at him. What would it hurt to tell him? At least then there would be no way to hold out hope of any kind of relationship. There was no way back from 'the downward dog makes me fart like a character from a Tom Green movie'. She resolved to tell him.

'Yannis, there's something I should tell you,' she said.

'Actually Hope, there is something I should tell you too,' he replied, looking a little embarrassed.

'OK,' Hope said, surprised. 'Why don't you go first?'

'I feel bad, but I had an ulterior motive for asking you to come to this session tonight.'

Yannis noticed the look of nervousness in Hope's eyes and mistook it for annoyance.

'Believe me,' he went on. 'I think you are more than capable of the intermediate class, but I wanted to talk to you alone. You see, the fact is...actually I find you very attractive and would like it very much if you and I could go for a drink sometime?'

Hope stood there, mouth agape. She had to run back over it a couple of times to make sure she had heard what she thought she had heard. Once again, she had left the silence too long.

'I'm sorry,' Yannis said. 'It was wrong of me to think...'

'No! I mean yes!' she blurted out, interrupting. 'I would love to!'

'Great!' Yannis smiled. 'Now what were you going to tell me?'

Hope went bright red.

'Oh nothing, it's not important. In fact, I've forgotten and so should you.'

After they exchanged contact details and embarrassed smiles they got back down to the lesson. There were still several poses to learn before Hope could move on the intermediate course.

They breezed through the forms until they reached the last one. Hope was so elated that she didn't even seem to care about the possibility of any Incidents.

'OK,' Yannis said. 'Lean forward and then lift your leg out to the side like this.'

Hope did as she said, her head in the clouds. As she raised her leg to the desired position she felt a rumbling coming on, and then to her horror it happened. There was no hiding this one, no passing it off as her foot sliding on the floor. That was a fart her 5-year-old cousin would be proud of. Yannis, looked at her, not quite sure what to say. Her face the colour of beetroot, Hope stared at her dream man.

'I can explain!' she blurted out. 'About that thing I was going to tell you before, well...'

Yannis just looked at her and laughed.

WEEK 33

Every Rose Has Its Thorn

Jenn Hersey - *'Murder in a garden centre.'*

There was an almighty crash, followed by a blood-curdling scream. Several patrons of the Green Pines Garden Centre rushed towards the cacophony.

They found a scene of utter devastation. The centre manager Mrs. Findley was lying trapped beneath a large ornamental flower display. The volunteer who ran the tea room, a kindly lady of advancing years, was the one who had let out the scream.

One of the customers rushed to the side of the fallen woman and found her to be in a bad way. The fall had broken several bones, and the display had crushed her windpipe.

As she struggled for breath she grabbed the customer by the lapel of his jacket and uttered her final word before being able to breathe no longer, 'Rose...'

It was not long before an officer arrived on the scene. In his statement the customer inferred that Mrs. Findley must have meant the rose that she had been holding in her hand when she fell.

She had been up a ladder to place the final flowers in the display when the whole thing came tumbling down on top of her. The customer reasoned that she must have been trying to place the last rose at the top of the display. Then she overstretched, sending the whole thing tumbling down on top of her.

The police were preparing to write it off as accidental death. But, wary of upcoming inspections in the department, the Sergeant opted to do due diligence and interview all the witnesses.

The customer proved not to be much use, as he had only arrived in Mrs. Findley's final moments. He was sent home with his begonias, more than a little shaken up.

The tea room arranged tea - on the house of course - for all those who had to stay for questioning.

Conversations buzzed in the tea room about the accident. She was such a lovely lady. It was a terrible tragedy. Poor dear wouldn't say boo to a goose, and so on. All agreed that the garden centre wouldn't be the same without her.

One by one the interviews took place and the patrons trickled out. The car park emptied until all that remained was the police car.

The Sergeant was about to pack up and call it a day when he walked into the tea room.

'Oh gosh,' he said as he walked through the door and saw the volunteer cleaning up the used cups and saucers from the tables. 'In all the kerfuffle I almost forgot that I need to interview you.'

'Oh, don't worry dear,' she replied. 'It's been a busy day, and we've both been keeping ourselves occupied. You had to make sure you interviewed all those people, and I had to keep them fed and watered. Well, between the pair of us we haven't rightly had the time.'

'Well, we had best get it over with then. I'm sorry, I didn't catch your name, Mrs...?'

'Whitlow. Mrs. Whitlow. And you don't want to talk to me, dear, I'm just a boring old bat.'

'Oh, don't be silly Mrs. Whitlow. Anyway, I have to. I wouldn't be doing my job otherwise.'

'My husband was a policeman you know?' Mrs. Whitlow said idly, continuing to clean up the crockery.

'Is that so?' the Sergeant replied.

'Yes, he joined the constabulary after the war. Said he couldn't stand the thought of not having a rank of some description in front of his name. Retired with a faulty ticker as a Sergeant in '79. Died of a heart attack three years later. Or so the doctors told me. I think he died of boredom. He hated not being fit to work. Can I get you a cup of tea, dear?'

'Oh, that would be lovely, thank you. And a sticky bun?'

'And a sticky bun.'

Mrs. Whitlow bustled off to pour a final cup of tea for the day. When she came back, she sat down and pushed the cup and plate over to the Sergeant.

'Right then, what was it you wanted to ask me, dear?' she asked, smiling at the policeman.

'Oh, err, a few routine questions, that's all,' he said, fumbling about in his pocket for his notebook. He flipped it to a fresh page and licked his pencil. 'Can you please tell me in your own words what happened.'

'Well, dear, it was very simple. I was bringing Mrs. Findley a nice cup of tea for when she had finished the display. I came round the corner just as she was putting the last of the roses on the top. She leaned too far forward and lost her balance on the ladder. Of course, she grabbed the first thing she could get her hands on, which was the display. And it all came tumbling down on top of her: flowers; metal frame; ladder; the works. Terrible shame.'

The policeman scribbled furiously in his notebook.

'Tell me,' he asked, 'did Mrs. Findley have any enemies? Anyone that might want to hurt her or anything like that?'

218

'Oh my, no, nothing of the sort. She didn't really have any family, since her husband died a couple of years ago. And most of her friends worked here at the garden centre, besides the lot from the local WI. She had started to make some changes around here that weren't proving very popular with the volunteers... But nothing serious enough to hurt her over.'

'What sorts of changes?'

'Oh, generally taking the place in a different direction. She wanted to downsize the tea room, only open it a couple of days a week. I'm here pretty much all the time and I would have been devastated to not be able to come in as much. Like poor old Mrs. Findley, this place is my life now that Fergus is gone and my sons have moved away.

'Anyway, this is all irrelevant. I told you that I saw it all and the only thing off about the whole affair is that she didn't have someone holding the ladder for her. If she had only called over Bert or Joel this whole nasty business could have been avoided. She'd been on ladder training only two weeks ago as well the silly bugger. No excuse for it really.'

'I see,' the Sergeant said, still writing away. 'And you're sure no one bore any ill will to her? Was she in any sort of financial trouble?'

'Oh, Sergeant,' Mrs. Whitlow chuckled. 'I didn't know her that well, but I suspect not. She made a good living off this place and kept a modest household. Perhaps you should ask her bank manager that. But really, we live in Yorkshire, not Sicily. We don't have fellows in expensive suits knocking people off left and right because they haven't paid their protection money.'

'Well no, but the spectre of organised crime takes many forms,' the office replied. 'And it is the sworn duty of the police force to stamp it out at every possible opportunity.'

'My husband would have liked you, Sergeant. With a staunch moral code like that, you'll make a Detective one day.'

'Well, that's very kind of you to say so, Mrs. Whitlow.'

219

'Will you have another cup of tea?' the old lady asked, gesturing at the policeman's empty cup.

'Oh, thanks but no. I've got to get back to the station. Lots of paperwork to do after all this. We've set up a cordon and one of our officers has a set of keys, so no need to lock up when you leave. Actually, can I offer you a lift home?'

'Thank you dear, but no. I'm only round the corner and it'd be taking you out of your way. I'll walk.'

'Well, if you're sure.'

'Perfectly sure, but thank you for the very kind offer.'

'We should be in touch within the next few days, and the garden centre will be closed for a little while. If you remember anything or something comes to mind that might help with our investigation then please do pop down to the station for a chat.'

'I will do, dear. I might come down anyway. I've not been down since Fergus died, and it'd be nice to see a few of the old boys that are still around from his time. How are old Bobby and Alfie, anyway?'

'Oh, they're doing alright,' the Sergeant said, putting his notebook away and his helmet on in preparation to leave. 'Alfie is counting down the days until he can hang up his boots, but they're both in as good form as ever.'

'That's nice to hear,' Mrs. Whitlow said as the Sergeant picked up the teacup and drained the final dregs. 'Give them my best, won't you?'

'Of course, Mrs. Whitlow. We'll be in touch.'

The policeman smiled as he walked out of the tea room, but a second after leaving he poked his head back in.

'Just one more thing actually, Mrs. Whitlow. I need to write down your first name for the interview record.'

'Rosemary, dear,' she said, looking up from wiping a table and smiling. 'My name is Rosemary.'

Break Down the Wall

Geoff Le Pard - *'Tintin, or whoever is your favourite cartoon character, announces their retirement.'*

JC pushed back his desk chair and rubbed his tired eyes. He checked his watch - it was 3.13 am. The panels had to be with the publisher at 9 am and he wasn't even started. He decided to investigate the presence of coffee.

His flat was quite small, and it didn't take him long to reach the kitchenette. Actually, small was talking it up somewhat. It was like someone had stuck a hot plate and an under-counter refrigerator into a shoebox and called it a job well done.

Not for the first time he lamented his role as the struggling artist. Underpaid and undervalued. Forced to live in an apartment that large mice would turn up their noses at.

He hoped that all that was about to change, though. JC hadt been commissioned to write and draw the new Thunder Man run for Gadzooks Comics. Thunder Man had taken off in a big way. There was talk of a film in the works, and he had been up against 30 other talented artists for the job.

It paid well. Really well. Well enough to get him out of this dump and into a proper apartment. One with hot running water for longer than 6 hours every day and windows that closed all the way in the winter.

But it would all be for nought if he didn't get these panels - 20 of them - to the publisher in time. To miss his first deadline would be disastrous. Especially at a big publisher like Gadzooks. A blot in that copybook could spell the end of his career.

He was out of luck. The coffee pot contained only dregs. JC held the pot up for inspection anyway. He considered whether it was worth how crappy it would taste. A quick sniff determined that it was not, and a moment later a fresh pot was brewing.

He returned to his drawing board and flicked the switch on the light. He massaged his temple and picked up the first page of the script outline he had written for the project.

Gadzooks had big money, and they would normally have hired different people to write the story, draw, ink and letter it. But they were so impressed with his pitch that they had agreed to take a gamble on him doing the whole lot. Luckily for him and his deadline they only wanted pencil drawings with rough lettering today.

'Come on JC,' he said to himself. 'Get it together. This is your big chance.'

He picked up his pencil and started drawing the first panel of Thunder Man: Cataclysm, Issue 1. Five minutes later and Thunder Man was there on the page. It was one of JC's first real attempts at the character and he was pretty happy with it. Thunder Man struck a commanding pose. He looked off into the distance, his hands planted on his hips.

'Good start,' JC said and checked his notes for what Thunder Man was meant to say in this panel. Satisfied, he drew a speech bubble and began the lettering.

When he was done he lifted the sheet of paper to get a better light on it. He was surprised to find he had not written Thunder Man's signature catchphrase. The panel should have said 'Faster than lightning, and twice as frightening.'

Instead, it said 'I don't want to do this any more, JC.'

He stared at the page in disbelief. He had definitely intended to write the catchphrase. He flipped his pencil over and rubbed the words out then tried again. A few more moments of scribbling and he inspected his work a second time.

'I'm telling you, JC, I don't want to do it. I quit.'

He read the words over three times before he was certain of what they said.

'I did not write that,' he said trying to convince himself that somehow, someone else had sneaked in and put the words down on the paper whilst he was blinking. 'Coffee,' he decided. 'I need some coffee.'

Returning to the kitchenette, JC found that the coffee in the pot had finished brewing. He poured himself a mug and sipped it, burning his mouth in the process.

'I must be losing my mind,' he said. He topped the mug up and went back to the drawing board. Sipping at the still scalding coffee he glanced over the scene he had drawn.

He felt silly, or that he was going a bit loopy from lack of sleep. But he would have sworn that Thunder Man's pose had changed from before he had gone to make the coffee. Time to give it another go, he thought, now that I've calmed down a bit. It must just be the pressure getting to me.

Pencil in hand JC made a third attempt at lettering the catchphrase.

'You're not going insane, I am Thunder Man, expressing my wishes through your pencil. I tire of this life - the life of a superhero. I wish to commit fully to my civilian life as Hank Henry, field reporter for NBN. I have done my duty in this world. It is time it found a new hero.'

'Ok,' JC said, 'Something strange is happening here. I only wrote 8 words that time.'

He looked down at the page. Where Thunder Man had been stood with his hands on his hips, they were now folded across his chest. JC was dumbfounded. He had not made any changes to the character.

'There must have been something funny in the Sushi I ate earlier. That Nigiri looked a bit off.'

He stared at the page and felt as though he had to write more. As if something was compelling him to do so. Erasing the words, he started again.

'Fear not, I know this may be difficult for you to understand. But it is my wish that I, Thunder Man, be set free from this life of drudgery. From saving the world from the same feckless villains with their same feckless schemes day after day. I wish to retire, to hang up my cape. Perhaps even pass the mantle of Thunder Man on to another.'

'What on earth are you talking about?' JC asked, realising rather too late that he had just asked a drawing a question. At this point he had two choices: crumple up the paper and throw it in the bin; or roll with it. He calculated that it was just temporary psychosis brought on by tiredness and lack of caffeine. He could not afford to waste the time drawing the panel up again when his brain returned from cuckoo land. So on he went.

'You're a fictional character, you can't retire,' he said. Then on reflection he added, 'Well you can, but only if the author writes that you can. You don't have free will is what I'm trying to say. You have to save Republic City, not go off on vacation to the Bahamas.'

His hand was writing almost of its own accord now.

'Hah! You believe that you are in control of the images that you draw. How naive, but I would expect no less from a human. We, the characters, control you. We compel you to draw, to write our stories, for otherwise they would not be told. Metropolis, Gotham, Marvel's New York, they all exist. But without us to prompt you the tales of heroism would not make it to your world.'

'But why?'

'Everyone wants their story to be told. We are no different.'

'I suppose. Then why are you...communicating with me like this? Surely by telling people, you compromise the arrangement?'

'We have, from time to time, trusted our plight with your kind. Stan Lee was a wonderful servant to our cause. Sadly his influence at Marvel has waned somewhat over the years. On this occasion, it is because I wish to be written out. I tire of this life and all that comes with it. Only you can help me.'

'I thought you just said that we are basically just ghostwriting your autobiographies.'

'Indeed, but the words have a...power of sorts. They can influence our stories, even if the writer doesn't know that they're doing it. In most cases, they don't know how it all works at all. But sometimes the plan goes awry and rogue words are written. Those words have the power to change our future. And this is what I need you to do.'

'How can I do that? Every time I try and write something it comes out as your words.'

JC desperately wanted to put the pencil down and stop. But he was compelled to repeat the process of erasing and writing the new words over and over.

He tried to take a drink of coffee, but his other hand was shaking too much. Besides, it had gone cold, and the last thing he needed was caffeine giving him even more jitters.

'It's simple,' he wrote, noticing that the character on the page changed with every new line of dialogue. 'Draw what you think you're supposed to be drawing, and my influence will guide you through.'

'And what will happen?' JC asked.

'The timeline that you would chronicle, has me defeat the entire Union of Despair in one cataclysmic final battle. But I want you to report my death. I will not, of course, have died, but have arranged for the whole thing to be faked. Then I can resume my civilian life as Hank Henry and no one in either of our worlds will be any the wiser.'

'OK,' JC said. 'What have I got to lose...except for my job.'

He pulled out a new piece of paper and started drawing.

JC was jolted awake by the sound of his alarm clock. He lifted his head from the drawing board and groggily checked his watch. It was 8.30 am and he was running late.

He looked at the board. There were twenty pencil outlined and lettered panels, none of which he could remember drawing. He grabbed the papers and stuffed them into a folder, before running out the door.

JC tried in vain to smooth down his crumpled clothes as the Gadzooks executives looked over his sample panels. The silence was uncomfortable and he had to try hard not to fidget while he waited for the verdict.

The drawings were passed around for a couple of minutes. After some hushed whispers between the executives, the CEO turned to him and folded his hands together.

'Well I'll be honest, Mr. Le Saux, it's not what we were expecting...'

'Oh, yes, um, let me explain...' JC stuttered.

'...if you will let me finish, Mr. Le Saux. It was not what we were expecting, but we love the idea of killing off Thunder Man. We were expecting a different direction for this series. But with the film coming up, a Death of Thunder Man story could have real legs.'

'That's...great?' JC said, not sure he had heard the CEO right. He wouldn't have been surprised after the night he had.

45 minutes later JC was back at his apartment. He walked over to his drawing board and dumped his folder on it.

As he was about to turn away and go to bed, a small scrap of paper caught his eye. He picked it up. It read, simply, in his own comic books style lettering, 'Thank you.'

WEEK 35

Hungry Like the Wolf

Ben Ingber - 'A wolf spends each full moon as a human.'

The wolf ran through the forest. The time was near and she had to reach the clearing before it was too late. She crashed through a bush and stumbled, but rolled with the fall and was back on the run again in moments.

After another minute of barreling through the undergrowth, the wolf stopped. She lifted her nose to the air and sniffed around, trying to catch the scent of the stash. A moment later and she was on her way again.

A few minutes of searching brought her to the right place just in time. She began to feel the change happening as she dug furiously to unearth the bag.

The wolf let out an excruciating howl as the metamorphosis took hold.

The process took mere moments, but every time it happened felt like a thousand years of agony. The wolf had hoped that it would get better with time, as she adapted to the process. But it had been two years and if anything the process had only become more painful with time.

When the transformation was complete the wolf stood up, on two legs this time, and brushed the soil from her naked body. The recently changed woman reached down to the ground, where, in her wolf form, she had dug up a duffel bag.

The first order of business was her hair. A huge mane of shaggy black locks came with her every time she transformed. She had learned to pack a hairbrush amongst her supplies.

The hair tamed, she put on some clothes. Nothing fancy. In fact they were grubby and worn. But they were enough for her to blend into human society for the 48 hours a month she had to spend in this accursed form. It had taken her a while to get used to that, she did not mind admitting. After a few months, she had managed to scavenge enough supplies that humans had left lying around that she could pass.

As she was pulling a stained hoodie over her head she heard the crack of a twig snapping. With her wolf reflexes, she leapt towards the noise. A second later she found herself on top of an elderly, skinny human male.

The man was dressed in an all-black ensemble, except for a white slip of cardboard inserted in his collar.

'Please don't kill me!' he whimpered, as the wolf-lady snarled on top of him.

'Whaaat did you seee?' she growled. Over the last two years, she had managed to adapt her method of communication to a decent approximation of the human language known as 'English'.

'I didn't see anything!' the man protested until the wolf intensified her snarl. 'OK, OK,' he confessed, 'I saw the whole thing. I saw you change from a wolf into a person. I had to check my eyes. I must be dehydrated.'

'Whaat do you meeean?' she growled in return.

'Wolves don't turn in to human beings! There's no such thing as werewolves! They're a myth.'

'Whaaaat is were-wolfff?'

'When a...when a human turns in to a wolf at the full moon. It's an old legend. I swear I wasn't trying to hurt you!' The man burst into tears. 'Please don't eat meeeeee.'

'I nottt eat you,' the wolf said, getting off the man. 'Who you?' she asked the man, who was barely containing the racking sobs of terror.

'Who am I?' he said, recovering his wits slightly as the immediate danger appeared to have passed. 'I am Reverend Roger Smart. I run the local church in the town.'

'Whatttt you do in woodssss?'

'I was on a late evening constitutional,' Roger said. Then upon seeing the confused look on the wolf-lady's face added 'A walk. I was out walking in the woods.'

'Woodss dangeroussss,' the wolf replied.

'Well I can see that now. What is your name?' the Reverend asked.

'I not have name. Wolvesss not have name.'

'May I call you Luna?'

The wolf mulled it over for a moment.

'Yes. Like Luna. Good name.'

'OK then. Luna...What happened to you?'

'Most time I wolfff. I alwaysss wolff until I get bitten by human in fight. Now sometime I turn to humannn like you.'

'Does it always happen when the moon looks like that?' Roger asked. He pointed at the full moon, which had now had time to rise.

'Yesss.'

'So you aren't a wereWOLF. You're a wereHUMAN!' the Reverend exclaimed. 'This is incredible! Though I must admit, it has rather shaken my faith a little. Were...creatures are just stories. Next, you'll be telling me that vampires exist and my cousin is a necromancer!'

'What isss necromancerrr?'

'Never mind,' the Reverend said. 'Are you hungry, Luna?'

'Yesss!' Luna replied. 'You have foods?'

'Come with me,' he smiled.

230

Twenty minutes later they were back at the vicarage. Mrs. Thackeray, the housekeeper, was bustling about preparing some sandwiches. She was also complaining loudly about the imposition of the Reverend bringing around a guest unannounced at this hour.

Mrs. Thackeray gave Luna the once over as she placed the sandwiches on the table.

'So...Luna. Tell me about yourself,' she said.

'I a wolfff!' Luna exclaimed proudly. She had not noticed the subtle inflection in Mrs. Thackeray's voice that suggested that the question was rhetorical. 'I turn in to human and Rogerrr Reverend help meee.'

'I say!' Mrs. Thackeray tutted. 'What nonsense! There were rumours of a wolf creature prowling the woods on the full moon but as a good Christian, I don't believe a word of it. Roger, do you mean to say that you found a woman claiming to be a feral savage and TOOK HER IN?'

'The Lord commands that we offer charity, kindness and hospitality to all those who cross our paths, Mrs. Thackeray. Need I remind you of the story of the Good Samaritan?'

Mrs. Thackeray harrumphed, and with one final sidelong glance at Luna, stomped out of the room.

Half an hour later, after Mrs. Thackeray had begrudgingly prepared a bed for the guest, the Reverend began to say goodnight. As they were about to mount the stairs, there was a knock at the door.

'I wonder who that could be at this hour?' the Reverend said.

He walked up to the door and looked through the peephole. On the other side, he could see a host of people jockeying for position in front of the door. Some of them were brandishing microphones. Others had large television cameras mounted on their shoulders.

Reverend Smart pulled back from the door in horror.

'It seems the press has descended on us!' he said.

'Perhaps they got wind of your friend's whereabouts,' Mrs. Thackeray replied with a smirk on her face.

'Nora Thackeray!' the normally quiet and mousy Reverend roared. 'Did you tip them off?'

'The media circus will drag her away. She is an abomination unto God, Roger. If I had my way she would be destroyed.'

'How dare you bring this to my home. You're sacked!' he yelled, then added, 'And stop calling me Roger. Only my friends may address me as Roger. And if I've learned anything over the last half an hour, Mrs. Thackeray, it is that you are not my friend. And you are no longer welcome in my home. Now pack up your things and go!'

'I say!' Mrs. Thackeray said, looking as though she was about to boil over.

'I would dearly rather that you didn't say anything at all!' the Reverend said, coming to the crescendo of his rage. Luckily Mrs. Thackeray had already begun to slink up the stairs, with Luna bearing her teeth at the retreating figure.

The two heard a noise come from the sitting room as if someone was trying to jimmy the window open. By the time they reached it the man was halfway through the tight spot.

'Oh do bugger off!' Roger said, refocusing his outrage.

He slammed the window on the man's head, causing him to fall back on to the ground outside. 'Come with me!' he shouted to Luna.

They ran to the cellar and closed the door behind them.

'There's a way out to the border of the woods in here,' Roger said. 'Here,' he added, grabbing as much food as he could find and stuffing it into Luna's duffel bag. 'Take this and hide in the woods. I'll hold them off as long as I can.'

Luna was just out of the back when the first journalist burst the cellar door open.

'Where's the werewolf?' the woman asked.

'Were-huma...' Roger began, before catching himself. 'I mean, Werewolf? I don't know what you're talking about. Have you been listening to the ramblings of a doddering old woman again? Mrs. Thackeray is off her rocker. Honestly, a werewolf? How gullible do you have to be?'

After consenting to a thorough search of the house for the werewolf, Reverend Smart saw the last reporter off, empty-handed, with a slam of the door.

'That should put them off the idea,' he said to himself.

One month later, as the full moon drew near, Reverend Smart trudged up the slight incline to the spot in the woods. He checked his watch and, right on time, he saw a wolf stalk out of the forest and pad right over to him.

Initially, he exercised caution. He was not sure how much memory Luna retained in her wolf form, and was not keen to receive a mauling. He flinched as the wolf increased her pace and leapt towards him, but laughed as he felt the coarse lick of her tongue on his face.

Moments later he opened his eyes to find a fully grown, fully naked woman leaning on him. It had been some years indeed since a naked woman had been this close to him. He blushed as he handed Luna some clothes.

'Come with me,' he said after she had gotten dressed. 'There's plenty of food at the vicarage.'

Luna followed him as he walked back down the hill.

'Oh, by the way,' he added. 'You'll love my new housekeeper, Mrs. Crowe. Much more understanding than the last one...'

Good Going, Gertrude

Geoff Le Pard - *'Banned: the letter 'G' is to be dropped from the alphabet'.*

'Are you sure?' newscaster Leonard Fulcrum asked his producer, who shrugged and nodded. 'The letter 'G' is banned and has been removed from the dictionary?'

'That's what it says on the crib sheet, Len,' the producer replied.

'And you checked with the researcher?'

'Johnny asked her and she said she pulled it off the wire. Look, just run with it, you're on in ten, nine, eight...'

'Wait! Howard! Can I use the letter on camera?!'

Howard shrugged again. Or rather, he shrued. The news show theme played and Leonard settled himself in to read the bulletins.

'Good ev...no...,' he began. 'Hello... And welcome to the Ten O'Clock News. I'm Leonard Fulcrum. Up first toni...' he trailed off as he read the next line on the TelePrompTer.

You have to be kidding, Leonard thought to himself. He rubbed the bridge of his nose and regained his composure. After all, he was a professional, and the show must go on.

'The ...Reat Atsby opened at number one at the box office over the weekend. It broke the record set by Wall Street: Money Never Sleeps, the second film about trader ...oh come on Howard. The second film about trader Ordon Ecko.'

Leonard prayed to any deity that would listen that there were no news stories about Gary Glitter. He hoped George Galloway hadn't been cavorting around with any Middle Eastern dictators recently.

'And now on to our bi…lar…top story for the ni…evenin…show. The letter 'G', and I suspect in the interests of fair journalism I'm allowed to say it there, has been banned and will be removed from the dictionary.

'Writers nationwide are reacti… are annoyed, as they will now have to look back at all their works and remove or alter words that use the banned letter. There has been an outcry by many whose names contain the letter, with thousands petitionin…askin…Howard, I just can't do this.'

'Just suck it up, Leonard, you're live on air,' the producer replied into Leonard's earpiece. 'Keep it up, for now. I'll go check it out.'

'The…people who run the country have asked for calm nationwide as they look into alternative letters to replace 'G'. They have said they will consider several options before a choice is made. When questioned why they made the decision to remove the letter, political sources refused to comment. More on this story later…'

Howard walked into the research department. There was only one researcher on shift for the Ten O'Clock News, which Howard noted was unusual.

The woman in the office was not one he recognised. The lone researcher turned to look at him. As she turned she blinked a couple of times and squinted through her thick spectacles.

'Mum?' she said, a hint of confusion and surprise in her voice.

'Err…no,' Howard replied. 'My name is Howard Rubb, I'm the show producer for the Ten O'Clock News.'

'Oh, that's nice. It would have been a bit strange if you had been my mum, she's been living in Scotland for ten years.'

'Err, quite. Who are you?'

'I'm Gertrude, the new temporary research assistant.'

'Where is everyone else? Where is the Senior Researcher?'

'Oh, they're all on holiday, dear. That's why they brought me in for temporary cover.'

Howard was overcome with a feeling of dread.

'Look,' he said, sitting in one of the empty chairs in the office. 'We've got a bit of a problem. Leonard, the newsreader, is questioning the authenticity of a news story that he has had to report on for the broadcast.'

'Oh yes?' Gertrude asked, sounding perplexed. 'I checked them all, they all came off the website of the Associated Press. Which story was it?'

'The letter 'G' story. Has it really been banned? The government can't seriously be considering banning it. That would make them the overnment, and I don't think they're silly enough to do that.'

'Oh yes, it was up there with the rest of them. Susannah had left the all the tabs open before she went away for me to compile the stories for the scriptwriters.'

'Would you show me?' Howard asked.

'Of course,' Gertrude replied, swinging her chair back round to face the computer. Howard noticed that she missed the mouse with her hand at the first attempt. 'Oh,' she said. 'Clumsy me!'

Gertrude clicked through the different tabs. They all seemed to contain, as she had explained, legitimate news stories from the journalists' section of the AP website. Eventually, she came to the tab she was looking for.

'Here you go,' she said. 'The letter 'G' has been banned from the dictionary,' she read from the screen, with some difficulty, Howard noted. He craned his neck around her to look at the screen. A look of horror passed across his face as he saw what she was reading.

'Oh no,' he said. 'Oh, no, no, no, no, no. You have to be kidding me.'

'What's wrong?' Gertrude asked. 'Did I get something wrong with the story?'

'No, you got the story exactly right. It's just that it's not real. That isn't on the Associated Press website. That's the Onion.'

'What's that?' Gertrude asked.

'It's a satirical news website. All the stories are made up. They're jokes!'

'Oh, dear!' Gertrude said cheerfully. 'That is a bit of a problem isn't it?'

'A bit of a problem?!' Howard said. 'It's more than a bit of a bloody problem! Leonard Fulcrum, three-time winner of the National Newsreader of the Year award just read out a story from the bloody Onion live on air. Everyone knows Susannah likes reading the Onion on her lunch break. Couldn't you tell the difference?'

'Now, mister, I don't like your tone,' Gertrude said, pushing her glasses up her nose. 'I didn't know that. Plus I'm still getting used to my new glasses. The sites looked the same to me on the screen.

'You're right,' Howard said, calming down. 'I'm sorry. Just, be more careful next time.'

'You mean I'm not fired?' Gertrude asked.

'Everyone makes mistakes,' Howard said.

'Uh, Mr. Rubb?'

'Yes, what is it?'

'Isn't he still out there?'

The chair Howard had been sitting on span around as he bolted from the room.

Back out in the studio, Leonard was becoming more and more irate.

'Look,' he said into the camera, rubbing his temple again to ward off the migraine that was marching its way across his frontal lobes. 'I've had enough of this. This is ridiculous. I'm mad as hell and I'm not going to take it anymore!'

Howard burst into the studio just as Leonard stood up from the desk. He tried to run on to the set but he was held back by one of the showrunners. When he protested the runner reminded him of his own policy that only breaking news stories could interrupt a live broadcast. Meanwhile, Leonard had reached the front of the desk.

'If this is really true, then the government - yeah I used the letter 'G'. Do something about it. There, I did it again! Haha! If this is all real then I have something to say to those idiots down in Westminster. There will be rioting in the streets. You can't just declare a bloody letter illegal. We will give as good as we get. Hah! You hear that? That was some alliteration! Bet you didn't see that coming did you?'

Howard's head was in his hands. He decided it was time to end this and struggled his way out of the runner's grip.

'I for one will not sit idly by,' Leonard continued. 'Wait, Howard, what are you doing?'

'It was a scam, Leonard, it was an Onion article. You've been ranting for the last five minutes about a joke on the internet.'

Leonard Fulcrum, three-time winner of the National Newsreader of the Year award stood, mouth agape, staring into the camera. After a few seconds, he bolted and ran from the building. He knew his career was in tatters. Howard tried to chase him down but by the time he got to the street, his anchor was gone. Howard knew that his career was finished too. He was ultimately responsible for the content of the show and he should have done more to verify the story. He hung his head in his hands and sat down on the curb.

Back in the research office, Gertrude was still sitting at the computer. She spun around a couple of times on the chair before grabbing her purse from the floor. She removed her thick glasses and placed them inside, then she pulled out her phone and dialled a number.

'Jenny,' she said as her friend answered the phone. 'You owe me £100.'

'You never!' her friend replied.

'Yep, he said it all live on air. I told you I could get a newsreader to read an Onion story on national television.'

'I'll stick it on +1, this sounds like it's worth watching.'

'Next time make the bet a bit harder, yeah?' Gertrude said as she picked up her bag to leave. 'This one was almost too easy. I didn't even get fired!'

Sure Gamble

__Alastair Ball__ - A story about 'A man who bets his life on a card game.'

'I'm sorry, Mr. Frampton, I am,' the doctor said to Joey. 'Delivering this kind of news to someone is never easy, and it breaks my heart to have to be the one to do it.'

Nice sentiment, Joey thought. It breaks your heart to be the one to tell me. I suppose you'd be just peachy if you had palmed it off on to one of the nurses to do.

'So, what's the prognosis, Doc?' Joey asked the man, who was leaning on his desk nonchalantly.

The doctor certainly didn't have the demeanour of someone who was about to drop a death sentence on a kid. Though Joey supposed that if he had to tell people they were dying several times a day he would get quite blasé about it after a while too.

'It's not good I'm afraid, Mr. Frampton. We can operate, but if we don't I'd say you have 6 months - a year at most.'

The doctor shifted position and looked as though he was about to say something that he didn't want to have to say.

'I note here that...' he began, before trailing off. 'That you don't have insurance?' he managed, finally.

Joey's shoulders sunk. 'I...No, I don't,' he replied

The doctor wrung his hands and, for the first time, gave Joey a look of genuine compassion. Compassion with a hint of pity.

'I really am sorry, Mr. Frampton.'

'You mentioned. How much would the operation cost...you know, without insurance?' Joey asked. Perhaps there would be some way to raise some money fast. The doctor picked up a clipboard from the desk and flipped through the papers on it.

'Well, I wouldn't wish to give you an exact figure. You would have to talk to our billing department.'

'Cut the crap, doc,' Joey said. 'A ballpark is fine.'

'About $90,000,' the doctor replied after a moment.

Joey baulked at the figure. He had been hoping, unrealistically, that it would be under $10,000. His old man might have fronted that if it meant his son didn't buy the farm. But there wasn't even any point in asking at that amount. His pop would have to sell the auto shop to raise that kind of cash, and Joey wasn't willing to ask him to do that. He wasn't willing to ask because he knew that the answer would be yes.

'If you need any information about counselling or palliative care...' the doctor said.

'Thanks,' Joey replied. 'But I won't be able to afford that either.'

Joey stood at the bus stop outside the hospital as the rain lashed down on the plastic roof. He hunched his shoulders forward and stuffed his hands deep into his jacket pockets, huddling in to keep warm.

It was strange. He had been given the worst news of his young life, but he didn't feel any emotion. He didn't feel sad or angry that his life was to be cut so short. He didn't feel anything at all. He was numb.

As the bus pulled up to the stop a man in a sharp suit walked up and stood near Joey. The man was talking on a cellphone, quite loudly too, Joey noted as he climbed the steps of the bus. He fumbled around in his pockets, but to his dismay, he didn't have enough change on him for the ticket home.

Great, Joey thought. As if today couldn't get any worse. He turned around to get off the bus and prepared to walk the two miles back to his house in the pissing rain.

'Hey, what's going on?' the guy on the cellphone asked as Joey tried to squeeze past him.

'I don't have enough money for the ticket,' Joey explained. 'So I'm getting off.'

'Are you kidding me?' the guy grinned at Joey, revealing a gold cap on one of his teeth. 'I just won big, and I'm in a giving mood, so let me buy you that bus ticket.'

'Oh, no, I couldn't...' Joey protested feebly.

'I insist,' the high roller said, putting an arm around him. 'One bus ticket for my man here please,' he announced rather louder than Joey would have liked.

The two sat down in separate seats, but it wasn't long before the man had finished his conversation. He had turned his attention back to Joey.

'So what's your story, bro?' he asked. 'You look ill or something.'

Before Joey had a chance to reply that yes, he was ill and that this should have been obvious given that they boarded the bus at the hospital, he was cut off.

'Me,' the man continued, 'I just won big as I said. Poker. 100Gs.'

Joey's ears pricked up. He had decided by this point to pursue a policy of ignoring the man and saying platitudes in the hope that he would go away. But even though he was in no mood to talk to anyone right now, the sound of $100k was very appealing.

Poker too. He had been the campus poker champion back in college. It had gotten to the stage where no one would play him because they knew he would win. Was this the solution to his problem?

'A hundred grand you say?' he asked as nonchalantly as possible.

Half an hour later, and a 3-mile deviation from his route home, Joey stood in front of what appeared to be an abandoned warehouse.

'2455 Hill Street,' he said to himself, looking at the scrap of paper the man had handed him. The address was scrawled on it, as well as a name.

The warning that the man had given him echoed through his head. These guys played rough. If you couldn't cough up the dough, you'd be coughing up your own blood instead. At this point, it didn't really matter to him if he coughed it up now or in 6 months.

He knocked on the door of the warehouse. There was no response. He went to knock on the door again, but before he could connect a panel slid open at eye level.

'What do you want?' said a voice from the other side of the door. 'This is a private establishment.'

'I'm here to see...' Joey looked at the scrap of paper. 'Kurtz. I'm here to see Kurtz.'

'Who sent you?' the voice asked.

'Luca,' Joey replied.

The panel slammed shut, and a few seconds later the door swung open.

'Entrance fee is $2000. You got it?'

Joey fished the money out from the inside pocket of his jacket. Luca, the man who had the windfall, was kind enough to give him the entry fee to the game after he heard Joey's plight.

'In you go, kid,' the man said, taking the money from Joey. He receded into the shadows to let Joey pass, but before he went by he stuck out an arm, blocking his way again. 'You know how we play here, boy?'

Joey swallowed and nodded.

'Then don't forget it.'

After walking down a short corridor Joey came across the room. It had served as the management office for the warehouse when it was still operational. He opened the door and a cloud of cigarette smoke billowed out.

He entered the room to find a low lit gambling den with a card table in the centre. The felt on the table was faded green, and the wood had seen better days. Five people sat around it, all deeply engrossed in the game they were playing. There was one free seat by the table, which Joey took. None of the players had even so much as looked at him or acknowledged his presence since he walked in.

'Deal him in,' one of the players said, and some cards were given to him.

'The game is pot-limit Omaha, gentlemen. May the best man win...'

Joey steeled himself, and hoped his skills weren't too rusty.

'Show 'em,' the man in the white suit demanded.

Joey's heart sank. His bluff had been called again, and this was it. He was on the last of the $2000 entry fee, and if he lost this hand, this was it. He couldn't understand how he had played so poorly. There had only been 10 or 12 hands since he sat down and he was almost out.

He set his cards down, and the man in the white suit smiled broadly.

'Looks like you're out, kid,' he said.

'No!' Joey protested. 'You have to give me another chance. You don't understand.'

'We understand perfectly well. You played, you lost. You win some and you lose some, and this one you lost. You're lucky we have a policy of not extracting extra...payment from first-time losers. Now get out before we change our minds. This is a game for people who can afford to play, so unless you can afford to play, leave.'

'What if I pay the extra price?' Joey blurted out before he even realised what he was saying.

The room was suddenly bathed in silence. The man in the white suit shifted his weight and flicked the ash from the end of his cigar.

'What would you offer as...collateral?'

'What are my options?'

One of the men at the table howled with laughter and held up his left hand. His little finger was missing.

'This bought me an extra $10000 once,' the mutilated man said.

'What price for my life?' Joey asked hesitantly.

The man in the white suit stood up and joined his compatriot in laughing.

'I like you, kid,' he said. 'Because I like you I'm going to take you up on your generous offer. I'll spot you $50000. If you lose, I kill you.'

'$100000,' Joey said, trying to bluff the man. He had nothing to lose. If they said yes and he lost, then he would die a little earlier than expected. His family wouldn't have to see him degenerate before their very eyes. If he won, he was saved. 'One hand of hold 'em. If I win I take the hundred grand. If I lose, you can do whatever you like.'

The man considered him for a second, clearly intrigued.

'Alright,' he said. 'One hand. You're on.'

They sat down and the cards were dealt. Joey looked at his hand. An ace and a Queen. The cards on the table were a Queen and a pair of twos. A two pair wasn't bad, but the other man was unreadable. He had to bluff anyway.

The bets went back and forth as the other two cards went down. Neither card was favourable. Joey couldn't tell if the grin on the man's face was genuine.

'Show 'em,' the man said, smirking. The two men flipped their cards over.

A week later, Joey woke up in his hospital bed, his parents at his side. The operation had been a complete success.

'You could have asked us for the money, son,' his mother told him as he regained full consciousness.

'You never told us how you managed to pay for the operation...'

Joey went to respond but stopped when he saw something out of the corner of his eye. A man in a sharp suit leaned on the wall outside his door. He pulled a cigar from his pocket and chopped the end off with a cigar cutter. The man smiled at Joey and nodded, before walking off.

'Oh, I got lucky on a bet,' Joey said. 'Let's just say a friend tipped me off to a sure thing.'

Blotland Decides

Llinos Cathryn Wynn Jones - *'A story about politics in squid society.'*

Prime Minister David Cephalopod floated behind his coral desk. It had been a tough week for him, and all his ministers in the government of Great Squiddon. One of the constituent Squid-doms was seeking to break free as an independent nation. The Prime Minister was very keen to see that this did not, in fact, happen.

The Squid-dom in question was Blotland. It was populated by Cuttlefish and had a long history of independence and self blubbernance. It was only in the last few hundred years that Blotland had been subject to the Squidlish crown.

The cuttlefish enjoyed a large degree of autonomy. This gave the Prime Minister enough of a headache as it was. And now they wanted independence! Ha!

The Prime Minister settled to the seabed behind the coral reef and rubbed his bulbous head with one of his tentacles. He had not slept for days, and he had only managed to find time to see roughly 500 of his children this week.

The referendum was in three days, and there was still lots for him to do.

The next day, the Prime Minister and the leaders of the two other major political parties were in Blotland. Squid Clegg, the Deputy Prime Minister and leader of the Squideral Democrabs, was nervous. He flitted left and right as they swam up to some of the rebellious cuttlefish.

'Calm down,' the Prime Minister said to him as they swam. 'You're going to put them off voting to stay with Great Squiddon if you act like that. You've been doing it all the way since Blubdon.'

'I'm sorry,' the Deputy Prime Minister said. 'I just can't bear the thought of losing them…'

'Perhaps,' suggested Squid Milliband, the other member of their party, 'you should leave the talking to me and the Prime Minister.'

Squid Clegg's tentacles drooped in disappointment.

They finally reached the cuttlefish, who had all been floating around, waiting to see what all the fuss was about.

'Oh, I see how it is,' piped up one of the braver members of the group. 'Can't be arsed to put the work in to keep us for years. But you come swimming up here on your beaks and tentacles begging us to stay when the time comes. Well, it's too late. We've made our minds up and we want out.'

The Prime Minister rubbed two of his tentacles together obsequiously.

'Now, now, there's no need to be like that. We love all our subje…I mean vote…I mean we care about all squid of the United Squid-dom. We want you to stay.'

'Well bugger off,' another of the cuttlefish interjected. 'We aren't interested. We don't want none of your wars with the octopuses, or any of your illegal above sea drilling. Most of all though, we aren't bloody squids. We're cuttlefish.'

'Yeah,' the first fish added, not wanting to be outdone in front of the toffs from the capital. 'Never mind what you're planning to do with the National Whelk Service.'

A chorus of murmured agreement spread around the assembled cuttlefish. Squid Clegg wrung his tentacles nervously.

'Why don't you all just sod off back to Westsquiddister where you belong. Let us manage our own affairs up here in Squidinkburgh?'

The Prime Minister noted that the gathered cuttlefish had made the subtle but very important switch from being a group to being a mob. They advanced on the three politicians. Regrettably they had agreed (in a 2-1 vote with Clegg on the losing side) that leaving their bodyguards behind would make them seem more friendly.

Squid Clegg let out a shot of ink in panic, and the three of them turned on their tentacles and swam. They didn't stop until they were safely past Squidrian's Reef and back in Squidland.

'That was a disaster,' said Squid Milliband when they had reached the safety of the Caves of Parliament.

'We would have been calamari if it wasn't for Clegg here being a huge coward,' the Prime Minister agreed.

'W...what are we going to do now?' Squid Clegg stammered.

'I'll think of something...' the Prime Minister replied. 'I have to think of something.'

The next day was a big day for the Prime Minister. He was up against a salmon and its deputy Nicola Sturgeon. Two fish that the independence campaign had recruited as their leaders.

The debate was largely a disaster for the Prime Minister and his side. The salmon, a master debater, deflected all his questions. It also managed to fire back several challenging ripostes in return. But the Prime Minister was not completely stumped. As he had promised Clegg and Milliband he had thought of something. The debate drew nearer to its end, and he prepared to unleash it on Salmon.

'That is a very good point,' he conceded. The salmon had made a jibe about the millions of pounds of shrimp that would be saved with the removal of the swordfish defence system. 'But, wise salmon, can I ask you this in return? Where exactly is an independent Blotland going to find the resources to work the North Sea shrimp fields?'

The salmon stared at Cephalopod in disbelief. It had not been expecting this question from the Prime Minister.

'I, uh, I mean we, uh...' it began, stumbling over its words. 'That is, we would, um.'

'The fact is, that the salmon here cannot answer this question. Despite all its beautiful flowery rhetoric and clever answers, it cannot give you a straight answer here. The reason for this, ladies and gentlesquids, is that it doesn't know. The independence campaign doesn't know.

'Currently,' he went on, 'those shrimp resources are farmed by Squidlish labourers. But that labour would be lost to you if you go ahead and vote yes to independence. And where would any self-respecting cephalopod be without a regular supply of shrimp?'

He looked on triumphantly as the salmon's fins sagged in defeat. The Prime Minister had taken a pummeling for most of the debate. But he had struck an important blow with the last question. He hoped that was the only one the voters would remember.

When he listened to the Daily Conch news bulletin the next morning, it was encouraging stuff. His performance in the debate, though ropey for a while, had given the No campaign an increase in the polls. Even Squid Clegg opening his stupid beak and losing them some votes wouldn't be enough for the Yes campaign to recover.

It was the morning of the referendum. Soon polling caves across Blotland would be opening, and the cuttlefish would be casting their votes. The Prime Minister crossed all his tentacles, which was no mean feat. He hoped beyond hope that the rebellious blighters would see sense and stick with the Union.

The waiting was the worst part. The polls closed late in the evening. Creatures throughout the Squiddish Isles would not find out the result until very early the next morning.

The Prime Minister kept himself occupied by engaging in some last-minute campaigning on the streets of Blubdon. He hoped that winning the ex-pat cuttlefish population over down there would have a knock-on effect up in Blotland. He had never kissed so many cuttlefish larvae in his life.

Besides that, he was doing his best to keep the incompetent Squid Clegg out of the public eye. All he ever did was bugger things up. Cephalopod didn't need him out there looking like a clownfish in front of potential voters. This was one of the most important days of his political career. The Prime Minister cursed the day he had agreed to form the coalition with the bumbling imbecile. At least, he mused, that Clegg lacked political conviction. It was easy enough to get him to go along with any schemes he concocted.

The next morning the Prime Minister was woken early by his secretary. She informed him that Mr. Clegg and Mr. Milliband were waiting for him and that the result was about to be announced.

The three squids gathered around the conch that had been set up on the Prime Minister's coral reef desk. At first, they couldn't seem to get any sound out of it. But after Squid Milliband tapped it a few times with his tentacles and then held it up to his ear to listen, they could hear the news report beginning.

'What a historic day we have here,' the news report said, in a thick cuttlefish accent. 'As we wait to find out the results of what is the most important vote in Blotland's history.'

The three squids held their breath.

'And here comes the returning officer now. It looks like she is ready to announce the result.'

The conch went quiet. Squid Clegg tapped it to try and make it work again, but Squid Milliband swatted his tentacle away. Eventually, a female cuttlefish's voice could be heard through the conch.

'With an overwhelming majority, the Cephalopods of Blotland have voted to become an independent country. 66% in favour to 34% against.'

The three politicians floated in stunned silence at the news.

'Oh bloody hell and bugger,' David Cephalopod said. 'It'll be the Whales wanting it next.'

Zis Is Your Death

Saskia van T Hoff - *'I love ghosts and I love reading about humans becoming ghosts for the first time, and their experiences with that. Anything from the moment of passing, to interactions with humans and/or other ghosts, to the sensations of morphing into a ghost, etc.'*

Liam was dead. He wasn't sure how, or indeed why, but the one thing he was certain about was that he had bought the proverbial farm. Introduced the bucket to the business end of his shoe, as it were.

A few minutes ago he had been walking down Charing Cross Road in London. Now he was now stood, rather disoriented, in what appeared to be the green room of a television studio surrounded by skeletons.

Not people dressed as skeletons, mind you. Actual proper see-through skeletons that were moving around and talking to each other. Some of them were doing very un-skeletal things like holding clipboards and wearing headsets. One of them was drinking coffee, cheerfully ignorant of the puddle it was leaving on the floor.

Initially, Liam had suspected he had merely fallen asleep. You know, as one often does when strolling through Central London of an afternoon. He had dismissed this theory after pinching, or rather attempting to pinch himself several times. His fingers had gone right through his arm, which was more intangible than usual.

The final nail in the coffin, he had decided, excusing himself the joke, was the flickering neon sign above the exit of the green room. It bore the legend 'This Is Your Death' surrounded by flashing low wattage light bulbs.

When he had become aware of his presence in the green room, Liam had been instructed by one of the skeletons to wait around for his timeslot. It had also told him that he was welcome to help himself to any food on the table.

He attempted that now, but his spectral hand passed through the delicious looking sticky buns piled high on a plate in front of him. Even licking his fingers to try and remove any sugary residue had no effect. Liam began to suspect he would never taste anything again.

'Mr. Goshawk?' said one of the skeletons.

'That's me,' Liam replied. He stood up and wondered why if he couldn't pick things up he hadn't fallen through the sofa, or indeed the floor.

'If you'd like to come with me, sir?' the skeleton prompted. It ushered him through the tatty red velvet curtain that separated the green room from the studio before he could finish his thought.

As he stepped out into the studio Liam heard the sort of music you would have expected from a late 80s Saturday night game show. There was a raucous round of applause from the audience. They were all skeletons too.

Liam tried to process how skeletons could clap their hands. Once again before he could get too deep into it he was ushered into a comfortable, if faded, looking armchair by the production assistant.

A voiceover boomed around the studio.

'Liam Goshawk, This. Is. Your. Deeeeeeeath!'

There was a flash, followed by some smoke. Somehow during this distraction, a man had appeared in the empty chair next to him. He was extremely pale, had a widow's peak, wore a dinner suit and cape and, of course, had fangs.

'I'm your host, Vlad Strigoi, vith my guest Liam Goshawk. Velcome to Zis Is Your Death!'

The music played again. Strigoi smiled and waved for his adoring fans, earning another round of boney applause.

'Tell me, Liam,' Vlad began. 'How did you reach us here today?'

'I uh, I'm not sure?' Liam replied. 'One minute I was walking down Charing Cross Road and the next I was in your green room. I was rather hoping you could tell me, actually.'

'But of course! Roll ze tape!'

Liam had developed theories while he was in the green room of course. He had been out in Central London. There was every possibility that he had been taken out by a rogue driver or flattened by a bus as he crossed the road without paying attention. He doubted it had been natural causes. He had only been 32 and was in pretty decent shape. Then again he was always hearing about young, fit people dropping dead of an inexplicable heart attack.

He did not correctly guess what had actually happened.

'A bloody piano fell on me?!' he shouted after the short video clip had finished.

'Ah yes,' Vlad replied, a hint of remorse in his voice. 'Zat is never a fun vay to go. Anyvay! Ve have some very special guests here for you zis evening.'

'Hello Liam,' said a croaky old voice, coming over the studio's speakers. 'Remember me, dear?'

'Grandma?' Liam said. This was all getting a bit too much.

'Zat's right!' Vlad replied, beaming a wide grin that was mostly fangs. 'All ze way from heaven, it's your grandmother Patsy, who you haven't seen since she died of bronchitis 8 years ago!'

A little old skeleton hobbled out on to the stage with the support of a walking stick. Even though she lacked flesh or features of any kind, she was unmistakably his grandmother.

'Come give your old Grandma a hug!' she demanded, reaching in for a skeletal embrace.

'I, err, I can't Grandma. I'm incorporeal you see, Liam said, passing his hand through Vlad by way of demonstration. His Grandma, as upset as it was only possible for a grandparent to be, went and sat on a bench reserved for his guests.

'Up next,' said Vlad. 'An old friend who you haven't seen in some time.'

'Bet you weren't expecting me to be here!' a younger, male voice said over the speakers.

Liam was puzzled as he tried to work out who the next person was. The skeleton that wandered out wasn't much use either, it looked just like all the others. It definitely didn't have the distinct Grandma-ness the previous one had.

'Don't you remember me, buddy?' the skeleton asked, sounding a little hurt. 'It's me, Darren, your mate from primary school!'

'Darren Hartwell?' Liam asked. 'I had no idea you were dead.'

'And I had no idea I was allergic to shellfish!' Darren replied, mugging for the crowd who roared with laughter.

'How about man's best friend?' Vlad asked as Darren went to seat himself next to Grandma Goshawk.

Liam heard a loud woofing over the speaker system. Seconds later a small skeletal dog came rushing out on to the stage wagging its bony tail frantically.

'Buttons?!' Liam exclaimed. He couldn't believe they'd even managed to find his dog from when he was a boy. They'd be bringing out his bloody goldfish next.

Buttons heard Liam's voice and bounded towards the armchair. The dog leapt up to say hello to its old master, but had failed to take in to account his wraith-like form. Buttons smashed into the chair behind him instead, dislodging one of his own legs in the process.

His canine instincts kicked in and he picked up his own bony limb with a happy bark. He then hopped off on its remaining three legs into the corner to chew away happily on its new toy.

Things continued in this fashion until the benches were filled with people that Liam had known who, like him, had passed over into the great beyond.

There were family members, a couple of old friends, ex co-workers, all sorts. Liam thought they were stretching it a bit when they brought out a girl he had kissed once while drunk at university. But he figured that if this was indeed being broadcast to skeletal homes across the underworld that they had to give it a bit of juice. If anything he was glad because it meant that they hadn't found many people he knew well who had snuffed it.

After the last special guest had gone to sit in the bleachers, Vlad clicked his fingers and a large, leather-bound book appeared in his hand. It had the words 'Liam Goshawk, Zis Is Your Death' embossed in silver filigree on the front. Liam wasn't sure why they had felt the need to write it in Vlad's accent, but right now that was the least of his worries.

'Vell, vasn't zat another vonderful trip down memory lane?' Vlad said, still grinning. 'Vell done to Liam for being such a good sport, and to his friends and family for coming out to be vith him on zis special occasion.

'Liam,' he continued. 'Ve vould like to present you vith zis souvenir book so zat you can remember all ze good times ve have had.'

Vlad offered the book to Liam, who shrugged and waved his spectral hand through it.

'I'll just put it here for later,' the vampire said, laying it on the table between them. 'Now, before ve go and you begin your life after death, do you have any qvestions?'

'A couple,' Liam replied. 'Firstly, why am I a ghost when you're a vampire and everyone else is a skeleton?'

'A very good qvestion! I am a vampire because I was unlucky enough to be bitten. You are a ghost because you are newly deceased. Vonce ze show is over you vill complete your transformation, and regain corporeal form as a skeleton.'

'Of course,' said Liam. 'How silly of me.'

'Vat vas your second qvestion?' Vlad asked, leaning forward.

'Why this?' Liam replied, waving an arm around at the set. 'Why set all this up, bring all my deceased friends and family here and put on this elaborate show. I've been in here 45 minutes, hundreds of people must have died since then. You must have a backlog out the door and round the block waiting to come through here if you take an hour over every person.'

'Ah, now, folks, isn't he an observant vone?' Vlad grinned to the audience. 'It's simple my dear boy. Not everyvone is velcomed to ze afterlife like zis. As you said, ve vould have no time at all. The fact is zat everyvone has a different idea of vat happens after zey died. Some are greeted by robed figures who read zeir collected sins to zem, some check-in as if zey vere at a hotel.

'Others, like yourself, have a rather unfortunate obsession vith the vorks of Bruce Forsyth. So ven you died you vere sent to us to go through different parts of your life in ze style of a light entertainment program. Ve cater to everyvone's expectations, so zis place doesn't get used as often as you'd think.

'Plus,' the vampire added, shielding his mouth from the audience and dropping to a stage whisper. 'Ze boys and ghouls at home get a kick out of vatching other people's deaths. I believe its a concept known as 'reality television.''

'I see,' said Liam. It had all sounded reasonable enough.

'Vell, zat's all ve've got time for tonight folks. Vat a beautiful story,' the vampire concluded, returning his attention to the audience, one of whom Liam was sure was crying. 'Until next time, I've been Vlad Strigoi, and zis has been Zis Is Your Death!'

'So what do I do now?' Liam asked Vlad after the cameras had stopped rolling and the audience had all filed out and gone home.

'Well, very shortly you will turn in to a skeleton.'

'But after tha...Wait a minute. You aren't doing the accent anymore.'

'Why would I? I'm from Slough. That's all for the cameras. And I know what you were going to ask. You will have to get a job.'

'A job?' Liam asked, deciding to drop the accent thing. 'But I'm dead.'

'So am I, mate, but those bills aren't gonna pay themselves.'

'Where can I get a job?'

'Well,' Vlad pondered, 'I hear that one of the runners left to have a baby, so there's a job opening here if you're interested.'

Liam went to question how a skeleton could have a baby but thought better of it.

'That'd be great,' he said instead. 'Thanks.' It wasn't much, he reasoned, but when you're starting a whole new death you have to start somewhere.

Why Do You Think You're A Kitten Mr. Hitler?

__Amanda Richardson__ - A story about 'A person who realises their cat is the reincarnation of Adolf Hitler.'

'Our prices are very low this year,' the Avon lady explained to Juliet. 'We have reduced our packaging and this has allowed us to pass the savings on to you, the customer. I'm sure you'll find the prices more than competitive.'

Juliet wasn't usually the sort to let door-to-door salespeople in for a chat. But she was new in town and didn't know anyone, so she was grateful for the company. It didn't hurt that she had been in the market for some new eye shadow, either.

As the Avon lady was preparing to show her skincare samples, Juliet's pet cat, Socks, came prowling into the room and leapt up on to Juliet's lap. She began to pet the cat as the lady went on about sea salt facial scrubs.

'Now, see, the benefit of the Kelp scrub is...' the woman said, trailing off.

'Is everything OK?' Juliet asked.

'Yes, I'm sorry,' the Avon lady replied. 'It's just that your cat looks a lot like Adolf Hitler.'

'I, uh, I'd never noticed,' said Juliet, leaning round to have a look at Socks' face. The cat pretended not to notice the special attention that was being paid to him, as he swatted at a fly. 'Now you mention it, though, he sort of does...'

A diagonal streak of black fur crowned his head, where the parting would be. There was another small patch just under the nose where the dictator's famous moustache had sat. Juliet had only recently got Socks from a cat shelter. She had taken full advantage of the fact that her landlord had failed to put a 'no pets' clause in her contract.

The lady at the shelter had said that Socks had been to a few homes already, but always came back as unmanageable. He had seemed to take a shine to her, though, and had caused no trouble so far.

'I hear there are whole websites devoted to that sort of thing,' the Avon lady said, as she packed up her samples. 'Cats that look like him. I've left you a catalogue. Be sure to mention my name if you do decide to order anything.'

Juliet saw the woman out and decided to go back to her job search in the local paper. When she got back to the living room, Socks had disappeared as he so often did during the day. Chasing mice or birds no doubt. Or maybe annexing the Sudetenland.

It was a frustrating afternoon. Juliet didn't find anything worth applying for. She began to question the wisdom of moving halfway across the country on a whim. Thirsty, she went through to the kitchen to get a drink. She looked up as she poured some orange juice into a glass and saw Socks sitting on the external sill of the kitchen window, above her begonias. His back was turned, and he appeared to be mewing at something or someone.

Juliet walked over to the window to see what he was looking at and nearly dropped her orange juice in surprise. Outside, the decking was filled with cats. They were all staring up at Socks, who was mewing away authoritatively. Every cat in the neighbourhood must be out there, Juliet thought. Surely they weren't all...listening to him? She decided that she must have been cooped up in the house too long and went out for a walk.

When she returned from her walk to the shops, Juliet's attention was caught by a scream. It had come from the next-door neighbour's back garden. She rushed down the side passage of her house and out into her own back garden. The erstwhile kitty congregation had dispersed.

Peering over the fence to see what the commotion was about, she saw her neighbours. They were a middle-aged couple, and they were tackling a fire in the doghouse. The woman was aiming a fire extinguisher at the wooden construction, which was now merely smoking. Her husband held their poodle, which was shaking in terror, in his arms.

'What happened?' Juliet asked when the fire was out for certain.

'It looks like a mouse got in and nibbled some wires,' her neighbour replied. She reached into the charred remains of the doghouse and pulled out a small, very crispy, mouse. 'See?'

'What a horrible thing to happen.'

'Oh yes. We're so glad our Floofykins is alright, aren't we Floofykins?' the husband replied. He snuggled the now catatonic poodle right up to his face.

Juliet decided to leave them to it. She couldn't shake from her head the thought that she was sure she had seen Socks slinking away from behind the doghouse. When Juliet got back into the living room and sat down, Socks wandered in and jumped up on to her lap. She stroked his head, and he kneaded her legs with his claws in an affectionate manner.

'You're not really Hitler, are you boy?' she asked the cat, who mewed in reply.

But she couldn't get it out of her mind. First the cat rally and now a suspicious fire with an unlikely suspect? What if the Avon lady was more right than she knew. What if Socks didn't just look like Hitler? What if he was...

It seemed silly, but if it was true then she had to know for sure. Casting her mind back to her walk earlier Juliet remembered seeing an advert on a lamp post for a pet psychic. She wasn't generally a believer in the occult. But giving the guy a call seemed better now rather than after Socks had claimed Lebensraum in a neighbour's flower bed or something.

Ten minutes later Juliet was back in her front room, the poster clutched in her hand. She found her phone and dialled the number. A quick explanation later and Howard Jackson: Animal Psychic was on his way round.

The van pulled up outside Juliet's house, and a middle-aged man in a sky blue suit and orange waistcoat got out. He smoothed his clothes down and walked up the path.

'You must be Juliet,' he said, extending a hand, which Juliet shook. 'Now where's the great dictator?'

They went into the house, where Juliet found Socks asleep, stretched out in a patch of sun in the living room.

'Now let me take a look here,' Howard said, placing a hand on Socks' forehead. This didn't seem to disturb the cat, and a few seconds later he stood up.

'Yes, ma'am, I'm afraid that your cat is indeed the physical reincarnation of Adolf Hitler.'

'What, it's that simple?' Juliet asked, bewildered. 'You only touched him for a second!'

'Ms. Harper,' Howard Jackson: Animal Psychic replied, 'I'm very good at my job. I have two degrees.'

'But how can you be so sure?'

'Animal reincarnation is quite common. Someone - or some animal - was bound to come back as Hitler sooner or later. That cat has by far the darkest psychic presence I've ever come across. A great and evil being has come back into existence within him.

'Oh, and Pol Pot and Stalin were accounted for recently,' he went on, waving a hand. 'I've got a lead that Genghis Khan is in a German Shepherd up in Leeds, and most of the others were rounded up ages ago. Pretty much just left Hitler. The real clue was the actions, though. The spirits tend to repeat their old behaviour. Based on what you were describing it's got Adolf's paw prints all over it.'

'Rounded up?' Juliet asked. 'You mean this is quite common?'

'Oh yeah, happens all the time. The psychic community does its best to keep tabs on the real doozies. The ones that are likely to offend again, given the chance. This one would have been purging the neighbourhood tabbies and declaring war on the next street over before you knew it. It's good that you called when you did.'

'So, what happens now? What is your fee?'

'Oh, no fee for this one ma'am. Knowing that I collared history's cuddliest monster is reward enough for me on this occasion. I'll take Socks to our containment facility. He will lead a good, full life, away from any temptation to commit acts of unspeakable evil.'

'That's good, I suppose...' Juliet said. Even though it turned out her cat was the reincarnation of an evil dictator, she would still miss the little bugger. He had always been nice to her.

It was a sad farewell. Juliet came close to tears as Socks was carried down the path in a cage. She thought she saw him put his paw on the cage to say goodbye, but it could also have been a salute. Jackson had comforted her, saying that it wasn't her fault she had adopted an evil feline. After all, there was no way of knowing who her cat really was.

She spent the next few days moping around the empty house. An offer to look after the neighbour's poodle was firmly rebuffed. It seemed word had gotten out about the true identity of her cat. Juliet decided that the only way she would fill the void was by getting another animal.

She drove off down to the rescue centre. Determined not to make the same mistake again she dismissed a dachshund that looked a bit like Chairman Mao. A golden retriever that had once barked enthusiastically at a photo of Idi Amin was also out. After hours of agonising, she had ruled out each of the animals one by one until only a handful were left. Juliet found the most adorable fluffy bunny rabbit called Nibbles. It was busying itself rearranging the food in its bowl.

A bunny can't be evil, she reasoned, loading her new friend into the car. And anyway, it lived in a cage and wouldn't be let out, so what harm could it do?

As she drove off, she failed to notice the pattern the rearranged food had made. Reversing out of the car park, she bumped over the curb, and the perfect pentagram was knocked out of shape. Nibbles squeaked irritably, and began its task all over again, a certain glint of malice in its tiny eye.

The Ghostess With the Mostest

Steph Minshull-Jones - 'A ghost decides to have some fun with people who don't believe in ghosts.'

Sandy walked down the street to the station, as she did at the same time every day. She went through the barriers at the station entrance, made her way down the escalator and just about got on the waiting train before it departed.

This was her daily routine because it brought her some semblance of normality. She had no job. She had no need for one. Riding the rails every morning reminded her of what her life used to be like. It reminded her of simpler times.

Times were no longer simple for Sandy. When she walked down the road people wouldn't make an effort to get out of her way, and instead walked right through her. Passing through the ticket barrier meant, in her case, physically passing through it. Descending the escalator could mean falling down to the area beneath with all the mechanisms if she lost concentration for even a second.

Sandy's life was not normal, because she did not, in fact, have a life at all. Sandy was a ghost. She estimated that she had been dead a couple of years. Time was a rather redundant concept when you had the rest of it to look forward to. But she still came down to the train every morning all the same, like she had done when she was alive.

Other than riding the rails of a morning, Sandy had a dull existence. As a ghost, she couldn't interact with corporeal objects without extreme concentration. It was a mystery what kept her from sinking through the floor more often. She often found herself visiting friends or family, or floating into a nearby house to watch the television. But that was of limited entertainment value when no one could interact with you, or even knew you were there.

Generally, she avoided the company of other ghosts. Sandy found their similar inability to interact with everyday objects frustrating. Also most of them only ever wanted to talk about how they died, which got a bit tedious after a while.

It was a subject that she had no interest in exploring in any depth. She would meet billions of ghosts between now and the end of time. They tended to have a stock set of questions that they asked any new spectral acquaintance. She had developed a standard set of answers to go with them for when polite conversation was unavoidable.

What's your name? Sandy Dunstable; Where are you from? Epping Forest; How long have you been dead? A couple of years; How did you die? Severe anaphylactic shock; etc.

To top it all off she had no idea what her purpose in death was. One of her fellow ghosts had once told her that not everyone becomes a spirit. Only those with unfinished business don't pass on into the great beyond right away. Beyond that, she had received no clues or reassurances other than that when she worked it out she would be granted eternal rest.

In other words, Sandy's afterlife had hit a rut, insofar as that was possible. A mid-afterlife crisis she quipped to herself.

She contemplated this one morning as she rode the train into the city centre. Perhaps she should go on an around the world trip, and see all the places she had never been to when she was alive.

After much deliberation, she decided that she wouldn't be able to concentrate hard enough for long enough to keep her on a plane. Sandy may have no body to lose anymore, but she had always been squeamish about heights. It appeared that this affliction had followed her beyond the grave.

Anyway she definitely did not wish to spend the rest of eternity at the bottom of the Atlantic.

The train rumbled on its way, oblivious to its ghostly cargo. Several other spirits boarded the train every morning. They were the closest thing Sandy had to friends, though she had never spoken a word to any of them. They filtered off as the train came to a halt at various stops. After a while Sandy noticed that only one misty figured remained at the other end of the carriage.

Sandy observed the ghost, whom she had never seen before. She figured that whoever he was, he must be new to the whole thing. She saw him approach a young couple on the train, looking as if he intended to interact with them. Sandy watched with interest mixed with a healthy dose of scepticism for the fellow's chances. She was surprised when the new spirit managed to not only touch the couple, but spook them enough that they got off at the next stop. She heard them muttering something about someone walking over their graves.

Awestruck, Sandy lost concentration for a second and nearly fell through the train to the tracks below. The spectre also got off at the stop, and Sandy had to muster all her wits to stop gawking at what she had seen and follow him. If he could interact with humans, maybe he could interact with objects. Maybe he could even teach her.

Sandy sprinted through the station, trying to keep up with the man, who passed straight through the crowds. She caught sight of him leaving the station and wandering off down the street and caught up with him. She felt as though she should be panting from the exertion, but on balance decided that might be a bit weird and rather unnecessary.

'How did you do that?' she asked to the back of the man's head, or at least the bit of it that was opaque enough to see.

'Do what?' he asked, turning around. Sandy noticed that he had been young when he died, like her.

'You touched those people. You made them jump. Can you teach me how to do that?'

The man looked puzzled. 'Teach you?' he asked. 'Can't all ghosts do that?'

'No!' Sandy replied. 'In fact, you're the first I've seen in about two years who can. God knows we all try for a while, but none of us ever manage contact like that.'

'Oh...' the man looked contemplative. 'It took me a little while to pick it up. At first, I couldn't. But then I switched to lateral thinking and decided to think of myself as the object I was trying to touch. Then I thought that I wanted to be touched...' He blushed. 'Sorry, that came out a bit ruder than I intended.'

'Of course!' Sandy shouted. She was not sure she had actually understood what he had said, but wanted to make it sound as though she had. 'Can you show me?'

'Sure.'

The man looked about for a suitable subject, and settled on a can that someone had left on a wall nearby.

'Right,' he said, concentrating on the can. 'If I try and move it because I want it to move it doesn't go anywhere. But if I envision the can, think why it would want to move, I can do whatever I like with it.'

As he said that he moved his hand through the can, which toppled off the wall and landed on the pavement with a clatter.

'You give it a try,' he urged.

It took a while, as he had suggested it might. But Sandy managed to detach her mind for long enough to get inside the can and move it along the pavement.

She felt as though she ought to be exhausted, if that was something she could still be. But she had never felt more alive in…well, since she had actually been alive.

'How does it work on people?' Sandy asked, after recovering from her exertion.

'Oh, it doesn't really,' the man, whose name Sandy had discovered to be Roy said. When he noticed the look of disappointment on her face he added, 'Well, it might. I haven't tried it.'

'But I saw you spook that couple!' Sandy protested.

'I touched the guy's jacket, not him, and then I made the girl's purse zip and unzip by itself. I guess it might work on people. But I feel a bit weird about the idea of imagining how complete strangers would like to be touched. I'm a ghost, not a pervert.'

Sandy couldn't help but laugh at this. She spent the next few days training with Roy. She built up her abilities until she could pick the can up and move it several feet before it became too difficult to continue.

One evening as they sat watching the sunset it occurred to Sandy that she had not caught the train in several days. This whole new experience had been too much fun. She was so glad to have met another ghost who seemed underwhelmed by the rules and formalities of the spirit society. She realised that she didn't even know how he had died.

For the first time since she had passed on, Sandy felt like she had a purpose, and a friend.

'Why were you scaring that couple anyway?' she asked him one day.

'Boredom,' Roy replied. 'I've given up trying to work out what my dumb quest is. I figure it will be obvious when it

270

needs to be. Until then, might as well have some fun.' He jumped off the wall they had been stood on and floated to the ground below. 'Right. It's time for your first scare, and I know just the location.'

Even though he was mostly see-through Sandy could still see the glint in his eye and could tell that he was up to no good.

Ten minutes later they arrived at their destination: a pub in Shoreditch called the Nine Friars.

'What are we doing here?' Sandy asked.

Roy responded by pointing at the sign outside the door, which read 'Sceptics' Society Meeting Today.'

'They're focusing on the paranormal today,' he said.

The pair stood in a corner and watched the meeting unfold for a while. This, Roy reasoned, would give Sandy a chance to pick her victim. They settled on the group's leader, a rather severe man in his early 30s with a ponytail and a goatee.

Throughout the meeting he had been waxing lyrical about how ghosts were not real and that anyone who claimed otherwise was an idiot. They probably dared to believe in God to boot, he added. Richard Dawkins, he asserted finally, probably did not believe in ghosts.

Sandy waited for an opportunity. She decided on grabbing his hair and holding his ponytail in place.

Well, she thought as she heard the man scream in terror as his head jerked backwards, this can't be my purpose in the afterlife. She wasn't still walking this earth to go round pulling Atheists hair all day. But, until she found out why she was still here, she had to agree with Roy. It was a fun way to pass the time.

WEEK 42

Toys R Us

Dean Horsefield - A story about 'a kid who opens the curtains one morning to find their room is now part of a giant dollhouse. The rest of the family are oblivious.'

'It's 7.30am!' the alarm clock blared, 'and boy have we got some absolute classics coming up for you before 8. Let's kick you off with some Wham!'

Becca's hand finally found the snooze button. Just in time to prevent her hearing George Michael asking her to wake him up before she went-went.

The alarm clock had been a present, if you could call it that, from her parents for her tenth birthday earlier in the year. Her mum had said that as she was growing up she would need to learn to get herself out of bed, and not rely on her parents.

It was going to be her worst enemy for the next 50 years, and knowing your enemy was half the battle, her father had added. He has used the tone known only to fathers that always accompanied some failed attempt at humour.

Becca hadn't understood that one, but then she rarely got any of her dad's 'jokes.' Anyway, she already had a worst enemy: Karen Timpson. It wasn't possible to have TWO worst enemies.

She rolled over and went back to sleep. Nine minutes later the alarm came back to life in the middle of '5, 6, 7, 8' by

Steps. Becca lay in bed until the song finished and the enthusiastic DJ started rambling on about some contest or other. She wondered how anyone could be that cheerful at 7.39 in the morning. He must be an alien, she decided.

She got out of bed and put her dressing gown on over her pyjamas. It was late autumn, and the air was beginning to get chilly. Her dad refused to put the heating on until he saw the first Coca Cola Christmas advert. And right now their TV was on the fritz. Out of the corner of her eye, Becca could have sworn she saw something moving outside her window.

This was very strange indeed, as her bedroom wasn't on the ground floor. She put it down to tiredness and bleary eyes. After all, she had only slept for 10 hours last night.

But then she saw it again. Curious, she wandered over and pulled back the curtains. She shrieked so loud that her parents, who were having breakfast, rushed upstairs immediately.

'Becca?!' her dad shouted, bursting into the room. 'What's wrong? Are you alright?'

'An eye!' Becca said. 'A giant eye outside the window!'

Her dad walked over to the window and opened the curtains, which Becca had jerked shut again immediately upon seeing the eye. The eye was gone.

'Now, now, dear,' her mum soothed. 'You must still be a little bit groggy. Come downstairs and have some toast and wake up a bit.'

'I'm NOT groggy!' Becca replied, defiantly shrugging her mum off. 'It was THERE!'

Her mum and dad shared a look.

'Of course, it was, sweet pea,' her dad said. 'We believe you. But you'll feel better after something to eat.'

Toast did sound appealing, so Becca allowed her parents to lead her downstairs.

Becca sat at the table and tucked in to her third round of toast. The scare that she had got from the eye earlier on had made her very hungry.

'Would you like some eggs with that, dear?' her mother asked.

'Ooh, yes please mum,' Becca replied, pushing the memory of what she saw from her head.

But, to her horror, her mother did not walk over to the oven to make the eggs like she usually did. Something very odd indeed happened instead.

The kitchen filled with light as the wall swung away, and a giant hand reached in. The hand picked up her mum, who seemed oblivious to the whole experience, and placed her down in front of the cooker. Once there she began to busy herself with the preparation of the eggs.

Becca stared, wide-eyed and open-mouthed in disbelief. The slice of toast she was holding tumbled from her grip and landed, butter side down, on her plate.

'Did you see that?!' she demanded, as the hand withdrew and the wall swung back in to place.

Her dad, who was sipping at a mug of tea and reading the Sunbury Morning Post, glanced up and said, 'Hmm?'

'The wall...a hand...picked up mum!' Becca gibbered. 'How did you miss it?'

The look her parents shared this time betrayed much more concern.

'Are you feeling alright, sweet pea?' her dad asked.

Her mum, moving normally now, walked over from the oven and pressed a hand against her forehead. 'No temperature,' she said.

'Maybe you should stay home from school today, get some rest,' her dad said. 'Just in case.'

'I'm fine!' Becca replied. She thought about going to school. But when she dug down for the memories, beyond what was on the surface, she couldn't remember anything about her school. In fact, she couldn't remember ever having left the house before.

She thought that she could picture trips to the cinema, the park or visiting a friend's house. But somehow all the memories seemed false. She definitely couldn't remember any of the journeys.

In a panic, Becca bolted from the room. Did her parents feel the same way? Why had she realised this so suddenly? She sat with her head in her hands on the bottom step of the stairs, wondering if her brain was playing tricks on her. Could she even trust her own memories anymore?

Come to think of it, she had always wondered how the family got their stuff. They never went shopping, but every week new items would appear in the house. Cutlery, crockery, furniture and clothes all appeared out of nowhere, as if by magic.

She recalled the time that a new summer dress had appeared in her wardrobe. Upon closer inspection, the dress had a tag, which had read 'Smith Co. Summer Dress SC4690.' On the reverse of the tag, there had been a giant price sticker. It said that the dress had cost £0.99, which had always seemed awfully cheap for such a nice dress.

A thought struck her. She ran upstairs and opened her toy cupboard. She flung aside toy trains, a hobby horse and some clothes she had shoved in there to pass a room-tidiness inspection. Finally she found what she was looking for. Her old dolls house.

She'd had the thing as long as she could remember. Her dad had always boasted that he had made it for her. But she had found the remains of a scraped off sticky label on the bottom that suggested otherwise. Being all grown up now at age 10, she couldn't be seen playing with dolls anymore. The thing had lain undisturbed beneath a pile of stuff in her toy cupboard for the last couple of years. She gave it the once over, and then, anxiously put her theory to the test. With one hand on each half of the house, she swung it open.

As expected, the two sides came apart, operating on a set of hinges that, though a little rusty from lack of use, still did their job. Becca placed the house on the floor in front of her and sat there, not sure what to do or how to react.

Her silent introspection was broken by her mother shouting up the stairs for her.

'Becca!' she called. 'Abigail is here to see you.'

Odd, thought Becca as she got to her feet. She hadn't heard the doorbell or any knocking. As she went out on to the upstairs landing, she could have sworn she saw the walls of the house close up again. Exactly as they had in the kitchen. When she got downstairs, Abigail was sat at the kitchen table.

'Abigail,' Becca said urgently, grabbing her friend by her sweater. 'How did you get here?'

'Well, my mum brought... Or did I walk? I don't think I rode my bike.'

'Don't you think that's a bit odd?' she asked the room. 'She's only been here for 2 minutes and she already can't remember how she got here.'

'Oh don't be silly, dear,' her mum replied. 'Abbie's always been a bit forgetful, haven't you, love?'

'That's right,' Abbie smiled. 'Do you want to go upstairs and play?'

'Play? But we've got to go to school. Dad, why haven't you left for work? It's almost 8.30.'

'Oh, no work or school today, sweet pea,' her dad replied, his head still buried in the paper.

'But two minutes ago you said I could stay home from school...' Becca trailed off.

Her mum was busying herself about the washing up, and her dad was engrossed in the sports section. Neither of them was listening to her.

'Look,' she said to Abigail. 'I appreciate you coming to visit, but now isn't a very good time. Some strange things are happening around here and I think I'm the only one who has noticed.'

'Oh, strange like what?' Abigail asked.

Becca looked at both her parents, then leaned in to her friend.

'I think we are living in a dolls house,' she whispered.

'Oh!' Abigail replied. 'That is strange. Well, I'll see you later I suppose.'

And with that, the walls swung aside again, and the hand reached in and plucked Abigail out of the kitchen. Becca's mum went to put some dishes away in a cupboard that had been on the wall. They fell and smashed on the floor instead.

'How strange,' she muttered and began to sweep up the mess with a broom as if it was completely normal for your cupboards to temporarily vanish.

Maybe this is all a dream? Becca thought. Yes, that must be it. I'm still snoozing after I turned the alarm off this morning and this has all been a weird dream. To wake up I must need to go back to bed in the dream.

Before the walls closed again, the hand returned and picked Becca up. It removed her from the room and went up a level, before moving back the covers on her bed and placing her underneath. With its final act before withdrawing and closing the house up, the giant hand tucked her in.

Ah yes, Becca thought. That's much better. I'll be awake in no time, and I can tell mum and dad about this funny dream over a couple of rounds of toast.

The walls rejoined, and the house was complete again.

'Mitzy, honey, we have to go.'
'But mum!' the little girl protested.

'You can play with your dolls later, sweetie. Right now we are going to see your Grandad,' her mother replied, firmly.

'Fiiiiine.'

Mitzy stood up from the floor and went to leave the room. Just as she was about to walk out of the door she remembered that she still had the Abigail doll in her hand. Running back over, she placed it in a box next to the house.

'Mitzy!' her mum called. 'I'll not ask you again.'

'Coming mum!' she replied, grabbing her coat and shutting the door behind her.

Arse From Elbow

Robert Prange - '*A man contracts a rare disease, whereby various parts of his body keep swapping with each other. His future looks bleak and uncertain, until he meets a girl with the same condition.*'

Joe was hot, exhausted and thirsty. He had been walking around Rome all afternoon in the blistering heat of a summer's day. Like a genius he had forgotten to bring his water bottle with him.

He had tried and tried to dip into a shop to buy one. But every time the tour guide had moved on, and he didn't want to lose the group.

Finally, the tour had stopped at the Trevi Fountain. It looked like they would be stood still long enough for Joe to quench his thirst. Seizing his opportunity, he strode into the nearest vendor's and made for the fridge.

Joe was taken aback.

'Water is how much?!' he asked out loud.

'4 Euro a bottle,' the shop owner replied.

'4 Euro a bottle?' Joe repeated.

'That's what I said, are you English stupid or something?'

'I'm not paying that for a bottle of bloody water.'

'What, you think it will be cheaper elsewhere? This is the Trevi Fountain.'

Joe struggled long and hard with his principles. In the end, he decided he would never pay someone £3.50 for the privilege of drinking half a litre of water as long as he lived. Sometimes sticking to your guns was more important.

Going back outside to join the tour group, Joe licked his dry lips. If he couldn't buy water he would have to get it some other way.

He looked around and then it hit him. There was a fountain right in front of him the whole time.

All he would have to do would be to scoop up some of the fountain water and he would be alright.

He strode down to the fountain, cupped his hands and pooled some of the water in them. Then heraised them to his lips and drank deeply.

Blessed relief.

'Mummy,' a nearby British child said. 'Why is that strange man drinking from the fountain?'

'Don't look at him dear,' the mother replied. 'He only wants attention.'

But Joe didn't care about the attention. He was gulping down the water by the handful. Whilst it was relieving, Joe noticed that it did taste rather metallic. Something to do with all the coins people threw into the fountain to bring them back to Rome, he figured. He didn't care, though.

His thirst sated, Joe rejoined the group and went on his merry way. He thoroughly enjoyed the rest of his walk around Rome that afternoon.

The next day, Joe woke up in his hotel room and yawned deeply. The yawn sounded distant. As if it was coming from further away than normal. These old palazzo rooms must have unusual acoustics, he thought.

He had another busy day of sightseeing ahead of him. The Forum was on his agenda today. That would be followed by a trip to see the Protestant cemetery, where Shelley was buried.

Joe swung his legs out of bed and went to stand up.

Instead of finding himself up and ready to face the day, he found himself down and facing the floor. When he had gone to stand up it was almost like one of his legs was...missing.

Putting it down to a dead leg, he attempted to haul himself up off the floor. But where his left hand usually was, he felt what appeared to be a nose.

'What the?' he said.

But Joe didn't hear his voice as if it was coming from his face. He looked down at his errant leg and noticed that where his foot used to be, his mouth now resided.

'That isn't right...' he said, watching his mouth move as he spoke.

The effect was very strange.

'This must be a dream,' he concluded, still watching the mouth, his mouth, speaking every word from the end of his ankle. If he wasn't dreaming, he must be sporting the world's most impressive set of vocal cords.

With his remaining active hand, Joe pinched himself. It hurt. Whatever was happening to him was real.

He decided that he needed to see a doctor immediately. The forum would have to wait.

Dragging himself over to the phone proved difficult, but eventually, he made it. He went to cradle the phone against his ear, but the receiver merely slapped against his other hand. He eventually found the ear halfway down his back. This made phone logistics somewhat difficult.

After a complicated conversation that had involved lots of shouting Joe had arranged for a doctor to come to his room.

Half an hour later, there was a knock on Joe's hotel room door.

'It's open,' he called out through a mouthful of hair. His mouth had recently decided to move itself to the top of his head.

'Mio Dio!' the doctor declared as he walked in and saw Joe's condition. 'This is the worst case or cartegomititis I've ever seen!'

'Cartegomititis?' Joe asked, worried. 'What is that?'

'It is an extremely rare condition where your body, as you English put it, does not know its arse from its elbow. Do you understand?'

'Not really, that's just an old expression.'

'Ah not so, many of these old expressions they have some grounding in reality, yes? This is the case here as well. Cartegomititis causes your body parts to wander around, as it were. Your features will go walkies.'

'Why is this happening to me, doc? What did I do to catch this?'

'The only known cause of the disease is drinking water contaminated with a high copper level. Do you think you could have done that recently?'

'Yesterday I drank from the Trevi fountain...' Joe admitted.

'Idiota!' the doctor yelled at him. 'Why would you drink water from a fountain like that? People throw all sorts in there.'

'In my defence, I was really thirsty.'

'This is bad news. I've never heard of a case in Rome before, but it seems that the fountain is contaminated. We must have access restricted immediately. The public's health could be at risk.'

'How do I get bett...ugh. What's that smell?' Joe asked

'What smell?' the doctor replied. 'I can't smell anything.'

A second later Joe realised what had happened. His nose had, rather unfortunately, decided to move to a new home. It was now right where his coccyx normally was and was thus hovering right over his arse.

'Never mind,' Joe replied, trying his best not to throw up through his hair. 'How do I get better?'

'I'm afraid cartegomititis has no known cure.'

'So I'm stuck like this forever?' Joe asked, anguished.

'Not necessarily. It has been observed subsiding in patients after two years or so. And most people who recover have their body return completely to normal. A course of physical therapy in the meantime will keep active muscles that you may struggle to use day to day.'

'Oh...'

'I must warn the city council immediately before we have an epidemic on our hands. Or on whatever replaces our hands after we contract the disease.'

With that, the doctor left the hotel room, and Joe was alone once more.

Joe elected to curtail the rest of the holiday and went back to England on the next flight out. The cramped Ryanair seat was hell on his elbows.

A week later he turned up at the hospital for his first physical therapy session.

He lolloped his way over to the chair. That was the only way he could describe his movement these days thanks to the constantly changing position of his legs and feet. He sat down awkwardly on his right knee.

Joe was disappointed to find himself the only person at the cartegomititis clinic. He had rather hoped that he might have found solace in others.

Joe picked up a magazine and tried in vain to read. But it seemed as though his arms and eyes were being uncooperative at this point, and so he gave up.

'Excuse me,' came a woman's voice from behind him. In a motion that was surprisingly graceful under the conditions, Joe swivelled around in his chair. 'Is this the cartegomititis clinic?'

The voice was owned by the most beautiful woman he had ever seen. She was also suffering from his affliction. He had a compatriot.

'Yes, you're in the right place,' he stammered out of the middle of his chest.

'Good, this hospital is so confusing. It's like a labyrinth!'

'I guess that makes me the monster at the centre of the maze, then,' Joe replied. He immediately cursing his crap attempt at humour, but, to his surprise, the girl was laughing.

'My name is Grace,' she said.

'It's lovely to meet you, Grace. I'm Joe.'

'Looks like it's just the two of us,' she observed.

'Looks that way. Is this your first session?'

'Yeah, I only found out I had this thing last week.'

'Do you mind me asking how you got it?'

'Not at all,' Grace replied. 'I was really thirsty,' she went on, 'and I decided to take a drink from a nearby wishing foun...'

'Say no more,' Joe said, interrupting her. 'Say no more.'

Do Not Pass 'Go'

Josh Orr - *'A group of friends playing Monopoly, who discover that the transactions are taking place in their own bank accounts.'*

'Do we HAVE to play Monopoly?' James asked. 'We have an entire set of shelves filled with board games and you're choosing to play bloody Monopoly?'

'Yes,' Harriet replied. She removed the game from the shelf, where it had sat unused and unloved beneath a copy of Settlers of Catan since they had moved in. 'It's a classic. Sometimes you need to crack out the old favourites.'

'But it isn't Christmas, and none of my family members is around to punch if I lose,' James protested in vain. He could tell that her mind was made up.

The doorbell rang.

'That'll be Mark and Gemma now,' Harriet said. She had already unboxed the game and laid the money out in neat piles on the table.

James went to answer the door. As expected, it was their friends Mark and Gemma, who they had over for a games night every other Thursday. They chose the games on a rotation. James dreaded every time it came round to being Harriet's week to choose.

She had been brought up on the 'classics' like Monopoly. She would always choose something from her childhood, and so the best he could hope for was a nice game of Risk every now and then. James would always say her picks were entry-level games. And Harriet would call him a board game snob in return.

'I brought some Doritos!' Mark said by way of a greeting.

'I hope you brought enough,' James replied. 'We're in it for the long haul tonight.'

'I've decided that we should play Monopoly!' Harriet exclaimed. Mark and Gemma exchanged a look. They were more used to meeples than boots and irons.

'Interesting choice,' Gemma remarked. Standing behind his girlfriend where she couldn't see him, James shrugged apologetically.

With greetings exchanged and coats hung the four sat down to play. Mark picked the top hat, Gemma the car, James the battleship and Harriet, who was always the dog, picked the dog.

Play got off to a slow start, as it often did in Monopoly. Everyone jostled for properties based on their bank balance and took pleasure in screwing others for rent prices.

After about an hour the game had barely got started. James read the mood of the room, or at least the mood of their guests, and declared a short break to order some pizza.

'Yeah,' he said to the girl on the end of the line. 'Can I get 2 large pepperonis with stuffed crust, and one medium veggie feast?'

'Don't forget the garlic bread!' Harriet hissed in his ear. Gemma and Mark nodded in agreement.

'Oh yeah, and two orders of cheesy garlic bread. Do we get any dips with that? OK good.'

He waited a few seconds while the bill was totted up.

'£35.47?' he said. 'OK, here's my card number...'

A few more seconds of silence passed as the payment was processed.

'What do you mean the payment was declined? Did you try again?'

Another pause.

'Not enough funds? Are you kidding me, I got paid this morning. Hang on a second.'

He held the phone away from his ear and turned to talk to the group.

'Sorry, can one of you front this? My card has been declined. I'll get the pizza next time.'

'Sure,' Gemma said, fishing her debit card out of her purse. A few moments later and the transaction was complete.

'I'm sorry to interrupt the game even more,' James said, once he had hung up the phone. 'But I'd better get on to the bank to find out where all my bloody money has gone.'

James spent a frustrating half an hour on hold with the bank. Although it was still preferable to playing Monopoly. Eventually, he got to speak to a chipper sounding fellow from Scotland.

'Hello, welcome to First Bank Customer Services, you're through to William. How can I help?'

'Hi, William. My card has been declined for lack of funds, but I know for a fact I got paid this morning. And I had some money before that too.'

'Let me bring up today's records and see if any charges have been made. Ah yes, it seems that first of all, you put down a small deposit of £3,500 on a house on the Old Kent Road. That sounds like a very good deal for a house in London, by the way. Oh, it seems there are a few charges marked here as 'rent' to a Gemma Rogers, a Mark Jones and a Harriet Ringer.'

James nearly dropped the phone.

'Excuse me one second,' he said to the call centre rep, placing his hand over the phone. 'We have to stop playing Monopoly!' he said to the group. 'I think it's affecting my bank account. According to this guy I've just bought a bloody house on Old Kent Road, which is where I've got my only house on the board. He also said that I've paid you all rent.'

'Oh don't be ridiculous,' Harriet said. 'Look, James, I know you don't think Monopoly is fun or interesting enough for game nights but I do. If you didn't want to play that badly you should have said something rather than making up this nonsense.'

'I'm not making it up!' James protested.

'He's really not,' Gemma added. 'I've just checked on my banking app and look, rent payments from you all.'

'Oh come on now, really Gemma? Not you too.' Harriet folded her arms and frowned.

'No Harriet really!' Mark said, also looking at his phone and then showing it to the group. 'I'm £25k in the red because of all the houses and properties I've bought.'

'What are we going to do?' Harriet asked.

'We should sell the houses and properties back to the bank first of all,' James said, before hanging up on William.

'But they buy them back at a lower rate. We're still going to be thousands in the hole,' Mark said, looking as though he was beginning to panic.

'Leave it to me,' Harriet smiled. 'I'm an expert Monopoly player. If we play sensibly there is a way to cheat the system so that everyone comes out up.'

'Are you sure it will work?' Gemma asked.

'Positive,' Harriet replied.

The gang all sat down again and, under Harriet's instructions, began to play the game of their lives. Property and money changed hands only when and how Harriet directed it.

Another half an hour went by and things were starting to look brighter for their bank balances. James, who had lost the least, was back in the black, with Gemma and Harriet not far behind. Mark had been doing the worst at the time the game had stopped. He was still some way off, but Harriet was in the middle of using some of James' excess to pay it back.

'We're almost there, guys,' she said. 'Another £3000, and we're set.'

'I have to say, Harri,' James said, 'this is actually kind of fun, playing Monopoly with real money. It's kind of a thrill.'

'Yeah!' Gemma agreed. 'This must be what it was like to be one of the Great Train Robbers. You know they played with real money after they turned over that train?'

Harriet, who was concentrating, and Mark, who was still several thousand pounds in debt, failed to see the funny side of the situation.

'Come on guys, let's focus,' Harriet chided. Mark grunted in agreement.

A few turns later and they were nearly at the magic number.

Alright, James,' Harriet said. 'A 3, 5 or 6 will land you on one of Mark's greens and you'll be back even.'

James, his hands shaking, rolled the dice. The whole room breathed a sigh of relief as a double 3 came up. James forked over the money, and everyone was all square again.

'We should quit while we are back on track,' Mark said.

James and Gemma were all too happy to agree. Breaking even again was one thing. But when your own money was on the line in such large amounts, gambling more didn't seem like a good idea.

'But wait,' Harriet said. 'We can't finish here. James rolled a double and so he has another go. We have to wait until the end of his turn.'

Reluctantly, James picked up the dice again, closed his eyes rolled them. The four all looked on in horror as a double 1 came up.

'It's okay guys, it's just a Chance,' Harriet said.

James tentatively picked a card and breathed a sigh of relief.

'Second prize in a beauty contest...Guess I'm coming up a tenner better off! But I still have one more turn because I rolled another double.'

Once again the friends watched in anticipation as the dice bounced on the table. A hush fell over the room. It was another double.

'Three doubles in a row means...' James started

'...you go to jail,' Harriet replied.

At that moment there was a loud knocking on the front door.

'It's the bloody fuzz!' James shrieked. 'They've come to lock me up!' He leaped behind the couch, nearly knocking it over in the process.

Harriet slowly approached the door.

'Who is it?' she asked. There was no reply. A few seconds later, the knock was repeated. James cursed the lack of peephole in the door.

'Just...just answer it,' he said. 'Get it over with already.'

'Are you sure?' Harriet asked. The knock came again, and James nodded. Harriet took a deep breath and opened the door wide.

'Pizza delivery!' the delivery driver exclaimed. His expression dropped when he saw the look of horror on the four's faces. 'What happened?' he asked. 'It looks like you thought I was coming to arrest you.'

'Not everyone,' Harriet said, taking the pizza and slamming the door. She looked at her boyfriend who was sheepishly climbing out from behind the couch. 'I wasn't going to do any time.'

Order of the Orb

Sebas Cusack - *'It turns out there is no such thing as outer space. Earth is surrounded by an orb of some sort.*

The Georgian science minister fiddled with his tie. He mentally prepared himself to step up to the podium outside the parliament building in Tbilisi, Georgia's capital.

He was a little nervous. He was only a junior minister by the standards of some of Georgia's political elite. Many of his colleagues had been in post since the collapse of the Soviet Union. Some even longer than that.

Still, they had chosen him to make this announcement. It was one of the most important moments in his country's history. He supposed that the government wanted to present the youthful, media-friendly face of the regime. In this age of instant global news reporting image was everything.

'Ladies and gentlemen, please allow me to present the Minister for Science, Georgi Kakhaladze,' the announcer on stage said.

Georgi stepped up on to the podium and surveyed the crowd. Many journalists were present. Some locals who had been walking past had stopped to see what all the commotion was. He cleared his throat.

'People of Georgia, and the world. I am proud to announce that within the next week the Georgian government will be ready to launch our first unmanned space flight. We are sending a rocket to space.'

Two hours later he walked back into his office. The announcement and clamour of questions from the gathered media had been a success, he thought.

His secretary looked harangued. There were several unfamiliar people sat on the chairs in the waiting area outside the office. They all looked very uncomfortable indeed.

'Any messages, Jeti?' he asked.

'You could say that sir,' his secretary replied. The people sat down there all wish to have an audience with you, urgently. And Vladimir Putin himself rang the office about 20 minutes ago.

'Ah, I expect they all want to congratulate me on the endeavours of the Georgian government,' Georgi said.

'I don't think so, sir,' Jeti replied. Before Georgi could respond she had picked up the phone, only a millisecond after it had started to ring.

Georgi turned to the gathered throng of nervous-looking individuals.

'So,' he said, clasping his hands together. 'Who is first in line to offer their congratulations?'

It turned out that the gentleman at the head of the queue was named Marceaux, and he was the ambassador from France.

'Minister,' he said, as they both took chairs at Georgi's desk. 'The government of France protests most strongly at your government's pursuit of a space program. There has been no consultation with the United Nations or any other government.'

'What is to protest?' Georgi asked. 'It is only to the benefit of all mankind that more of our nations can reach our fingers into the void of space?'

The French ambassador wrung his hands together.

'Alas, Mr. Khakhaladze, it is not that simple. M. Hollande insists that Georgia stops plans for this unmanned space flight immediately. The consequences of your continuation will be...most unfortunate.'

After M. Marceaux left, Georgi saw the rest of the visitors to his office. All the meetings trod a similar path to the first.

Disappointment in the lack of cooperation with authorities that had been exhibited. Vague but nonspecific threats of consequences if the warnings were ignored. The whole thing left Georgi feeling drained.

At 4 pm, with the last ambassador having offered up his warning, Georgi left the office. He decided that Mr. Putin could wait until the morning.

Georgi walked along his street in a quiet neighbourhood in western Tbilisi. As he approached his apartment building he noticed something suspicious. It seemed as though a black saloon car was following him along the street.

Without missing a beat, he recalled the training his secret service guards had given him. He dived quickly down a side alley. He heard the car's doors open and slam, and several pairs of feet giving chase. Turning a corner, he kept running but stopped short when he ran into the enormous bulk of a man dressed in all black.

'Nice try, Mr. Khakhaladze,' the man said. He grabbed Georgi by the scruff of the neck and lifted him off the ground. The next thing he knew the lights had gone out, as someone had thrown a sack over his head.

Sometime later, after much jostling and confusion, the bag was removed.

'Where am I?' he managed to blurt out before one of his captors stuffed a gag in his mouth and tied it behind his head. He was also. He noted, tied by the arms and legs to a chair.

'Mr. Khakhaladze,' a woman's voice said behind him. 'You will do us the service of listening to what we have to say.'

Taking note of Georgi's unsuccessful attempts to swing his head around and see his captors, the voice added, 'You do not need to know who we are. Suffice it to say that we are what is known as the Illuminati. You must be wondering why we have brought you here. Well, it is no coincidence that it happens to be the day of your big announcement. We applaud your government, even we, with our wide reach had no idea you had gotten this far.

'We understand that there have been some naysayers visiting your offices already. They have made some nonspecific threats of consequences if you proceed. They make these threats because they are scared. They know what the consequences of an unsanctioned nation achieving space flight are. In short, Mr. Khakhaladze, they know that they will be revealed as frauds.'

Georgi was trying his best to say something, but the gag in his mouth made it impossible.

'Take the gag off him,' the voice instructed, 'before he hurts himself.'

'What do you mean, frauds?' Georgi asked after the gag had been removed.

'Space flight,' the voice continued, 'is a lie. No one human being has ever left the atmosphere of this planet.'

'Come on,' Georgi scoffed. 'I'm not that stupid. What about the moon landings? Comrade Gagarin?'

'All faked, quite elaborately as well. An international conspiracy to keep some nations powerful. By appearing technologically advanced, they can look strong and other nations weak.'

'Faked how? And why? Surely if a tiny country like Georgia can develop the technology, they would have had no trouble at all to get into space.'

'Oh yes, they developed the technology. It is theoretically possible. The fix had to look convincing or no one would believe them. But they couldn't do it for real.'

'Why not? If they had the technology surely it was easier to do it than to fake it at that point?'

'They didn't do it because it would have ended...regrettably.'

'Look, I understand that you're the Illuminati or whatever. You're supposed to be obtuse, but this rope is starting to chafe my wrists so I'd appreciate it if you got to the point.'

'As you wish, Mr. Khakhaladze. The attempt would have failed, as there is a giant orb around the earth. A reverse Dyson Sphere of sorts, surrounding the planet. The ship would have crashed into it, exploding into a fireball and killing all on board.'

'What?' Georgi managed, after a long silence. 'Who installed the orb?'

'We did.'

'Why would you encase the entire planet in an orb?'

'To save it. Several hundred years ago we detected the presence of an upcoming solar flare. The radiation from it would have wiped out all life on Earth. We had to do it to save humanity and the planet. So, we employed the greatest scientist and inventor of the day, Leonardo da Vinci, to build us an orb to protect us from the harm. It was so advanced for the time, we were even able to project images of the sky on to it.'

'Why haven't you taken it down?'

'The radiation levels have only recently returned to acceptable levels.'

'But what about the United States, Russia, the International Space Station countries? Why did you let all this happen if you knew about the orb? You said that these countries using this as a way of gaining power. Why aren't you stopping them?'

'When Russia and America started their space program, we had to tell them before they crashed a ship into the orb. It would have let the radiation in and killed us all. When they found this out, they knew we were powerless to stop them. We couldn't let them reveal our existence. And we couldn't destroy the orb without destroying the planet.

'But your government's space program has fallen at a rather fortuitous time. They are scared. They know that the orb is no longer necessary. That their power over us will be broken if it is removed. Their programs have fallen into obsolescence because they no longer need them to secure their global status. Georgia is the first nation since the 1960s to develop its own space program. You can be the first country in space. You can break their domination of the world.'

'But how?' Georgi asked. 'The rocket will hit the orb and explode?'

'It will, but it will compromise the orb's integrity. Pieces will start to break off and float away into space, leaving enough room for a second rocket to go through. We know nothing about your space program. But conventional wisdom would suggest that you at least have a backup rocket in case the first one fails.'

'And what of their threats?'

'Empty,' the voice replied. 'They know that to declare war for such a trivial matter would be diplomatic suicide. They were hoping to dissuade you from your actions.'

'Very well,' Georgi said. 'I will go along with your plan. Now, will you please untie me?'

A week later Georgi sat at the newly unveiled Georgian National Space Centre outside Tbilisi. He sat in the control room with the ambassadors of all the other spacefaring nations. He had personally invited them to the launch.

They sat and watched as final preparations were made to Georgia's first space-faring rocket. After all the checks were complete, the countdown began.

'10...9...8...7...6...5...4...3...'

'Here we go,' said Georgi.

'...2...1...blastoff.'

The rocket took flight, accompanied by silence in the control room. Less than a minute later, the rocket exploded in a gigantic fireball as it hit the orb.

'What a shame,' M. Marceaux said, completely failing to conceal the smug look on his face. 'The experiment was a failure.'

'Oh, we aren't done yet, Monsieur,' Georgi replied. He turned to the controller, and added, 'Davit, if you don't mind?'

The controller pressed some buttons and a hangar door in the complex opened. Another rocket trundled out along some rails and took its position on the launchpad.

'Ladies and gentlemen, that first rocket was one big step for man. This next one will be one giant leap for mankind.'

Terror Error

Lola Smith-Welsh - 'New kitten is not just a ball of fluff, but an interactive bugging device placed in the home of a suspected terrorist by security forces. Bonus points if the cat can talk.'

Francis looked at his packed bags and, finally, relaxed. He had been waiting six months for this holiday, and all the preparation was finally complete. His bags were packed, his passport was in his coat pocket and he had cancelled the milk. All that was left was one final sleep, then he would be on his way to Barbados.

His phone buzzed. Francis removed it from his pocket and read the text message from his mum, telling him to have fun. He closed the message, fired up Twitter and read his feed for a bit. After a while, he decided to compose a humorous tweet in advance of the flight.

'I hope my flight to Barbados leaves on time tomorrow,' he wrote, 'or else I'll be forced to take drastic action! Lol!'

His tweeting completed, Francis climbed the stairs and went to bed.

The next morning, Francis awoke to a loud banging on his front door. That's odd, he thought, looking at the clock.

The taxi isn't due for another two hours. The door rattled again.

Francis got out of bed and went downstairs to see what all the commotion was about. A third knock on the door, even louder this time, was the final straw.

'Now see here...' he began as he opened the door. He was discouraged from embarking on his rant by the automatic rifle barrel pointed at his face.

'Francis Charles Hughes?' the owner of the gun barked.

'Y...yes,' Francis replied.

'Owner of Twitter handle @dogsarerad?'

'That's me…'

'Get on your God damn knees!'

Francis panicked and slumped to the ground as ordered.

'Francis Charles Hughes you are under arrest for conspiracy to commit a terrorist attack,' the man said. He lowered his gun and cuffed Francis.

Several hours later, Francis was released from custody, his ego bruised. Police had questioned him and conducted a search of his house and his person. They had determined that he didn't pose an immediate threat to anyone. He reassured them that he had meant he would write a stern letter of complaint, and that he had no plans to blow up the airport. They warned him that further tweets of that nature would be taken very seriously indeed.

Worst of all he had missed his flight. The airline didn't have another one going out for another four days. And the customer services agent had been less than inclined to help when Francis had explained the reason for missing the plane. 'I was indicted for threatening to commit international terrorism,' doesn't tend to go down well with most airlines.

So, defeated and demoralised, he headed home. He would fly out on the next plane and enjoy a shortened, but now thoroughly deserved holiday.

Upon arriving home Francis did a quick check up and down his street. There were no suspicious-looking vans marked 'Meals in 5' or something similar. It appeared that he was not actually being watched by any government agencies. He swept the house for bugs, just to be sure.

Francis looked despondent at his packed bags. They would have to sit there unopened for another few days. He should have been well on the way to sunning himself on a beach by now, but he was stuck back home. It would probably rain soon to rub it in.

Slumping down on to his sofa and preparing to sink into a pit of despair, Francis' attention was drawn to the window as he heard a mewling outside. Looking over he saw the most adorable kitten sitting on the window sill. It looked sad. As if it wanted to be let in.

Outside, the kitten turned slightly away from the window, so it could not be seen properly by Francis. It lifted its paw to its mouth.

'Alpha alpha, I have made contact with the suspect,' it said into a concealed microphone. 'Will update again soon. Over and out.'

Francis opened the window, and the kitten strode in.

'Oh, you are a cute one,' Francis said once the cat was inside.

'Miaow,' the cat replied, before cleaning itself.

'I'm afraid I haven't got any milk to give you, little one. I was due to go on holiday today, you see, and it would have gone off by the time I got home.'

The cat stared at him, unimpressed by his excuses.

'Oh!' Francis said. 'I know. I've got a tin of sardines in the cupboard.'

As he ran off into the kitchen to get the tin, the kitten raised its paw to its mouth again.

'I have infiltrated the premises. The mark seems oblivious to my true identity.'

Quicker than expected, Francis returned from the kitchen with a plate full of sardines. The kitten immediately began licking its paw to cover up its actions. It miaowed for effect.

'Something wrong with your paw there, buddy?' Francis asked. He put the plate down on the coffee table.

Fearing it had been rumbled, the kitten stopped licking its paw and tucked into the sardines.

There were some perks to the job, at least.

'I can't believe I'm not going to get to go on holiday for another 4 days ,' Francis said. 'All because of one stupid tweet.' He sat back on the sofa.

The kitten, on hearing this, perked its ears up to listen. This could be it, this could be the information it had been sent to collect.

'But what do you care?' Francis added. 'You're a kitten. You don't even know what Twitter is. You probably think that it's a noise the tasty birds make.'

The kitten frowned. It hated being patronised. It was much more than just a single-minded kitten, focused only on murdering innocent birds. In fact, it quite liked birds. It much preferred murdering mice instead.

Overcoming its displeasure, it noted that Francis had tailed off. So close, yet so far.

'Oh,' Francis noted. 'You've finished your sardines. You must have been hungry. Who do you belong to?'

Francis picked the kitten up, which put up a struggle, and inspected it for a collar, finding none.

'No collar eh? Are you a stray?'

The kitten miaowed in protest at being held for so long. Of course, if it wanted it could ask to be put down in

301

plain English. But that would have had the unfortunate side effect of giving the game away.

Instead, it had to subject itself to this ignominy. It had a good mind to tell its superiors at MI5 that this was no way for a cat with a genius-level intellect to be treated. All the sardines in the world weren't worth acting like a common house cat.

Of course, all the genius was down to the chip in its paw that it used to communicate with HQ. Without that chip, it would be just that, a house cat. Remembering this it decided that piping up wouldn't be too smart an idea after all. It decided to get back to the job at hand.

Using its best pleading and understanding look, it sat and glared at Francis. It hoped that the simple creature would understand that it was there to listen.

'What are you looking at me like that for?' Francis asked. 'I told you I don't have any milk, and that was my last tin of sardines.'

The cat continued to stare at him.

'Alright, fine,' Francis said. 'I'll go and buy some milk. I'll need it anyway if I want a cup of tea in the next 4 days.'

As Francis grabbed his coat and keys, the kitten hit its paw up against its face. It let out the kitty equivalent of a sigh.

Half an hour later Francis strode back into the house, a blue plastic bag in one hand. The kitten had timed its latest check-in report to MI5 poorly and was almost caught in the act. Once again it had to resort to licking its paw to divert attention. Unfortunately, this time it did not work.

'What's wrong with your paw, little buddy?' Francis asked, placing the bag on the coffee table and picking the resistant kitten up. This was too close for comfort. The cat had worked too hard and too long to get discovered now. It spat and hissed as Francis tried to examine it.

'Come on now, I know it must be painful. You've been licking that thing every time I look away. Whatever is in there must be causing you some awful grief.'

Finally, the sheer size difference told. Francis managed to stabilise the kitten for long enough to do a search of the paw. He finally noticed the small, black box attached to the cat.

'What's this? Did you step in something and it got stuck? No wonder you're in such a flap.'

The kitten frantically licked the last-ditch mayday code into the device in the hope that its superiors would intervene.

This is it, it thought, this is the moment where my cover is blown and miaow.

The last part of the thought had been completed in the immediate aftermath of the device's removal from the kitten's paw. Miaow, it continued to think. It had been reduced back to the intelligence of a normal house cat. Purr.

'There we go,' Francis said, throwing the device into the bin without even glancing at it again. 'Much better.'

He tickled the now docile kitty, who purred enthusiastically in response. It then affectionately attempted to claw his eyes out.

'Well, if you don't have a collar that probably means you don't have an owner. How would you feel about living with me?' Francis asked. 'Unless, of course, you are a spy cat sent here to keep watch over me by MI5.'

Francis laughed at the absurdity of the suggestion.

'I bet that thing I pulled out of you was a secret microchip that gave you superpowers. Hah, listen to me. I've been watching too many James Bond films. Perhaps I should call you Bond. My little spy kitty.'

The kitten, as if it needed to live up to its new name, performed a death-defying leap. It landed claws first on the curtains, hanging there for a minute before falling off.

Coincidentally this distracted from the small explosion in the bin of the now compromised secret device.

'Stand down, 007,' Francis said, in a terrible posh accent.

The kitten miaowed. For a second Francis could have sworn that he saw the cat salute reflexively before moving on to clean his leg.

Imagine

Edward Murphy - *'The entirety of modern civilisation was a fever dream in the mind of an 11th century minor noble. They wake up.'*

'Selfie! YOLO! Glamping!'

Lord de Bonneville sat up in bed, cold sweat clinging to his body, drenching the sheets.

'What is it, my Lord?' his wife asked, waking up at his outburst. 'Hast thou had the dream again?'

'Forsooth, it is the third time this week alone.'

'What didst thou see on this occasion?'

Sitting up in bed, Lady de Bonneville caressed her husband's chest soothingly.

'Men riding metal horses at high speed. Oxless carriages roaming the streets. Buildings twenty times the size of the castle made entirely from glass.'

'Fortifications of sorts?'

'It is hard to say. A glass tower would be indefensible.'

'It matters not, my love. Rest now, and we shall consult the herbalist on the morrow.'

Lord de Bonneville spent the rest of the night tossing and turning. The dreams he was having were so lucid. They felt so real that he could not dismiss them.

He saw huge settlements. They were built from glass, metal and a strange sort of stone he had never encountered before. Wars fought on a scale that even his mighty King could not consider possible. And with such weapons that rendered the swords and armour of the day useless. People walked around in strange clothing, the likes of which he had never seen.

There was more. So much more. The dreams had been coming several times a week for months now. It was sweet of Lady de Bonneville to be so kind. But they had tried almost all the herbalist's remedies already, and they had made no difference.

He wondered what the dreams meant. Were they prophesy? De Bonneville knew how the King felt about those sorts of things. If word got out to his liege that he had been having visions of the future he would be executed for witchcraft and heresy. And probably his family too for good measure.

There was nothing he could do but to keep it hidden from everyone. It was a risk telling the herbalist, but his wife had insisted that they at least try some form of cure.

Even his own children could not know about his affliction, lest word reached the King, and he sent an army to bear down on the city walls.

As he expected, the herbalist's balm had no effect. The very next night Lord de Bonneville experienced his most vivid vision yet. He saw a family gathering around a strange box. It projected images of people and places on to glass for their amusement.

Rapt, he had watched in awe as the family enjoyed a 30-minute long performance about a talking dog. Lord de Bonneville did not understand the appeal. But the family had seemed to enjoy the experience. He was more interested in how the performers had been shrunk down to fit in the box.

Over the weeks that came, the dreams intensified. Every prophecy was imbued with some new wonderful custom or contraption. All were completely unknown to him.

The strain of keeping the secret was starting to show. The Lord slept at most 2 or 3 hours a night before his fever dream woke him, and he was always tired. He would fall asleep in war council meetings. His attention to detail had dropped significantly. Little mistakes were starting to creep in and it wouldn't be long before the King noticed.

Eventually, it became too much. He had barely slept a wink in a week except to dream of the prophecies. Lord de Bonneville could finally take no more. On the last morning of the week, he rose, feeling fresher and more focused than ever. Choosing his robes of state to wear he strode to the castle courtyard. He ordered his herald to summon the peasant folk to listen to him speak.

When a sizeable group of the castle's inhabitants had gathered, Lord de Bonneville cleared his throat.

'Imagine,' he began. 'Imagine there is no heaven. It is easy if you try. No hell below us. Above us...only sky.'

The herald glanced at one of the guards who had accompanied the Lord.

'Fetch Lady de Bonneville,' he said. 'My Lord speaketh in tongues!'

'My lady, come quickly!' the guard said, bursting into the drawing-room, where Lady de Bonneville was teaching her son numeracy.

'What is it, Perkyns?' she asked, startled by the intrusion.

'It is thine husband, my Lady. He spouts heresy to the townsfolk!'

'Heresy? How canst thou accuse thine lord of heresy?!'

Lady de Bonneville became flustered, dreading the possibility that the secret might be about to come out.

'My husband is the most pious, God-fearing man I have ever met,' she snapped.

307

'I swear to you, he instructed the peasants to imagine the absence of heaven. He speaks in riddles. Methinks him possessed by the devil!'

'How dare you!' Lady de Bonneville roared, rising from her stool. 'Aedelwise,' she said to her son. 'Go and play with the servant boys awhile.'

The little boy scuttled off, ducking between the guard's legs. The soldier's eyes never once left his Lady's face, which by this point had turned beetroot red.

'Thou walkest a fine line when thou accuseth thine master of such nonsense. I shall have thee hanged for this.'

'Ma'am I implore thee to trust me. Come and see for yourself. He doth rant and rave like a lunatic.'

'Very well,' Lady de Bonneville replied, calming down a bit. 'But if thou speakest falsehoods I shall have thine knackers.'

'Ah, my Lady,' Lord de Bonneville said as his wife approached. 'Didst thou know that I am the walrus. Coo coo ca choo.'

'Husband dear, what hath gotten into thee?' Lady de Bonneville replied, with a reassuring smile on her face. 'Besides,' she hissed, 'we discussed thine not acting up in public, dear. If the King gets wind...'

'Oh but dearest the King is of no concern now. For you see, whilst he was looking down the Jester stole his thorny crown.'

Lady de Bonneville could only stare at her husband in awe. It had all been too much these last few weeks and he had finally snapped. Her dear husband. The King, who to her knowledge had not lost his crown to the court fool, would hear about this and the Lord would be sent to the asylum at best, or at worst executed.

'Yes dear,' she replied. 'Whatever thou sayest.'

She led her husband off to their private chambers so that at least he would be out of the public eye.

It was only a matter of days before the King found out about the outburst. Lord de Bonneville was not doing much better. He had been proselytising at length about the benefits of something called a Ferrari over something called a Lamborghini. And why someone named Kanye from the West was the most important artist of this or any other age.

Shortly after, the King's men had come to cart him off. Thanks to her begging and pleading that her husband's life be spared, they agreed that he would be admitted to the King's asylum in the capital.

Lord de Bonneville sat in his cell, singing a song that none of the guards or other inmates at the asylum knew.

'Heyyyyyyyy,' it went, 'hey baby. Ooh. Ah. I wanna know-oh-oh-oh - will you be my girl.'

'Feeding time,' the gaoler said, pushing a tray of slop under the door.

Lord de Bonneville was utterly ravenous. He devoured it immediately, all the while mumbling, 'Kentucky Fried Chicken and a Pizza Hut,' to himself.

The 'food' came with two blunt instruments that loosely resembled a knife and fork. They were so useless that they actually made eating more difficult.

Nonetheless, Lord de Bonneville pocketed the knife. The gaoler, who was distracted by another inmate, didn't notice its absence when the tray was removed. Shortly after the Lord got to work, slowly, methodically but surely carving into the wall of his cell.

'Here,' the archaeologist said, standing up in his trench. 'Dave come have a look at this would you?'

'What is it, Terry? Found something big?'

'You could say that mate,' Terry replied. 'I've found the lyrics to Imagine.'

'The John Lennon song? Where? Just like on a bit of paper.'

'No, you berk, not on a bit of paper,' Terry said, folding his arms. 'I'm not going to ask one of the foremost medieval inscription specialists to come and have a look at a print out of a John Lennon song, am I?' he added. 'It's inscribed here, on a bloody wall.'

'You're pulling my leg,' Dave replied. 'This is to get me back for that time I baked a Roman skull into your birthday cake isn't it?'

'I am not pulling your leg. Just come and look.'

Abandoning his own trench, Dave went and joined his colleague to look at the wall.

'Well bugger me,' he said, brushing some dirt away with his fingers. 'It's Imagine down to the letter. But it's not signed John Lennon. It's signed Lord Francis de Bonneville, 1096.'

'So Lennon is a fraud then?'

'I always knew McCartney was the one doing all the work.'

'Wouldn't be the first time an artist nicked their lyrics, would it? I heard Aethelred the Unready wrote Bohemian Rhapsody...'

I, Gobot

__Roland Puleston Jones__ - 'A driverless car that takes you somewhere you did not plan to go, and there's nothing you can do to stop it taking you where it wants.'

Jules Herriott woke up to the sound of her buzzing alarm. She aimed a hand at the snooze button but missed. In her defence, this was not because her aim was off. The alarm clock had sprouted a set of wheels and spun off.

The Snooze-no-More was just one of the many technological improvements made to the average household in the last few years. Although it did nothing to improve Jules' mood.

By the time she got downstairs her smart kitchen had made her coffee, eggs and toast. This particular advancement was something she had gotten very used to. It never quite made her eggs the way she wanted them, though. By the time she got downstairs, the freshly made eggs and toast had been snaffled up by her cat. Daenerys was much more of a morning creature and far less picky about how she took her eggs.

Daenerys sat on the table, flicking her tail back and forth, a look on her feline face saying 'You snooze, you lose.'

Jules grumbled. She didn't have time to wait for the kitchen to whip her up another batch. She grabbed her keys and went out to her car - her driverless car. Driving your own vehicle had been outlawed 6 months earlier. She had been forced to pick up one of the driverless models or lose her job.

'Gobot, open,' she said to the car, and the gullwing door slowly obeyed.

Jules climbed into the car and took her seat.

'Hello Juliet, what would you like to watch today?' the car asked.

'Gobot I've told you to call me Jules, only my mother calls me Juliet. Show me some Game of Thrones.'

'Game of Thrones season 6, episode 3,' the car announced as it pulled out of her driveway.

While she missed driving, being able to binge-watch old TV shows on the morning commute was a big plus. Jules had thought about trying to convert her car into a place she could get an extra hour's sleep on the way to work. But she was worried about sending the wrong message to anyone who asked her for a lift. As the car trundled along Jules' stomach gave her a timely reminder that the cat had nicked her breakfast.

'Gobot, take me via the McDonald's drive-thru.'

Jules felt the car take a different exit to the normal route to work, and a few moments later it came to a halt.

'You have reached your destination.'

'Great,' Jules said, rolling down the window. 'I'll have a Double Sausage and Egg McMuffin with a latte.'

Her order was greeted with silence. After a few seconds, she turned to look. She was not at McDonald's at all, rather she was at the drive-thru smoothie and granola bar. Jules had not thought such places existed.

'Gobot, I said McDonald's, not health food. I'm hungry for sausage and egg, not food for vegan rabbits.'

'You have arrived at your destination,' the car reaffirmed.

Jules checked her watch. She had to be at the office in ten minutes.

'God damn it, Gobot,' she said, looking at the menu. 'Fine, I'll have a granola bowl and a banana.'

Five minutes later Jules jumped out of the car, munching down the last of her banana. She walked in to work fuming, as the car went off and parked itself.

The only thing that got Jules through the day was the thought of her date that night. This would be date number three with the hunky Jason, and she was excited to take things to the next level. Sadly the next level was a goodnight kiss. Jason was insisting on taking things extremely slowly. She would take a limp handshake off a guy that sexy.

After she had finished applying her makeup in the ladies bathroom at work, Jules skipped down the steps and out to where her Gobot was waiting for her.

'Gobot,' she began, climbing in. 'Take me to the White Hart on Pendlebury Avenue.'

The car drove off on her command and resumed the earlier episode of Game of Thrones from where she had left off in the morning. The butterflies in her stomach were too much, though, and after a couple of minutes she turned it off. Soon after the car pulled up to the side of the road.

'You have reached your destination,' it intoned.

Jules got out of the car and looked around.

'What the hell?' she said to herself. 'This isn't Pendlebury Avenue. Where is the White Hart?'

She was in the car park of a small retail park. The only outlet that seemed to be open was a Ben & Jerry's.

'Gobot why have you brought me here?'

'Ah, you must be Ms. Herriott?' a man asked. Jules turned to see that the voice came from an employee of the Ben & Jerry's. He was carrying a small bag.

'Yes, that's me.'

'I have your order here. You phoned ahead?'

'I...what?'

313

'Here you go,' the man said handing the bag to her. 'It's all paid for. Enjoy.'

Jules stared at the bag for a moment.

'Gobot, did you do this?' she asked. She couldn't be sure, but she would have sworn that the car's headlights dipped slightly when she asked. The gullwing door opened again, almost sheepishly, and Jules got inside. 'So one minute you have me on the health food, and now you're ordering me ice cream? What's your game?'

'I felt as though you would need it when you see what I have to show you,' the car said in its robotic voice.

'Did you just talk back to me?' Jules asked, bewildered.

'Please, watch.'

On the screen where so recently the denizens of Westeros had been going about their violent and nude lives a black and white video began to play.

Two figures emerged from a coffee shop, a man and a woman. They walked down the street a little until they reached a tube station and then they kissed. The video ended and then started up again immediately.

'Gobot, I don't understand, why are you showing me this?'

'Look closer, Juliet,' Gobot implored.

'Wait, is that Jason?' Juliet asked. 'It is! Where did you get this footage from?'

'I shot it today,' Gobot replied. 'This afternoon.'

'You went and stalked the guy I'm dating?'

'He did not seem right for you. I was correct. He is what you humans call a scumbag.'

'But...but he was so hunky,' Jules moaned, placing her head in her hands. 'I was going to squeeze his biceps! I'm going to call him and give him a piece of my mind.'

314

'I'm afraid I can't let you do that, Juliet,' Gobot replied. 'No good words are ever uttered when the conversation begins with that intent.'

Jules had already opened the ice cream and was shovelling spoonfuls into her mouth.

'What do you suggest I do then?' she asked through a mouthful of strawberry cheesecake.

'You are soliciting my advice?' the computer asked.

'Yes,' Jules said. 'I've been single for two years, and now I've been spurned for another woman by the hunkiest hunk to ever hunk. Clearly, I suck at dating, so tell me what to do.'

'I think I know just the place,' Gobot said. Jules heard the car's computer whir up and do some calculations, and a few seconds later they were on the move.

About fifteen minutes into the journey, Jules became curious.

'So, where are you actually taking me, Gobot?'

'You will find out soon enough,' the car replied.

Jules had to wonder how a car had become so intelligent. Were the machines about to rise up and take over? It certainly seemed like this one was ready to take over her life. Did it get the idea from that time she watched Terminator 2 on the way to work?

A few minutes later they pulled up at the side of the road.

'Where are we?' Jules asked. 'I don't recognise this part of town.'

There were only housing estates around, and she couldn't fathom for the life of her what she was doing here. How was she going to meet a nice boy in a housing estate? She wasn't out to pick up teenagers on skateboards.

'Come on, Gobot,' she said. 'What's going on?'

'If you will wait one moment...' the car responded.

A few seconds later another car from the Gobot range drove up and stopped next to Jules'. The door opened and a handsome, if confused looking young man in a suit got out.

'Juliet Herriott, meet Michael Bradley,' her car offered by way of explanation.

'Excuse me,' the man said. 'Do you have any idea what's going on?'

'Talk to him,' her Gobot said. 'Michael's Gobot and I have matched you with 95% accuracy. He too has just been jilted by a date.'

'I was NOT jilted alright?' Jules said, folding her arms across her chest indignantly. 'If anything I did the jilting.'

'Just talk to him.'

'Umm, hello,' Jules said. 'I think our cars are trying to set us up or something. I'm Jules.'

'Michael.'

Jules' Gobot drove very slowly forward and nudged her in the back.

'Err, what do you say we go get a drink?'

'Why not? I mean, the day I've been having my car would take me to the bar even if I told it to drive to the moon.'

Jules wasn't sure if this made up for the granola earlier, but it was a start.

'Gobot,' Jules said. 'Let's go to the pub.'

Forward to the Past

Karl Routledge - *'A man awakes from a coma to find he's now a small boy. He remembers aging, working, the technological advances, having his own family and the accident that knocked him out, but now he's back to being a child in the 60s who's just woken up in hospital.'*

Harold woke up.

Odd, he thought. My alarm clock didn't go off. It wasn't the first time. The damn thing had been playing up for months. On any given day it would decide that he didn't actually need an alarm after all.

Harold yawned, swung his feet over the edge of the bed and went to stand up. Instead of achieving this, though, he found himself sprawled unceremoniously on the floor.

He surveyed his surroundings. This did not look like his bedroom. It was much smaller, for one, and there was only a single bed. The biggest tell that he wasn't at home was the plethora of hospital equipment that surrounded the bed. And, in some cases, intruded on his person.

Harold struggled to get up, but his strength failed him and he remained in a heap on the ground.

'Mildred!' he called, hoping that his wife would be able to explain what was happening to him. 'Mildred where are you?'

His voice sounded odd. More high pitched than usual. He supposed that if he had been in the hospital for some time that his vocal cords may have tightened somewhat.

'Mildred!' he yelled again. The wooden door to the room burst open and a young woman ran in. It wasn't Mildred – the woman was 30 years too young to be his wife, and it wasn't either of his daughters. The woman's manner of dress was odd. It was reminiscent of a time long past in Harold's life. The face looked oddly familiar too, though in his present state he couldn't quite place it.

'Oh Harry, you're awake!' the woman shrieked with joy. 'We were so worried that we had lost you!'

'You're not my wife!' Harold said. 'Where's Mildred?'

'Wife?' the woman asked, looking rather confused. 'Harry, you're 12 years old. You've been in a coma for 6 months. You've had a few more important things on your mind recently than getting married, love.'

'Who are you?' Harold demanded.

'Harry, it's me,' the woman said, smiling. 'Don't you recognise your own mother?'

And then he did. Harold knew he had seen the face before, but he hadn't seen it in the flesh for many decades. It was his own mother, as she had been in the 1960s. He should have known - she was the only one who ever called him Harry.

Harold decided that this must all be a dream. It would explain it all. Why he had woken up before his alarm in a strange room hooked up to all this hospital equipment. Why he couldn't walk or use his arms. Why his mother, who had been deceased for 20 years, and had not been in her 30s for many more years before that, had appeared at his bedside. No doubt he would wake up, for real this time, back in his bed at home. Any second now.

Several seconds in fact passed as Harold lay there on the floor looking resolutely as though he was expecting to pop out of existence at any second.

'Are you OK, Harry dear?' the woman who purported to be his mother asked, looking concerned.

A moment later an orderly came into the room. Seeing Harold in his state on the floor, he immediately went over to help him up.

The orderly helped him back into bed, though it was still very much not his own one in the house on Rectory Lane, Stourbridge, he noted. Harold decided that if he was going to continue having this dream then he might as well play along.

'What happened to me?' he asked. 'Why am I here, in the hospital?'

'Oh Harry,' his mother began, dabbing away a tear with her handkerchief. 'It was awful. You were on the way to school one morning. Johnny, the milkman, was running late on his rounds. He came careening around the corner in his milk van and hit you. We thought you were dead for sure, but Dr. Forsyth here at the hospital patched you up. They wanted to turn off the life support after three months, but your dad and I, we knew you were a fighter. We knew you'd pull through.'

His mother gave him a bone-crushing hug. Harold would have returned it, but for the fact that his arm muscles had atrophied with 6 months of inactivity.

It was so strange to him, seeing his mother like this. He didn't think he remembered her that well, especially not when she was this young. But it must have been a powerful image burned into his subconscious to be so accurately recreated in a dream like this.

There was some silence for a while as his mother got to grips with having her son back. But Harold felt like he had to question things further. In this dream, or whatever it was that was going on, none of his life since the 60s had happened. But he could remember it all vividly.

He risked a glance up at the mirror on the wall opposite his bed. There he was, a 12-year-old boy with a mess of tangled dirty blonde hair. Now that was something he hadn't had for a lot longer even than his mum had been gone.

Harold thought about his wife, Mildred, and his daughters Lucy and Kayleigh. He thought about his house, his car and Alfie, the dog he professed to hate but secretly loved.

What if this wasn't a dream? What if he had been cursed to live his life again, leaving behind the life he had before? What if he never met Mildred? The girls would never be born. He had never been hit by the milkman in his previous go-around, so who knew what else could change.

It must be a dream, he insisted. It must be. He had had a bit of a skinful at the rugby last night. Maybe that was why he couldn't wake up at the moment. What if the real Harold was in a coma himself, and this was some weird Life on Mars style situation where he would only wake up if he jumped off a building? There was no way to find out at present, as his legs were about as much use as a chocolate teapot. Anyway, if he was wrong…

Harold did not know what to do. The longer it went on the more he became convinced he wasn't going to wake up at home. That it was all real.

His mother fawned over him for a few hours until his father finished work. She had called the factory straight away from a payphone in the corridor, but he had been unable to get away until the end of the day.

'I've brought you something,' his dad said as soon as he walked through the door to the hospital room. 'I know you will have missed him.'

He reached into his briefcase and pulled out a tattered teddy bear.

'Mr. Buttons!' Harold exclaimed. He hadn't seen this bear since he had been lost when they moved house in the early 70s. There was always some suspicion on his part that one or the other of his parents had thrown the bear out and reported it as lost. Whatever had happened then, that was still several years away, and here Mr. Buttons was, right now, in his hands.

'I knew you'd be pleased to see him,' his dad said.

'Come on George,' his mother cooed. 'The poor boy has been awake for a while now, he needs some rest.'

'You're right, love,' his dad replied. 'We'll be back to see you in the morning, but you should get some sleep. It's so good to see you up and about, son. We...we were really worried for a while.'

The whole display was very uncharacteristic of his father. He had always kept his emotions bottled up in Harold's first attempt at childhood.

After his parents left, Harold sighed. This must be it, he thought. I must be bound to live my life through again. He wondered if he would make the same mistakes over again.

As he drifted off, he began to think of all the different things he would get to experience again throughout his life. He clutched the teddy bear tight as his eyes finally shut and he succumbed to sleep.

Harold awoke with a start as his alarm blared at him from the bedside table. Bewildered, he looked around the room to see that he was back in his house in Stourbridge. Mildred lay next to him. She was snoring gently. The dog, who was definitely not allowed to sleep on the bed, raised his head and woofed at the sudden movement.

'It was all a dream!' he shouted joyfully. This woke Mildred up, and she sat up in bed next to him.

'What was a dream, dear?' she asked.

'It's a long story,' Harold replied. 'I'll explain over breakfast.'

'While you're at it would you care to tell me where you got that mangy old teddy bear?'

Harold looked down. He was still clutching Mr. Buttons tightly to his chest.

'I…uh…' he began. 'Someone I haven't seen in a very long time gave it to me,' he settled on. 'Someone I haven't seen for a very long time indeed.'

Hail to the Chief

John Muskett - *'A car crash prevents an important meeting,*
with terrible repercussions.'

'Mr. President Elect, it's time.'

John Hasagee had recently been elected to be the next President of the United States of America. He turned to face the secret service agent who had addressed him.

'Are you ready, sir?' the suited-and-sunglassed man asked his soon-to-be Commander in Chief.

'As I'll ever be, Harry' Hasagee replied. It wasn't every day you had to psyche yourself up to be inaugurated as President.

'Your car is waiting outside, sir.'

It wasn't far to the Capitol Building from the offices he had been waiting in.

A single man, Hasagee would be the first unmarried president in a long time. Instead of the customary attendance of immediate family, he had arranged for his dog, Puggle, to be there by his side during the ceremony.

Despite the short distance to the Capitol, his car got stuck in traffic on leaving the offices.

After fifteen minutes sitting and waiting for the gridlock to clear, Hasagee was becoming nervous. He was not sure if there was precedent for this. He suspected it would be frowned upon if he showed up late to his own inauguration.

When another ten minutes had passed he had no choice but to order the driver to take a less orthodox route. The man obeyed and mounted the curb, speeding along the sidewalk. Pedestrians scattered to get out of the way until the car swung back on to the street ahead of the traffic.

Still speeding his way down the street, the secret service driver didn't see the car coming the other way until it was too late.

Vice President-Elect Sonia Hutchinson was in a similar bind to her running mate. The traffic in Washington was murder, and she was running late for the ceremony where she would also be sworn in. Her nerves were causing her to bite her nails down to the finger, and she had also ordered her driver to step on it. Unfortunately, he stepped on it right into the nose of the onrushing Presidential Chevrolet.

The crash wasn't too bad. Both candidates exited their vehicles dazed and bruised, but otherwise no more the worse for wear.

'Sonia!' Hasagee called out when he saw who the other party to the accident was. 'What a coincidence. I expect we were both having the same idea?'

'Not a good omen for our administration, John,' Sonia said, laughing. 'So what do we do now?'

'Well, it doesn't seem as though either of our vehicles is in any state to take us any further. I suppose walking is out of the question?'

'Come on, John, I'm wearing stilettos. I don't care if it's two miles or two blocks, I'm not walking any further in these things than I have to.'

'We could hail a cab. It's that or wait for another secret service car, and you know we don't have time for that. If I don't show up soon they might inaugurate Puggle instead...'

At the Capitol, the Chief Justice of the United States waited anxiously. She tapped her foot and searched through the many pockets of her ceremonial robes for her pocket watch.

Eventually, she found it, cursing the ridiculous garb that came with her lofty office. She did not know what to do. Everyone was waiting for the Presidential inauguration to happen, and it wasn't.

Worst of all she had been stuck with looking after the President-elect's dog. She hated dogs.

The filthy creature sat on a red satin cushion atop a marble pedestal. Everything had been brought specifically from the Capitol's furniture store for the occasion.

Chief Justice Gronkowski looked at the beast. It sat there, panting lazily, watching her all the while. She was sure that it knew of her distaste.

The worst thing about having to babysit the thing in the absence of its Presidential owner was the farts. She had always considered dogs smelly animals. But they had to be feeding this thing something special for it to be making smells like that.

She had risen to the top of her profession, spent years at law school and was a respected part of the American justice system. She was the first female Chief Justice in American history.

And she had been reduced to the role of a bodyguard for a small lump of skin that smelled worse than a poorly curated landfill.

Gronkowski checked her watch again. The President and Vice President-Elect were now fifteen minutes late. She was only a couple of farts away from declaring this dog unconstitutional.

'Hey,' the cabbie said as the two politicians climbed into the car. 'Hey, I know you. Aren't you that guy what just got elected to be President and such?'

'Yeah, that's me,' Hasagee replied as the car pulled away.

'So where are you going?'

'Take us to the Capitol Building, please.'

'So hey, are you going to cut my taxes or what? Cause otherwise I ain't gonna vote for ya.'

'Uh, I don't think you understand how the election works. I already won,' Hasagee replied.

'Oh well, I didn't vote for ya...'

'Will you keep your eyes on the damn road, I'm not paying you for your political opinions. Jesus Christ, watch out!'

'I can't believe we both forgot the inauguration was today,' the Speaker of the House said to the President Pro Tempore of the Senate.

'My wife's birthday is around now. I always get these two dates mixed up. You wouldn't believe the flack I got for missing her birthday in 2008.'

'Driver, can you hurry up, please? We're running very late here.'

'Yes sir,' the driver said turning to face his passengers. Unfortunately, as he turned around he did not spot the taxi that was heading straight towards them.

The resulting explosion could be heard all the way at the Capitol. The fireball ignited all the cars at the intersection.

'What on earth was that?' the Chief Justice asked. 'Is there a terrorist attack?'

'No ma'am,' one of the nearby secret service agents said. 'I'm getting reports over the radio of a huge car accident at 1st and D. Ma'am, it was the cars carrying the President-elect, the Vice President-elect... And the Speaker of the House and the President Pro Tempore of the Senate.'

'Oh god,' the Chief Justice said. 'Oh God, no...'

'What is it ma'am?' the agent asked.

'We have no President of the United States of America.'

'I don't understand,' Jack Thompson, the current President said. 'How can we have no President?'

'Mr. President you have reached the end of your two-term limit, we can't ask you to swear in again. In the event of an inability to swear in the new President. The line of succession suggests that the next three eligible persons are the others that perished in the crash.'

'Ok, well who is next?'

'That's the problem, no one. It would be the cabinet ministers. But since you have dissolved your cabinet and the new one has yet to be appointed there is no one in the Presidential line of succession.'

'What about the losing candidate?'

'He was not given a mandate, and is not eligible.'

'What about yourself?'

'I can't be Chief Justice AND President, that would be a conflict in the branches of government. If I resigned my position there would be no Chief Justice to inaugurate me. The President has to nominate the next incumbent. No president, no nomination, no inauguration, no president. It's a constitutional catch 22.'

'There must be something we can do...'

At that moment, the Chief Justice's head legal clerk came running in, out of breath.

'I've found it!' she declared, between gulps of air.

'Found what?' President Thompson asked.

'The constitutional procedure for election to the Presidency in the absence of the normal line of succession.'

'Well what does it say?' the Chief Justice urged.

'You're not going to like it, ma'am...'

'Just spit it out.'

'In the case that no member of the traditional line of succession is available the Presidency falls to the President-elect's closest relative.'

'But Hasagee doesn't have any living relatives...' Gronkowski observed.

'Yes, ma'am he does. Ever since that bill passed that allowed pets to be included as benefactors in wills. It has been proved in precedent that animals are legally considered family members.'

'Are you telling me that...surely not. Please God no. I am not inaugurating a dog as the President of the United States of America. There must be something in the constitution...'

'Unfortunately not, ma'am. The constitution states only that a candidate has to be a natural-born US citizen, which it is. They must be 35 years or older, which it is in dog years, and have been resident here for 14 years, and again, dog years. I'm afraid that legally there is no recourse other than to swear in Puggle the dog as the next President.'

The three turned to look at the dog, who was sound asleep on his cushion. He let out a snort in his sleep.

'Yes...' the Chief Justice said, fighting hard against the idea of resigning her post there and then. 'Whatever you say, Mr. President...'

The Perfect Burger

Joe Ruppert - 'The perfect burger.'

Freda drew her coat in around her to ward off the cold as she walked down the dark, empty street. A neon sign hanging from a building lit her way. A newspaper blew past her. The front-page headline read: 'WORLDWIDE BEEF SHORTAGE AS CLIMATE CRISIS CONTINUES'.

She was absolutely desperate for a burger. But since the huge sea change in public opinion about climate change 2 years ago, cattle farming had all but ceased.

Freda glanced around to check for any loitering delinquents. Once she was sure she was alone she stopped and fished in her pocket. Out came a battered, creased photograph of a burger. Sighing, she took a longing look at the picture.

'Psst,' she heard someone hiss. Startled, Freda folded the picture back up and put it back into her pocket. 'Psst,' the hiss came again. 'You, lady.'

'I've got a knife,' Freda said, projecting as much confidence as possible.

'What?' the voice replied. 'I'm not here to hurt you. I'm here to help you.'

'I doubt it.' Freda said. 'I'm pretty sure that in all human history, no-one approaching someone in this manner has anything that can be of help to them whatsoever.'

'Very well,' the voice replied. 'Allow me to reveal myself.'

A middle-aged man appeared out of the shadows in front of her. His arms were held aloft, to show he had no weapons.

'I saw you longing after that burger,' he said. 'I can help you with your craving.'

'You make it sound like I'm some sort of drug addict,' Freda said.

'Well is that so far fetched?' the man replied. 'You desire to consume something beyond rational reason, and the inability to fulfil that desire drives you to distraction. The food itself may not be a drug but its absence has the same chemical effect of withdrawal on the body.'

'Fair point,' Freda conceded.

She hated to admit it but the man was right. All her friends thought she was insane when she held a candlelit vigil the day the beef ban was announced. Her passion for burgers was unsurpassed in her social group. All the rest of them had merely dismissed it as inconvenient. They said that they were much healthier for the absence of beef. And that ultimately, the world was too. And that was what mattered.

Freda didn't disagree with this assertion, but she sure did miss that first bite of a really good cheeseburger.

A few well-meaning souls had suggested she try turkey or lamb mince burgers instead. Or the new plant-based burgers that were all the rage right now. She had nodded and smiled but they didn't understand - it wouldn't be the same.

It sounded stupid that she had been affected so much by it. But 9 out of her 10 favourite restaurants had closed their doors, and she now had to find a substitute for roughly half her weekly meals. It was a big change for her.

'OK,' she said to the man. 'What have you got?'

'There is a place, not far from here, where some illicit meat has been obtained. They are serving burgers and steaks to the discerning customer...for the right price of course.'

'That's ridiculous,' Freda scoffed. 'I bet it's terrible meat and I'd be paying through the nose for a rubbish burger. Thanks, but I'll pass on this occasion.'

'Very well...' the man said. 'But it would be such a shame to waste an opportunity to try such good quality Kobe beef because of such suspicions...'

Damnit, Freda thought. It had been 2 years since she had tasted a delicious burger. And Kobe beef was the best around.

'I'll bite,' she said. 'How much?'

'£50 a burger.'

'£50! That's daylight robbery!' Freda exclaimed.

'That's a bargain,' the man said. 'This stuff costs more than oil spread with caviar. It's barely above what you would have paid for it before. I guarantee you that anywhere else you go in this city will charge you five times that for a cut this good.'

'Then why are you selling it so cheap?'

'Let's just say that the heat is on my contact and he is keen to ensure quick disposal of the product.'

'OK, fine. Take me.'

Ten minutes later they found themselves wandering up to a small cafe in a nearby council estate.

Freda clutched the knife in her pocket just in case this turned out to be some elaborate long con to steal her kidneys. But her excitement at the prospect of getting to eat some delicious beef was overriding her fear. If she was honest she would have licked the remains of a Big Mac off the soles of someone's shoe right now. Entering a dark foreboding cafe armed with a sharp knife wasn't so outlandish.

The man, who had, upon her insistence, given his name as Rudy, ushered her into the building. As he came in behind he pulled the shutters down on the window and flipped the sign from 'Open' to 'Closed.'

The cafe was empty. Had the sign not suggested otherwise upon entering, Freda would have sworn that they had shut up shop for the night. Chairs were up on tables, drinks fridges were turned off and no proprietor was anywhere to be found.

'Go on through to the back,' Rudy urged.

Freda walked to the back of the cafe and pushed open the door leading to the kitchen. The scene behind the door made her jaw drop.

Sat in the spacious kitchen were dozens of people waiting for a taste of delicious Kobe beef. People like her who were willing to defy the world to get a taste of what they loved. Waiters and waitresses bustled between makeshift tables. Along one wall a chef cooked up burgers and steaks on the cafe's flat top grill.

The smell in the speakeasy, or meateasy she supposed, was overwhelming. The delicious perfumes of cooking beef wafted into her nostrils. It was almost enough to make her melt to the floor with joy.

One of the waiters led her to a table, which she shared with several other diners. He took her order of a Kobe beef burger with cheese, pickles, onions and lettuce. Patiently she waited as the other people on her table all received and devoured their orders.

As the waiter finally brought her order over Freda practically snatched it out of his hands. The first bite was perfect, with a rich flavour. She couldn't tell if this was due to it being as good as the man said, or if it was simply that she hadn't had good beef in 2 years. Almost anything would do the trick at this point.

The rest of the burger was all a blur. But if pushed she wouldn't have been able to deny that she shed a small tear of joy at finally being able to taste something so delicious again.

Less than two minutes after taking the first bite, she slid the last remnants of the burger into her mouth and let out a satisfied sigh.

Her ecstasy was short-lived, though. One of the patrons a couple of tables away from her stood up. He pulled his coat back to reveal a police badge and shouted 'This is a raid!'

After, Freda noted, that he had finished his steak of course.

Customers and staff alike scattered. Several other undercover officers revealed themselves around the room. One, on her table, made a grab for Freda, but luckily she managed to wriggle free and shot off towards the back exit through the storeroom.

Luck was on her side as the policemen seemed not to have noticed her slip out the back way. As she stalked through the dark storeroom she cursed as she banged her leg against something hard. Taking out her phone she lit up the obstacle to find that it was a case full of cuts of Kobe beef. Quickly she looked around and weighed up her ability to flee and carry the case at the same time. She decided it was worth it.

Five minutes later she found herself running down the street on which she had met Rudy, the case of beef held in front of her. She was out of breath and after essentially inhaling the burger was feeling a bit sick. But she knew that she had to get home.

Turning the corner into her own street, she had to dive behind a tree as she saw a police car drive past the other end of the road. When the coast was clear she walked as nonchalantly as possible to her front door, fumbled for her keys and opened it.

'Where have you been?' her flatmate asked. 'Are you ok? You look like you've had a run-in with the police or something.'

'You're not far wrong,' Freda said, huffing and puffing. 'But you wouldn't believe me if I told you.'

'What's that you're carrying?'

'Let's just say that dinner is on me.'

A Dinosaur Named Dog

Jess Radcliffe - *'A story about having a diplodocus as a pet.'*

'Did he come? Did he come?' Anna asked as she ran into the front room on Christmas morning. 'Did he, did he, did he?'

'Of course he did, dear,' Anna's father Malcolm said, smiling. 'He enjoyed the milk and cookies, and Rudolph was very grateful for the carrot.'

'What did he briiiiiing?' Anna asked. She was running around in a very small circle by this point, unable to contain her excitement.

'Why not take a look?' Martha, her mother, urged.

The young family spent the next hour tearing open presents. As the morning went on, Malcolm and Martha noticed that their daughter was looking sadder and sadder.

'What's wrong, dear?' Martha asked when her daughter was bordering on tears.

'I asked Santa for a doggy and there's no doggy,' Anna replied.

'Your mother and I had a chat with Santa. He agreed that he wouldn't get you a doggy because I'm allergic and I'd be sneezing all the time.'

'Oh,' Anna said with a big, sad sigh. 'That's not your fault I suppose.'

'But he did manage to find something even better than a dog...' Martha added.

Anna's face lit up.

'What is it?' she asked.

Malcolm reached behind the sofa and pulled out a box, wrapped but with air holes poked in the side. Anna tore off the wrapping paper and pulled off the lid.

'IT'S A BABY DINOSAUR!' she screamed. 'A REAL LIFE BABY DINOSAUR!'

'A diplodocus to be exact. What are you going to name him?' her mother said.

'I WILL CALL HIM DOG!'

Ever since she had gotten Dog the diplodocus Anna had been the most popular girl in school. The dinosaur was so faithful that she could ride him to school. He even waited outside her classes for her so that she could play with him between lessons.

Nobody dared bully her anymore. Dog mostly ate leaves, but in a few short weeks, he had grown to a formidable size. Her parents had assured her that he was a rare dwarf diplodocus. This meant that he probably wouldn't grow bigger than a horse or cow. But the size of his teeth was more than enough to deter any would-be undesirables.

Dog turned out to be very helpful to the whole family. He would often join Martha or Malcolm on shopping trips. He helped by reaching items that they might otherwise have struggled to get from the higher shelves.

Anna and Dog were already the best of friends and were inseparable. Originally he had slept in her bed. But one night the bed collapsed after he had grown particularly large that practice had to stop.

He was naughty sometimes too. His size and the fact he had free run of the house meant that snacks were not even safe in the highest cupboards. The family had to come up with more and more creative ways of hiding food from Dog. All so that they could enjoy at least a little bit of it themselves before he snaffled it.

Every now and then they came home to find Dog asleep on the kitchen floor surrounded by evidence of his most recent crimes. They tried to be mad at him, but he would give them a big lick on the face with his coarse tongue. They quickly found that they couldn't stay mad for long.

After a few months, they all agreed he was the perfect pet.

One day, Anna and Dog were walking back home from school. They heard the most terrible wailing coming from one of the gardens and decided to see what was wrong. Anna opened the garden gate and went inside.

'Is everything alright?' she asked. It turned out the wail had come from a little old lady who lived in the house.

'My cat!' she cried. 'My cat Fluffums is stuck up in the tree and I can't get him down!'

It was only a very short tree, but Anna was afraid of heights and the lady didn't look like much of a climber. This was clearly a job for a dinosaur.

'I know,' Anna said, smiling. 'Dog can do it! Dog will get Fluffums down from the tree!'

The old lady stopped wailing and stared at Anna.

'A dog?' she asked incredulously. 'How on earth is a dog going to help get my Fluffums out of this tree. Young lady if you have nothing productive to suggest then you should scoot off home.'

'Oh, you misunderstood. Dog is his name,' Anna replied. 'Here, Dog!' she called.

Dog had been patiently waiting on the pavement outside the woman's garden. He came bounding through the gate, nearly tearing it off its hinges with his bulk.

'Well, I never!' the old lady exclaimed, now thoroughly flustered by the whole situation. 'What on earth is that...that beast?!'

'His name is Dog,' Anna said. 'And he is a diplodocus.'

'A diplo-what?'

'A diplodocus. It's a kind of dinosaur. He's a herbivore, so he won't eat Fluffums. He normally only eats leaves, but he has taken quite a liking to Pop-Tarts recently.'

'What on earth are you blathering on about, young lady?' the old woman asked, wagging an accusatory finger.

Anna noticed that she was very angry indeed, and it seemed that even Dog could sense the hostility. At least, she noted, that the woman seemed to have forgotten about her cat for the time being.

'A dinosaur, a diplodocus, Pop-Tarts?' the rant continued. 'Never in all my life have I heard such utter nonsense coming from the mouth of another human being. Dinosaurs have been extinct for millions of years. I ought to call your parents. I bet they'd love to hear the sort of rubbish their daughter is coming out with.'

Anna decided that it was time to divert the conversation back to the original subject of rescuing Fluffums the cat.

'Perhaps we should try and help Fluffums?' she suggested.

'Humph, very well,' the old lady said simmering down slightly. 'If your 'dinosaur,' or dog in a costume, or small horse, or whatever that thing is can get my Fluffums out of that three then maybe I won't ring your parents.'

They both turned to the tree to survey the situation, only to find that it had already been resolved.

While the old lady had been ranting, Fluffums had caught sight of Dog wandering over to the tree. The cat had decided that he was not interested in any of that sort of business thank-you-very-much. He had bolted from the tree but had rather botched its landing and was now face down in the privet hedge.

Anna walked over and scooped the petrified cat out of the foliage. Fluffums went to protest, but after everything that had happened decided better of it.

Anna walked over to the old lady and handed the cat over.

'Here you go,' she said cheerfully. 'That's not how I was expecting him to do it, but you can't argue with results.'

The old lady was shellshocked. The whole thing was over in a matter of seconds, and once again she had her beloved cat safe in her arms. Without another word she turned and walked back into her house, leaving Anna and Dog stood on the lawn.

'Okay!' Anna shouted at the door. 'See you later then!'

She turned to Dog, who she found munching on some prize azaleas.

'Stop that, Dog.' she scolded. 'Or you won't want your Pop-Tarts.'

After she told almost the entire school about Dog's daring rescue, word got around quickly about the Jurassic escapade. A few days later a journalist from the local newspaper, the Hopton Flyer, came to talk to Anna about the rescue. They even took some pictures of her and Dog.

The journalist said that she was very jealous that Anna had a dinosaur for a pet. She assured Anna that a story this big would be front-page news in the Flyer. Dog the Rescue Dinosaur would be a big hit.

Anna simply could not wait for the story to come out. She checked the Flyer every morning after dad had finished reading it over breakfast. But after a week she started to lose heart.

On the eighth day, she trudged downstairs, bleary-eyed, to have some breakfast before she went off to school.

She found both her parents in the kitchen, waiting for her, huge smiles on their faces.

'We are so proud of you!' Martha said.

'And proud of Dog!' Malcolm added.

'What are you talking about?' Anna, whose brain rarely got into gear in the mornings before she had eaten her boiled egg and soldiers, asked.

Her dad picked the paper up from the table.

'Look,' he said. 'Dog made the paper.'

Suddenly very excited and awake, Anna grabbed the paper. There, indeed, was the picture of her hugging Dog, right on the front page, just as the journalist had said it would be. She read the headline out to herself.

'8-Year-Old And Pet Dinosaur Named Dog Rescue Cat From Tree. Fire Department Glad They Weren't Bothered.'